# Praise for *Rain*

"[An] exquisitely written first novel . . . [Gunn's] language is pitch-perfect; on almost every page, she expresses familiar feelings in ways that are unsentimental and entirely original."
— *New York Times Book Review*

"What impresses most is Gunn's sure evocation of the way children feel and think . . . Partly because of this finely modulated tone and partly because this book is about loss and haunted by waters, *Rain* is reminiscent of Norman McClean's classic *A River Runs Through It*." — *Guardian*

"It's a beauty . . . Gunn tells a story that's very sad and simple, though her methods are not unsophisticated. The confidence with which she interweaves the twelve-year-old Janey's perceptions with those of Janey the fully mature narrator; the expert modulation of lush, lyrical voice; the precise use of physical details to suggest psychological states — these are signs of a talent built to last." — *Mirabella*

"Taut, beautifully written; a fresh look at the volatile world of childhood." — Edna O'Brien

Pr~~ai~~

"Devastating." —

"To crack open Ki~~rsty~~ ~~is to~~ rumble unwittingly with the lid ~~of~~ ~~the box~~ . . . Its figures of speech, lovely on the page, turn unholy once they have taken on life . . . [but] go ahead, open it, it's worth the risk."
— *New York Times Book Review*

"Daring . . . the gossamer sensuality of Kirsty Gunn's prose makes the most elegant of horror stories." — *Boston Globe*

"Gunn creates a sensation akin to drifting under the influence of a powerful drug. The writing flows beautifully and deliciously, gradually revealing a tale of obsession, addiction, and abuse." — *Library Journal*

"Very rarely do books come along that make you gasp with their strangeness and beauty . . . Reading this book, you will realize you have forgotten to breathe." — *Vogue Australia*

"Kirsty Gunn has the originality of a poet . . . [This is a] page-turning horror story . . . irresistible." — *Times* (London)

"Kirsty Gunn writes like a dream and her short but perfect novel crackles with poetic energy." — *Elle*

"A dreamlike mixture . . . shot through with jewel-bright imagery." — *Times Literary Supplement*

## Praise for *This Place You Return to Is Home*

"A haunting debut collection . . . weird and remarkably affecting . . . A small gem." — *Kirkus Reviews* (starred review)

"Lyrical . . . These melancholy tales impress the mind's eye like delicate watercolor paintings." — *Entertainment Weekly*

"Like Raymond Carver, [Gunn] sketches scenes from the lives of ordinary, unhappy people with thin but vivid strokes that make the reader pause and think about what has happened." — *Boston Phoenix*

"Her pacing is hypnotic. She lures the reader with images that are mere brushstrokes, lines that deftly say everything by refusing to say anything." — *City Pages*

FEATHERSTONE

# Featherstone

### KIRSTY GUNN

A Mariner Book
Houghton Mifflin Company
Boston • New York

First Mariner Books edition 2004

Copyright © 2002 by Kirsty Gunn

Published in Great Britain by Faber and Faber Limited

For information about permission to reproduce
selections from this book, write to Permissions,
Houghton Mifflin Company, 215 Park Avenue South,
New York, New York 10003.

Visit our Web site: www.houghtonmifflinbooks.com.

*Library of Congress Cataloging-in-Publication Data*
Gunn, Kirsty, date.
Featherstone / Kirsty Gunn.
p.  cm.
ISBN 0-618-24692-4
ISBN 0-618-44660-5 (pbk.)
1. Missing persons — Fiction.
2. City and town life — Fiction. I. Title.
PS3557.U4864 F43  2003
813'.54 — dc21    2002032290

Printed in the United States of America

MP 10 9 8 7 6 5 4 3 2 1

For the memory of my mother

# Acknowledgements

The author is grateful for the assistance of the Scottish Arts Council in the completion of this book.

om the
e ascent
ide by a
mencing
e village
tions are
u inform
e before

.06, map
fs of the
ceessible
compris-
t measur-
d 110 ft
rnational
ng in the
familton-

ap 4, 14.
stand of
town of
by road to
capital of
uth-west.
700. The
argely in
the late
of access
pted new
on of an
the port.

Ref. 431,
rving the
eastern
s since at
826 pop.
famous
h Street is
e original

063, map
p of over
e. Access
uth end

---

PASTNEL, South Ref. 771, map 13, 5.
1. Village 6 miles north of CARRTOWN,
on the River SHAWN. 1911 pop. 80,
curr. pop. 950. The village, which grew
up around the glassworks established in
c.1830, is now inhabited mostly by
skilled workers who commute to the
engineering works in Carrtown.

**FEATHERSTONE**, North/Central. Ref.
127, map 13, 4, 3, etc. Orig.
Fether's/Feather's town; farming, crops;
1826 pop. 120, curr. pop. 1,500–1,600.
An attractive small rural town serving
outlying estates; bank, post office,
school; EC: Wed; fishing, shooting, golf.
River FERNLEIGH: 2 miles, sit. in public reserve, orig. forest planting.
Approach from south into Main Street,
outlying streets, 6 miles radius; many
orig. wooden dwellings. To the north,
hill/mountain range, it's colder, and to
the east and west is the sea. The south
you know already as the place you've
come from, come so far only to be here,
in this small town named for a feather
and a stone. The feather drifts on the air,
and the stone is a tiny thing you would
remove from your shoe, throw down the
street to hear the sound of it touch the
earth. Ref. map 2>NC.

FENN, East/Central. Ref. 442, map 28.
Village 4 miles south of the market town
of SPENFIELD, pleasantly situated in
the Minden valley. Curr. pop. 230. The
village was the birthplace of the explorer
William Stanwick in 1854 and his childhood home until he emigrated at the age
of 19. A small museum, originally built
as an annexe to the village school, houses a collection of original documents
relating to the Stanwick family.

FENWOOD, West. Ref. map 10, 13.
Market town in the Iver valley, best-
known for its race-course. 1859 pop.
900, curr. pop. 2,700. The Fenwood
Festival has been held annually in

---

great sto.
FEVERS
Ref. 041,
River B/
lage of S
joined b
Stone. fir
by fire in
tion of th
FINGAL
6, 4. A st
of Line
manufaci
tural ma
pop. 2,7
founded
town is
mental w
FINPER
Village
Bay. A n
extends
dunes an
arranged
No. 6, S
FLAXT
13. Villa
40 miles
as the 'C
940. Ca
camping
FLETC
784, ma
road cro
Newton
east. In
tin-min
Fletche
several
hotel so
mines
lulls. Re
FLORE
3, 8. I
COWF

# Contents

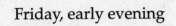

Friday, early evening

# ONE

He looked up and thought: *I know you.*

His hands were still in earth, where it was warm, but he withdrew them, brought them up to shade his eyes. He looked, with his hands at his forehead that way against the light, and he thought he did know her, though the light was bright on her, and around her bright, and at her back, like foil. It was late, late afternoon.

The sun, however, that was a thing he hadn't noticed before. Though he had been out in his garden for most of the day, Johanssen had no reason to be looking at the weather. To kneel on the stiff, sweet-smelling sack he always used for work, to sift with his fingers through the freshly dug flower beds – this was all he had to do: no need to worry then about the light and time around him. Yet now, in the moment of bringing his hands up out of the earth, and the late summer sun suddenly low in the sky and too bright to see, and with the air on his thin, naked arms cooling to cold, though these weren't his thoughts – coolness, the slight damp chill of the open air – though these weren't his thoughts, when the voice came across to him out of the light he registered then, in that moment, the small drop of temperature and his body felt old then, he became very old when he heard her voice coming across to him from out of the light:

'Uncle Sonny, it's me.'

Thurson Johanssen was an old man, he didn't need cold air to tell him. Of course he was old, he had an old man's name, but

3

no one called him it. He was old but still they gave him the other name, a great name he could figure, a name for someone who was only a boy.

'Hey, Son,' they said to him.

'What's up, Sonny?'

That was how they were with him, and he always enjoyed it. There was a lightness in their voices when they said the boy's name.

'Great garden again this year, Sonny Jim,' they said, and they gave him such pleasure then, with their friendly voices.

'Your flowers, Sonny. They're always the prettiest in town.'

It was true that he did so love the garden. He loved it in all its parts because, he could figure, all old men must love their gardens, though he'd had this one since he was a boy. He had been young like a boy when he'd begun with it, when Nona had helped him with the tiny branches and the blossom, yet still he loved the garden now like it was new, loved it in all the parts he could come to because, he supposed, it was a reminder of her, this place where his sister had first showed him how to let things grow. There was the part where the flowers had been thick, waist-high all summer in a kind of cloud, the forget-me-nots and Queen Anne's lace, and the tall pale-coloured poppies he favoured best, pale like skins with their dark in the centre like a mouth or an eye, with their black dust. He was in that part now, where they had grown, making the earth soft again for a new planting, smoothing down the ground as if smoothing down paper to draw, the lines and shallow dips for flowers, marking with his fingertip a place for a seed.

Of course, Francie would know he'd be in his garden this time.

She would remember, even after all these years.

'There's no skill to a garden, there's no talent in it' – that's what he always said to anybody, if they talked to him about it. 'It's just a question of timing.'

There was spring. Summer. Then autumn again. The long

4

winter again . . . Certain times of year held certain things to be done, that was all, and she would know that, Johanssen could figure. She would remember. That with the poppies long gone and the little dry roots of lobelia weightless in the palm of his hand, he'd be somewhere in the garden now, digging over the beds, pulling out the dead plants free.

Francie would always know the way he did things, where he would be, in what part. She might have been down the back already, to look for him there, because he did love that part too. This time of year he could easily have been working there, where the grass was flat and soft and the roses grew so thick over the fence that they covered the tiny barbs in the wire that could cut you. Or further down, where the small orchard went into woods, into the willows, those trees familiar and dense and known to him but even so, when he went out there at night sometimes, after he got back from the pub, say, went out into the willows for a pee he might get lost, kind of, for a little while when it was dark, or late, or if he'd had too much to drink, maybe. Rhett would be with him, sniffing around, he might growl a little just at some small sound, and Johanssen would watch him, thinking all the while he knew exactly where they were both standing. Then, after he'd buttoned himself up, he'd be looking around and see only the thin trunks of willows on every side, there would be no pattern in them, and that's when he'd be lost then, like a boy might get lost, or a young man might. All the same, he loved it down in this part of the garden too. Even as the willows kept growing, green stalks that kept coming out of the ground every spring, like wands, and he couldn't stop them. It was because he was home there. Of course she would always know he'd be home there.

And yet . . .
There was this part of the garden where he was now, where he was kneeling, and there had been her voice, then his looking up . . .

And though she must have known that all the time he was looking and looking into the light to see her, he was looking to see but he couldn't see. Only the sun, printing gold into black into gold against his eyes, only a dark shape against the sky, like a dear shape cut clean out of the light and laid against it . . .

*I know you.*

And then she was gone.

Slowly Johanssen got himself up from the ground. Stood himself up, straightened, and behind him somewhere Rhett shifted then was up on his feet like a young dog to follow. Together they walked the few paces over to the hedge at the side of the road, and stood, waiting at the hedge, but nobody there down the road, nobody. Perhaps she had turned the corner already, down at the end by the petrol pump and round the hotel into Main Street. Or maybe she had run the other way, past Bryson's, past the Grahams', down past Nona's old place and then round the corner by the pine trees and gone.

Even so, they stayed, Johanssen's eyes along the road, up and down, Rhett with his muzzle pointing up into the slight breeze as if he, too, was waiting.

'Where did she go, eh?'

Johanssen put his hand to the dog's soft head, touched an ear that was soft.

'Where did she go just when I could have got up to meet her?'

He fondled the dog's ear, like a fold of soft cloth between his fingers.

'Where did she go, eh? Old boy? Where is she now?'

And in time, the dog sat, lay down, a great sigh escaping from him, like from a bag, and still there was an old man, standing, looking into nothing, just the same empty road, but it was warmer there, out of the shadow where he'd been kneeling, now that he was standing in the light the sun seemed warm again on his back, on his dirt-stained arms.

◇

Johanssen could guess there were any number of places a person could run to in this town. Not even a town, most people would say, but you wouldn't call it a village either. That wasn't the right word. Village would make it something different again, so town would have to do it, though the place was small. People said they were going 'up town' like they were going into London or New York, a queer way of putting it when you were just after the milk, or a packet of tobacco papers, but people said 'up town' just the same. There was the main street, the Railton Hotel on the corner and the stretch of shops beyond it, a few streets going off either side. Even so, the place was big enough that you could be private if you needed. Big enough that you wouldn't have to leave.

Johanssen had never felt he'd had to leave.

He was someone who had lived all his life in this one town. He had never gone away. He had been born here, gone to school and grown up here. Found work and retired, and even though he'd never married, stayed fixed in his ways, maybe, with his sister's house up the road he could go to, and young Francie coming to him every day with her songs, and her stories from school, still he could tell anyone anything about the place they might want to know, the different ways to get around. Like where the roads were good, for example, if you had a car, or if you were walking along then he knew where the grass verges grew thick enough that you could climb up onto them if a big lorry came by. He could tell you where fences were broken, or where there were cracks in the concrete where the gravel showed through. Or where there were cattle grids that were hard to walk on, or drains where you could lose money . . . plenty of places where you could lose money.

A person returning to town might need to know about that kind of thing, Johanssen could figure. They would want to be reminded of where they could safely walk, and of shops where they could spend their money. Like Dalgety's on the main street, where they had the smart clothes and the packages of books ordered in from the city, with silken threads to mark where you'd stopped reading and the thick, shiny paper covers. They might need to know about places like that, or like the post office and the bank and how they were also in the main street of town. That was a well-kept road. If you went along it to the end you came to the hall where they sometimes had dances, and then there were the showgrounds over the bridge just beyond, and that was somewhere that always had plenty going on, rugby games, the country A&P in summer. There was everything here, everything. So why feel it wasn't enough to stay, that you'd have to leave, go searching out for more?

And yet, that's what Francie had done, and as Johanssen stood waiting, the memory returned to him from all those years ago, of the town suddenly being full of streets and roads that instead of taking you to places that you knew, only took you away. They were paths and exits and routes marked 'To the North', 'To the South', and they were like a map of little scars, like the lines rubbed with dirt on the palms of Sonny's hands that showed how you couldn't bring people back, not even when Nona was buried, and flowers and earth piled over her like a bed yet still she was cold and wanted Francie there . . . No, by then Sonny knew there were certain roads you could lose yourself if you wanted, you could hide. You could be deep in the high country on a twisting, empty, unsealed track, or lost in traffic on a four-lane highway. Either way, you weren't coming back. Even the little slip-way out of town Johanssen had helped seal, from his days as a working man, was somewhere you could disappear if you wanted. You would simply drive down that tiny road to the gate, open the gate, close it behind you, and it would be like you were nowhere in the world. You'd go deeper and deeper into trees, following a grass towpath all the way down through the Reserve to the river. It could get muddy there in winter, and dangerous to drive if the water was high, but still the council kept the undergrowth back so there was always a clear path and space enough amongst the trees to park a car. It was somewhere Ray Weldon often went, Johanssen knew, and he was fond of Ray.

That wasn't a place, though, for most people. It was too dark, even in high summer, and shadowy mostly with water and leaves. Johanssen himself would never go there. He would just carry on down the sealed road half a mile past the river turn-off, ignoring that sign; he would just keep going straight ahead to where the road eventually brought you back again to the outskirts of town. Bob Alexander's garage was along that way, a nice place sitting outside in the sun, where he did the mechanics and electricals, and the Carmichaels' lumber yard opposite, though Johnny Carmichael always said he was going to move from there, because he was too near the holy cross of the church for his liking, didn't want the minister hearing him swear.

'Too damn near,' Johnny Carmichael would say, proudly, and it was like Johanssen could hear the scream of the cutting timber in the background whenever Johnny shouted, whisky on his breath.

'For the Carmichaels,' he would shout. 'Too damn near, and their wild ways.'

Johanssen laughed a bit, just then, thinking about Johnny and how he talked so big.

'Got a load on today . . .' His eyes would be blue as blue, and his hair still black from where he used the grease. '. . . but nothing my horsepower can't handle.'

It was like Johnny and the Carmichaels thought they were princes of the place sometimes, the way they might swagger about, and give on as if they knew things other people couldn't, about strengths or weights, or money, when all the time they were just like everybody else and probably guessing.

Even so, as he stood there by the hedge in the last of the afternoon sun, Johanssen thought he might ask Johnny tonight, if he'd noticed anybody new arriving in town, a young woman. He could ask Johnny or Gaye, or any of their boys. The boys would probably be the best ones to ask, always out on the lookout for things happening, driving around in their father's beat-up old trucks and pick-ups, doing all the picking up anyone could handle. Johanssen laughed again a bit, at that, a kind of a joke he'd made, and thinking of those Carmichael boys. He would see them tonight, no doubt, and their father; he'd ask them all when he saw them at the Railton Bar tonight.

Had they seen . . . he would ask.

And he'd ask Margaret behind the bar, too.

'Funny thing,' he might say then, when Margaret had his glass put out before him, and when his first sip had been taken from it. 'Funny thing . . .'

And he would wipe the wetness of the beer from his mouth with the back of his hand, or with a handkerchief even, but all the time keeping it casual, acting very casual.

'This afternoon,' he would say, and he would take another small sip of beer.

'Thought I saw someone I haven't seen in a long while.'

'Thought I saw Nona's little girl.'

# TWO

In the bar, Margaret smiled, even though she was alone. She often experienced these small moments of pleasure and always she gratified herself with them. She might smile, smoothing a strand of hair back from her face. Or she might run her hands lightly down the sides of her body as though a man could be watching or anybody could be watching, and yet all the time she was alone.

Strange, people thought she was so friendly, that she would put out for them that way. It came from running a bar, Margaret knew, that people thought of her as a local by now, after two years, as a person who took note of the comings and goings in town and was clever in that way, detailed in her interest in others when really she had little time for them, mostly, and thought of herself always as someone on her own, different from the rest.

Standing here now, in the cool, grey-lit emptiness of the hotel bar, Margaret could feel this knowledge deep in her, this secret about herself, and how much she loved the secret too. It was like a trick she'd pulled off, a sleight of hand, that she'd been able to make herself completely the woman who would stand and patiently serve when all the time her life was quite removed from that of any other woman. So Margaret smiled . . . for nothing. Just for the pleasant way the last pale rays of sun fell through the windows of the bar this time of day, late afternoon. To know that no one else was here, but that she was the only one in the large, empty, high-walled room, that this could be enough for her now.

She was very clean, that was part of the feeling. Clean like a maid, like a young girl was clean. Five o'clock and the hotel wouldn't be open for another hour, the lunchtime crowd long gone. Three hours between, and in that time she had been able to bathe and put on fresh clothes and feel enough that it was like arriving somewhere, to be able to come down the stairs into the bar again, like she could do anything, change anything. In clean clothes she had been able to go around the room and tidy, in minutes, it seemed, gather up all the empty glasses where they had been left, drained and dirtied and half-filled, clustered together on the small tables and lined along the window sills. She'd washed them, dried them and it was like it had taken no time at all. Minutes more to go about the room filling the rubbish bag with empty cans and paper napkins and straws, with cellophane wrappers still salty from peanuts and crisps, minutes to stack up the ashtrays that were full of stubs and ash and litter, to empty them, wiping them out clean with a damp cloth so the messages were clear again, printed in bright coloured letters on the base or around the rims:

'Drink DB – to your health!'

'Cheers!'

'Johnnie Walker is in town this Christmas!'

She had rinsed them, and the dirtied cloth, in clean water so no grey remained to streak the colours, so that even the little black-and-white dogs on the glass ashtrays showed as freshly washed, their noses shiny, their little eyes gleaming.

'Whyte and McKay. The only blend at home in the Highlands, and in the World.'

Really, it had taken no time at all. Easy then to run the hoover over the green patterned carpet so it looked new, so she couldn't see, at first, the beer stains and frayed holes burnt into the rubber backing. Easy in all ways to work at these tasks, to make the bar hers again, to arrange it, like an image of herself, to lay out the beer mats on the tables in neat patterns of three or four, as if people would notice, would remark upon it if she hadn't done it just right.

This was all part of her pleasure, this afternoon; no one else could own it. The particular pleasure of this one place, of chairs arranged, carefully in little groups, a room with its burnt, spill-stained carpet bare and clean as though it were a lovely hall. These thoughts were part of the space around her, they seemed to inform the air, give to furniture, objects, their own definition. It was as if even the glasses themselves were thinner and more beautiful in this light, at this time, like ornaments for Margaret of all the things she knew about, how people might speak or lay a table or serve, fine empty ornaments of all the memories she alone in this one small town could hold.

She stepped back now from the bar to admire her work.

*Yes.*

There the last glass had been replaced on its shelf, the last pitcher set beside it. The smile came to her again, touching her like a little nerve.

*Everything, yes.*

In certain parts of the room the sun had highlighted an area, a wall, a corner. There was a polished table top, the long, gleaming brass rod running the length of the bar. There was the cracked glass lampshade in the corner, catching the light from the window and scattering it like a thousand coins all over the floor.

*A pleasant room.*

Despite everything, pleasant. Despite all the men that had been in it, overweight, the sweating bodies of farmers and farm workers. Despite their heavy tramp of boots, their thick, damp workshirts smelling of meal and blood, of machinery oil . . .

Despite them all, the men who came in early unchanged from a day's work, and the others who arrived later, fixed up with hair oil and cheap aftershave for the women who came

in with them . . . Despite the shouting voices that would fill
the room soon, and on through the night, loud and relentless,
the men's voices and the shrill competitive voices of the
men's wives . . . Despite them all, a pleasant room, and quiet
now, with the fading afternoon sun coming through the partly opened windows and touching the folds of the curtains
with pale dust, like velvet brushed with gold.

*Yes.*

Margaret took in everything entire.

*Yes.*

Then she turned back to face the long mirror of the bar.

Usually, when she worked, at night or on the lunchtime shift,
the mirror was behind her. Usually, Margaret did not turn.
There would be too many people about her at night, the faces
of thirty, forty, fifty people crowded in around her at the bar
and the electric bulbs burning upon them all like suns. Nor
could she do it any earlier than this, when daylight cast its
searching light all through the room and would show too
clearly the lines on a woman's face, the shadows, the dark
hunter look in her eye. Never then, Margaret knew it, like a
piece of the daylight lodged in her, to remind her. No one
should ever see her then.

Now though, this minute . . .

With the feeling of contentment welled up in her, with the
creamy grey light pooling in the mirror's surface . . . Now she
could turn, and look, and she smiled . . .

And someone smiled back.

And she liked that woman, with her little smile.

The relief was like a sigh. Like something Margaret had been
holding back and now she could let it go.

*You* . . . she whispered, to herself, to her reflection. Once
again she had proved it. That the face she remembered was
the face that she could see. Once again she could believe.

*Beautiful.*

She was still there, all of her. She hadn't been thieved from or ruined. She could still recognise . . . that face, that mouth. She could still see in herself . . . that thing. Margaret looked, held her gaze directly, looking deep into the mirror, into herself. She was there. She watched herself take a cigarette from the pack on the bar before her, and bring it up slowly to place it between her lips. She watched herself do it, slowly, as though a camera were rolling, slow roll upon roll of dark colour film, recording her, watching her . . . her nuance, her breath. Watching her watch herself, bring the cigarette slowly to her lips, slowly, with deliberation, as if for a lover but with her eyes fixed on the woman in the mirror as though she herself were that lover . . .

*I see . . .*

And, keeping hold of herself in that way, looking deeply at her own reflection, with the cigarette between her lips, and her head inclined at a lovely angle against the light . . .

*I see . . .*

She was about to take up the matches from the bar and light the cigarette . . . when there was a sound. A tap on the door.

'That's it for now.'

Then the door was pushed open and Renee was stepping in.

Margaret should know by now. It was always the same way. There would be a slight shuffle in the hall, that shy tap on the door . . . Then Renee herself standing there, a dishcloth in her hand.

'I did the steak and kidney,' she was saying. 'Like you said, only I used a packet pastry, but just as good . . .'

Of course Margaret should know to expect her by now. The kitchen shift was finished for the day and though there would be some talk about some job or other, all Renee was really there to say, beneath her words, with the tilt of her body, with her eyes flickering around the room, was *May I go now, Miss Farley? Please now will you let me go?*

15

Her eyes never looked into Margaret's eyes. Though she had been employed for nearly a year, ever since Margaret knew she could afford the extra help, even though they saw each other most days, Renee never looked into Margaret's eyes when she spoke. Instead she would glance around the room, at the floor, at the corners and surfaces of the walls as though all the time she were looking for something. Nor were her hands still. Every now and then she would rub at them, or at the cloth she held, as though she'd seen something on her hands, or on the cloth, some mark. She was doing it now, rubbing at her hands as if to work flour or vegetable juice or nothing at all off the skin.

'And beans,' she was saying. 'Not cabbage, because Horace had beans fresh he wanted to get rid of . . .'

She looked down at her nails, intently, as though she was looking under the rims of the nails for dirt, but talking all the time, still talking, as if the two women were so familiar that they would go over and over these details together and care about them. As if Margaret would care.

'The lorry was full, the driver said, with turnips from up north . . .'

'Horace was too late . . .'

'So he has beans, if you like, we can get them all week . . .'

Slowly, bit by bit as she spoke, Renee edged further into the room. She would come a certain amount towards Margaret, for friendliness, to describe that she was comfortable, relaxed with the woman who paid her, but she would never come fully in. She stood now against the wall, the door and the hall to the kitchen beside her, talking and talking to Margaret as though she were communicating something urgent and important when it was only words that didn't mean anything between them, only space, words in the air, and emptiness.

'The potatoes are done,' she was saying. 'The water's on. There's parsley for them, if you want to use parsley . . .'

These poor, uncertain sentences. Margaret thought how they

went on and on. On and on into the air and nothing definite in them, these weak and foolish words for bits of chores and jobs already used and soiled, as if the sentences themselves were only tasks for Renee to identify, then complete, tidy away to their proper place of silence.

'Parsley's nice, or mint, perhaps . . .'

It was crazy, Margaret thought, that she was here now, with this woman. This woman with her busy hands and restless eyes that couldn't even look into Margaret's eyes . . . crazy. Margaret tried to smile at her but she could barely smile . . . How, when only a few minutes ago there had been that other woman, with her lovely smile? That other one, with her soft hair tied up off her neck, with her sweetly, darkly made up mouth . . .

Still, there was nothing for it.

Margaret stepped away from the mirror.

'That's lovely, Renee.'

The woman had something that Margaret did need.

'Thank you,' she said, and she took a few steps towards her.

'And so quick today, too . . .'

Margaret let one heartbeat pass, and another.

*Yes . . .*

Then, drawing on all the strength of the mirror, though the mirror was behind her, drawing upon all the strength and loveliness of the image in the mirror . . .

She spoke again.

'And even without Mary Susan to help,' she said. 'She's not . . .?'

'No,' the older woman interrupted, and for a second, for one second, her eyes looked Margaret full in the eyes.

'No, she –' and then her glance was away again, flickering, flickering.

'Not again,' Renee said, 'for the work in the kitchen, I mean. Not again for that, she says. She doesn't mind serving up, later on, if you –'

'No, no . . .'

Quickly Margaret turned back, back to the mirror again, but it was too late. Already the colour was rising to her cheeks. She put a hand up to cool them, but too late, the burn was there, and the jump of her heart behind her breast-bone like fear or shame. Too late, too late. She waited, for a second, two seconds, and then she turned to face Renee again.

'I can do that myself,' she managed to say. 'Tell her, she doesn't have to come in at all if she doesn't want to. I could perhaps just . . .?'

She was trying to be calm, like before, like the woman in the mirror was calm, but there was only the heat in her skin to feel and a heart trapped inside her like an animal in a cage of bone.

'I'll let her know,' she managed to say, 'if I need her. But please tell her –'

'It's just that –' Renee's eyes were on her apron now, at the hem of patterned cloth, her fingers working the hem.

'No, no . . .' Margaret looked up and down, the length of the bar, for her cigarettes, but she couldn't see her cigarettes. 'Of course,' she said, 'I understand.'

Margaret looked again at the bar and now she could see the cigarettes there on the bar, of course they were there on the bar, and she took one cigarette out from the packet, but not at all now in the slow way like before. She put the cigarette to her mouth, but it was nothing like before, with the glass and the cool grey of an empty room and her own sweetly, darkly made up mouth.

'Of course I understand . . .' she said.

Nothing like.

'It's because I'm her mum, I suppose . . .' Renee was saying, and her hands were still moving at her lap, twisting, fiddling, as her eyes cast wildly about the surfaces of the room. 'You've made it all so nice again in here,' her voice was saying. 'I don't know what it is, did you get the curtains cleaned, or is it the brass? Such a pretty room. No, I don't know what it is, really, Miss Farley. Growing up, maybe. Thinking she might be a bit too old now to be here doing dishes in the holidays with me. In a kitchen all afternoon, maybe, with no one to see her . . .'

Margaret didn't say anything. She lit her cigarette, and inhaled deeply from it, letting out a channel of grey smoke thick into the air. She smoked. She tipped ash, gently, gently, into a saucer she kept behind the bar, and everything she did she saw reflected in the mirror in front of her, but everything was different now. The woman she'd sought before there was gone. The face, the curious unknown expression of that other face, the darling little smile . . . gone. Only Margaret left. Only the crimson colour of a blouse or a dress at her front and too much of her skin showing from it.

She pulled it together, to cover.

She might as well have been wearing a thick knitted jumper or a house-smock, like the house-smock Renee wore, as this lovely thing she had chosen.

Margaret pulled the blouse again, buttoned it at the top and smoothed the front pleat in her skirt.

'Of course I understand,' she said again.

'It's not you, not the place . . .' Renee's voice in reply was louder than before. 'She's fond of you, Miss Farley, I know that. It's just . . .'

'No, no.'

Margaret inhaled from her cigarette.

'Tell her not to worry . . .'

She walked towards the other woman again, walking briskly now, as if nothing had ever happened to stop her.

'I was the same myself at that age . . .'

She took the last few paces and stood there, side by side with Renee in the doorway, as if she were so relaxed, her long cigarette still burning between her fingers.

'Tell her, really, not to worry.'

Margaret put her hand on the woman's arm, and the cigarette end was still burning.

'Tell her everything's fine. We can manage, you and I . . .'

The hand holding the cigarette remained there, pressed down upon the woman's arm, and a fine spread of ash dropped upon the other woman's sleeve. Margaret brushed it away.

'You know, I'm fond of Mary Susan, too,' she said. 'She knows I am. Tell her, will you, how much I miss our talks, now she's not working here any more . . .'

She brushed ash away again although there was none remaining. 'If you could just tell her . . .'

But Renee was already out the door.

Margaret stood motionless in the empty room, the colour still burning in her skin. All she could hear was silence. Nothing. The silence of her own heart. Then, through the partly opened window she realised she could hear . . . footsteps. Renee's footsteps on the rough gravel drive. Voices.

'Thanks, Mum.'

'Shhh . . . she'll hear . . .'

'Don't care.'

'Quietly, love. She'll think . . .'

And the voices fading away into the fading air.

Margaret closed her eyes.

The girl had been there all the time.

Right there, the girl had been right there just outside the window, all the time, listening. Waiting for her mother, standing in the gravel of the car park, leaning against a car perhaps, her long legs bare against the warm metal.

There all the time.

While Margaret had been alone, while she had been looking at herself in the mirror, the girl had been there. Leaning on a car, or walking up and down the gravel drive . . .

*Head up . . . Shoulders back . . .*

Picking her way through the gravel in her high and golden shoes, practising for herself the special walk Margaret had taught her . . .

*Look at me . . .*

Margaret could see her behind her closed eyes, as if she was right there. Her girl's hips swaying, walking unsteadily towards her mother . . .

*Look at me . . .*

Reaching for her mother, to steady herself, to let her mother take her, take the soft weight of her in a way Margaret herself had not been able. Allowing her mother's care for her to take her into her arms and wanting it, leaning in towards her mother in a way Margaret so longed for her to lean, and smiling for her, a beautiful smile, all over her beautiful young face.

## THREE

The shoes were so beautiful. There'd been someone looking at them before, a quite glamorous lady. She'd looked and looked and even though she'd had no make-up on and her hair wasn't exactly what you'd call 'styled' . . . She was still pretty, Mary Susan thought, kind of. She would have suited the shoes.

*Head up . . .*
*Shoulders back . . .*

Mary Susan would quite like to have talked to her, about shoes, maybe, and how learning to walk in heels was hard. She'd seemed to be the sort of person who might know about things like that. Only the lady hadn't stayed long enough to speak. She'd just hung around, scuffing her bare feet in the dust like she was a kid, and then she'd gone off someplace like she'd never been there at all . . .

*Head up.*
*Four paces forwards.*
*Turn.*

Still, Mary Susan felt, it had been nice having someone watch her practise walking, even for just a little while. Having some stranger watching her, only her, Mary Susan Louise Anderson. It had been like being someone who was really special and not from around here at all.

*Shoulders back.*
*Pull your stomach in and hold your back straight.*

*Keep walking that way as if walking that way doesn't feel queer, even though it does.*
*Hold your back straight.*

It was really difficult to do.

Elena from the modelling agency had been brilliant at it. She'd said she walked that way all the time, and it was like her shoulders were a coat hanger and her beautiful clothes just hung from the coat hanger, like clothes hanging in a shop window. That had been an amazing day, that day Elena had come to school to talk to the girls. Usually on Careers Elective it was just some teacher or policeman or dentist who came to talk, some secretary or other. Yet there had been this one time, this one special day at the end of summer term and it had been like a gift for Mary Susan, a surprise of an idea that she'd never even thought about before. To live in the city, to wear beautiful outfits all day and have someone take your photograph . . . Mary Susan couldn't think of anything in the world more wonderful. Elena had told her modelling was something to seriously think about, as a career, and she'd talked about diets and clothes and the proper way to walk in heels so your body showed the clothes hanging from it, straight and clean. That was what a model's job really was, Elena had said, that's what she had to teach all her girls. To use their bodies like beautiful hangers for the clothes.

*Head up.*

Elena knew everything, more than about modelling even.

*Shoulders back.*

It was because she was foreign.

Now that she had the right shoes, Mary Susan had to keep practising walking every chance she got, they were such beautiful shoes. Gold and with straps and the most expensive in the catalogue . . . Mary Susan had to wear them during the day even though they were for evening, just so she could get used to them, so she could get used to walking in heels. Like even now, even though her mother had finished her job and come outside to meet her, she still had to keep her head up, keep her body straight. She and her mother were just walking down the gravel drive but even so Mary Susan tipped her head back slightly like she'd seen Elena do it and imagined someone was watching her, like that lady had been watching her before.

'Do you think she could have been a model herself, Mum?'
    'Shhh . . .'
    Her mother was always tired after work.
    'She reminded me of Elena, you know,' Mary Susan said. 'She was quite a glamorous lady. When you consider round here. You know . . .' Mary Susan pointed out one foot and wiggled it into the air. 'I think she may have liked the look of my shoes.'
    'Shhh . . .'


Renee wasn't even hearing what the girl was saying. Model, something. It was always model talk.
    'Not so loudly. Now what is it?'
    Always model this, model that.
    'Aw, Mum . . .' Mary Susan sighed, too loud to be a real sigh. 'You never listen.'
    'What then?'

Actually, Renee was hoping that Margaret couldn't hear them. They were far enough down the drive by now, but she just hoped her daughter hadn't been chattering on about the hotel all this time, and about Margaret, she just hoped she hadn't been chattering on about her.
    'That lady, Mum. She wasn't from around here. Do you think she may have been a model once herself, checking out that I was walking right?'

'Shhh . . .' Renee said again.

Seemed she was always afraid these days, that Mary Susan would be on about Margaret, the way she had been lately, using the posh voice:

Don't you know, *darling* . . .

Oh, how utterly *gorgeous* . . .

*The way you do your hair is so-o-o di-vine* . . .

It made Renee laugh sometimes, but even so she just hoped Mary Susan hadn't been on about her now, about not wanting to work in the kitchen any more, not wanting to do anything for Margaret any more . . . And yet in the past hadn't it always been Margaret, Margaret? And wasn't she supposed to have been a model once too?

'Mum?'

Oh, but the air was lovely! Now she was here outside, and away from the hotel and all that business with Margaret in the bar, now she was here, she could breathe again, into this lovely air. She could feel the sun still warm, and golden everywhere. On the leaves. Golden like a red gold on the leaves and branches, yellow gold in the streaks of clouds.

'Mum?'

'It's beautiful out here!'

Renee stopped, put down her bag. Now they were at the end of the drive, she could take her cardigan off, and stand for a moment in that lovely air.

'It's still warm enough, it's lovely . . .'

It was only for a moment, but with her bag set down, and her apron off, and her cardigan, Renee felt as if she was a girl again, her daughter's age, to feel this warmth in the air, the light. It was as if she really was a person standing all alone in the sunshine and her life spread out around her like thickly woven cloth. There were the bright leaves, the grass, the red, warm earth . . . and nothing to worry about. Nothing to worry about at all. Then the kitchen business came back into her mind again and the lovely feeling was gone. Why, anyhow?

'I really don't understand you, you know.'
She picked up her bag and started walking again.
'I thought you used to like Margaret . . .'

But Mary Susan had gone on ahead. She couldn't hear anything except her own thoughts, concentrating, practising. She put one foot in front of the other pointing outwards and did the little half-turn she'd learnt that special day at school. Then she spun fully around, keeping her back straight and her arms out. If only, she thought, her mother could see the way she was, the person she truly was. If only Mary Susan could describe to her the feeling of what her life was like, how she wanted so much more for herself than her mother could imagine. No one had any idea how hard that was, to want to make yourself into someone different from the person you're expected to be. When Elena had finished talking that day she'd handed out leaflets and brochures and a form to fill in if you wanted to attend special classes that Elena herself would teach. Some of the brochures were thick as magazines and full of things you needed to know about skin and hair and how to make sure your body was in the right proportion for your height. Mary Susan kept all the information together in a folder at home and she looked at it over and over to memorise and learn.

She so needed to learn. All kinds of things, needed. Like about underwear, the right kind of clothes. What colours suited her, about cuts in clothes, so they wouldn't look cheap . . . These were things other girls would know about already, girls who'd grown up in the city and had the kinds of families who could help them, who could teach them from the start. Nothing for them like coming from far away and having to start over. Mary Susan had only even been to the city twice, once when when she'd been just a kid and then six weeks ago when she'd asked and asked and her mother had finally agreed to take her as a special birthday visit. That was really the only time. Everything else she had to find out in magazines and books, or in the brochures Elena had given her.

That was why the lady who had been watching her before had seemed so special, Mary Susan realised now, because it was as if she might have known about magazines already, like the kind of young and beautiful mother who could really teach her, pass on to her that special thing. Much more than the coat hanger.

'No way', she said, 'could that lady have been from around here.'

They had been walking quite quickly away from the hotel, Renee not looking back because she feared Margaret's face in the window. That white face, the way the dark mouth opened in it, to speak, to smile . . .

'Mum?' Mary Susan was calling.

It was only because of Mary Susan that Renee was worrying so much anyway, she knew that, it wasn't Margaret herself. And it wasn't the end of the world that Mary Susan didn't want to work at the hotel any more, why should she? There was no reason she had to give. Renee saw her there now, walking on in front with those long legs, tall and gold in the lovely light, yellow and red gold. Her own girl.

'Mum?'

Why should she have to do anything at all she didn't want to? Be kept in a job, inside a dark place? She'd spent far too much time in that hotel as it was, Margaret filling her head with nonsense about clothes and fashion and Mary Susan just young with this fully grown woman . . . If you thought about any of it, it wasn't right.

She must consider the girl more, Renee thought; she was at that age she would need to rely on her mother. Renee would have to concentrate more, notice more. Like now, for example. It was like she'd only just this minute seen her daughter for the first time, and she was out here in the open wearing next to nothing and it was the damn silly shoes on her again.

'And what have you got those things on for?'

27

It was like she'd only just this minute noticed.

'You'll break your neck.'

'But I've got to practise, Mum . . .'

Mary Susan did a little turn, picking up her feet with the silly great heels attached to them, and her arms out like she was on a tightrope, like any minute she might fall. Like the shoes might tip her clean over into the gutter.

'For goodness' sake be careful . . .'

But Renee put down her bag and watched all the same, as Mary Susan did the special walk all the way down the road, walking very smoothly, very nicely, really.

'I've just got to . . .'


No one understood how important it was to practise.

If you wanted to make it, you had to practise and practise like Elena from the agency had said:

'Girls, not all of you will have what it takes. Only those who put their hearts into this business will be the girls who will win.'

It made Mary Susan clutch her own heart, just to think of it. Being a winner, on a stage in a bikini someplace. On the cover of a magazine. She turned and rushed back to her mother and kissed her all over her face.

'Oh, Mum, Mum, Mum, Mum, Mum . . .'

If her mother could just see her once, like she could see herself.

'I've got to do this, Mum. To practise. Elena said . . .'

'Oh, Mum, nothing.'

Renee picked up her bag and started down the road again.

'Practise my foot. In three-inch heels in gravel, down a country road, that's practice, I suppose . . .'

But Mary Susan had to. No one like her mother would ever understand.

In silence, the two of them walked down the empty road. Past the petrol pump, the spare paddock for the school pony. Past the old hall that Mary Susan remembered used to be a cinema, boarded up now and with weeds growing in the cracks on the concrete front. How could anyone imagine what it was like growing up here? Mary Susan could remember, sometime, being taken to a film once, in that boarded-up old building, with someone showing her to her velvet seat with a flashlight, and a little shop in a corner where you could buy ice creams in the interval . . . But she must have been young then, in the memory, and happy with anything, and besides it was probably just a dream like she'd had so many thoughts about things that she wanted to believe were real. Looking at the place now, with the front closed over and something wrong with the roof so that it was half coming down, you'd sure never believe it had ever been open. And that was what it was like here, what all of it was like.

She hated the empty streets too, the way there were never any cars going anywhere, that feeling you got in cities this time of day. Right now Mary Susan could imagine everybody would be leaving work and going home and getting changed to go out again. And it wouldn't be like summer there like it was still summer here. There, it would be a new and exciting season with different things in the shops to buy, different clothes.

Here, no one dressed up to do anything, always it was the same old clothes. Girls in their dumb print cottons, little baby skirts, and it was every day, every day the same. Mary Susan swore an oath she would never be like that. Like today, she was wearing shorts and a T-shirt with stars – printed silver . . .

*Head up.*

It had been her birthday present, that day with her mother when they'd got off the bus and in front of them had been a big department store all decorated with stars and silver flowers and the T-shirt right there in the window and they'd just gone straight inside and bought it. Same way she'd chosen her shoes – catalogue, sure, but still nothing like them round here. They were expensive too, but you needed to buy nice things, if you were planning some kind of future for yourself, you needed them. When school started again in two weeks' time she'd get some shift work at the supermarket, and maybe another job as well, and she'd save and save until she'd bought so many clothes no one would ever notice the difference between her and city girls, and by then she'd have saved enough to do Elena's modelling classes too, maybe, and Elena had said you could make three hundred a day, once you'd graduated – and that was just for starters. Mary Susan couldn't believe she'd worked that dumb kitchen job at the hotel for so long. That was a year ago she'd started doing stuff with her mother: potatoes, potatoes . . . What a stupid idea that had been anyway.

*Shoulders back.*

She was walking way ahead of her mother now, but she knew her hips were doing the right thing, that she was walking right and that the T-shirt was sitting properly on her front like it was supposed to.

*Shoulders right back.*

Elena had said she was the sort of girl who could really carry herself in that way, for bra work say, or any kind of under-wear. Mary Susan walked ahead a few more paces, very smoothly, and stopped, as if a photographer was there. She held herself quite still, while he took a picture.

*Click.*

Like she wasn't wearing anything underneath.

'A pretty little body . . .' That's what Elena said. And her mother, something like it. And Robbie Campbell, who could be her boyfriend if she wanted.

   'Give us a peep, Susie . . .'

Rolling his tongue around his mouth like he had a sweet.
'Go on . . .'
Only she didn't want to. With him.
'A pretty little body . . .'
And Margaret from the hotel had said it too.

Mary Susan felt goosebumpy thinking about it, how her shape might seem to some people. Like Margaret had always noticed her that way, like she knew how Mary Susan felt sometimes, standing alone in her bedroom undressing, seeing herself full-length in the mirror.

*A pretty little body . . .*

At least there was nobody at home who would want to look. Only a little brother, and he was too young to know anything. She could practise at home for hours if she wanted, down the hall, around the kitchen into the sitting room and back into her bedroom. She could practise modelling wearing nothing at all, only the shoes, Mum and Eric never knew she did that. Around and around and around, wearing nothing at all but the high thin shoes made of gold.

*'Pretty, pretty girl . . .'*

She imagined that feeling now, the feeling of modelling in her room. Certain words touching her, like Margaret used to sometimes come up behind her in the kitchen.

*'Look at you . . .'*

Just to remember made the goosebumps come back. Margaret with that dark lipstick of hers . . . everything about her so fancy. Like her stockings came from Paris, Mary Susan knew, from a special shop that only sold stockings. All Margaret's ways were fancy, so why come and live in this town? She stayed in rooms above the bar – lousy, tiny rooms – yet Margaret knew about the whole world. She had all the cities to choose from, but she chose here, she never left this place.

'I can teach you things,' Margaret had said, and she had taught her, how to walk, stand up from a chair. And she had shown her how to put that lipstick on.

*'Look at you . . .'*

Coming up close and filling in the colour, dark and wet like peeled plums . . .

Yuk.

Mary Susan would always feel goosey thinking about it. She was scared of Margaret now. She hadn't turned up for work for three weeks, got her mother today to quit the job for her entire. Anyway, too bad. She shouldn't be that scared. Margaret was old. Not like Elena, or her girlfriends at school. No real friend had that way of coming up behind you, that queer, quiet way.

Mary Susan turned, spinning on her heels. She saw her mother crossing the road to go up town, her bag already heavy-looking, even with no shopping in it, like it was full of stuff someone else had got her to carry. Mary Susan wished her mother wouldn't always carry something: bags, bags. She wished her mother would wear something pretty, didn't have to work in the first place in that dumb hotel. She saw that she had stopped now and was talking to Mickey Parsons, still holding that heavy bag, and Mickey was nodding his head, yes, yes, yes please, like he always did when people talked. Poor Mickey, like a little boy, and he was a man. Drooly stuff always coming out of his mouth.

'Yes, yes. Yes, please, Mrs Anderson . . .' she could see him saying.

'Yes, please . . .'

Mary Susan took three steps, like on tiptoe, and did the little spin again, and now there was Evelyn Parsons coming out of the post office and someone else behind her, Ray Weldon. He stopped to talk. He was wearing a faded red shirt, with the sleeves pushed up so his brown arms showed, and all the little golden hairs. Ray Weldon, him.

Mary Susan forgot the walk and ran up to meet them.

# FOUR

Ray knew.

Something in the smell, or the quick bits of sun flicking in and out of shadows down in the bush. Something in the wet smell there, of leaves going bad, but fresh growth, too, coming from under them, in little seeds under the damaged twigs, flowers even . . . He knew, there, down at the Reserve that morning, with the shift of heavy air like a body of air pressed close against him and the shade and light amongst the trees a pattern he wore as a mask on his own face.

He'd had no reason for being there. Driving down the narrow track that early in the morning great pieces of gauzy darkness were still lifting out of the dense tangled heart of the bush, even the birds in the trees quiet . . . He'd felt like a crazy man then. *Like night can't bear to leave here*, he had thought, and there was no fishing rod with him as an excuse, no gun, with the birds and animals sleeping, no reason at all to be down at the river that dark, secret time.

Even so, he'd found himself stopping the truck where he always parked it, getting out, standing in that dark. His shoes had sucked slightly, into the wet ground, and through his shirt he could feel damp from where small trees and branches had touched him. His eyes took in their shadowy forms, the thick slow flow of the river, but he didn't know in himself why he should be there in that place so full of memories. Then the smell had come up, that bad, sweet smell, and he'd caught the beginnings of sun forming tiny pools on the shallows of the water, pieces of light amongst the leaves overhead

. . . and then he knew all right. Francie was back. It was like he tasted the knowledge. She was back there amongst the sweetness, in the leaves, in the smell. At last, after all this time, she'd come home.

Ray had kept the knowledge in him during the long day that followed, kept it in, fresh knowledge. He didn't say a word or act differently in any way to anyone. Even now, standing outside the post office with Renee Anderson and poor Mickey Parsons and his mother, standing out here in the bare light with these people, he could still talk normally, could smile or laugh when their words required it.

'That's your girl over there, and so grown . . .' Evelyn Parsons was saying.

'How old is she, Renee, to be so tall?'

'Not old enough,' Renee said, 'as far as she's concerned . . .'

They laughed, Ray laughed.

'Kids seem to be that way,' he said.

Yet all the time, when he spoke any words, he felt in himself how to be there wasn't easy. Not easy to be standing there with the women when he was a man with such a taste in his mouth for memory, and the memory like having her now, gathered into him now, into his heart that was like a great moving, turning machine saying:

*Francie.*

*Francie.*

*Francie.*

'She's too skinny, mind,' Evelyn said. 'But a beauty, isn't that right, Ray?'

Sure nothing was easy when all he was thinking was so far from sentences and talk, but only how he used to be with her and how it was like music then, her bones and muscle like a web of string and keys around him, plucking, humming . . .

'Don't you know, she's to be a model soon?'

Her body moving, turning . . .

34

'What do you think of that, Ray?'

Like touch, like the vibration of sound . . .

'Ray?'

Like everything he could ever need.

There was the shift of someone beside him, one of the women moving a bag from one hand to another and he realised at that moment he hadn't heard anything anyone was saying.

'Ray?'

He'd listened maybe, but he hadn't heard.

'What's that?' he said now, and the effort of speaking the two words was like wrenching himself out of himself, so tightly had he been holding his face impassive, his arms so tightly folded against his chest to keep his loud heart in.

'Already a pretty girl . . .' Evelyn was saying, 'but a model, what do you think of that?'

Ray took a breath, quietened himself. He looked across the street to where they were all looking, to where a girl was standing.

'I don't know what she's telling everyone,' Renee said. 'Ignore it, I'd say. Anyway, models and nonsense, it can't be what Ray wants to hear about on a Friday afternoon.'

'Still,' Evelyn said, 'a pretty girl.'

'Yes, yes. Pretty, pretty,' said Mickey Parsons, his heavy head swinging from side to side.

'Pretty, pretty,' he said again, poor Mickey. A boy of a man in little boy shorts with his enormous body straining at the waist. He nudged Ray and winked.

'Yes, yes, eh? Eh, Ray?'

Ray nodded to him: 'Sure thing.'

He looked across the street again and there was the girl they'd been talking about, Renee's girl, and she was pretty enough, he supposed. She had the long, skinny legs that she would, in time, stretch out in front of a man as they lay down together on the ground, lean bare legs that would run towards a man to greet him. A man would enjoy those legs, as the girl would bend down to retie her shoelaces in front of him; or as she would bang a satchel against her legs as she walked beside him, he would enjoy the idle bang of the satchel against her calves. She might scratch an insect bite on her leg as she talked to a man, not even noticing the speck of blood that welled up on the skin like a tiny jewel. She could grow in time to be that girl who would lie beside someone she loved while behind her the river was a thick slip of blue amongst the trees, a girl so close you could see the lines of sun-oil going down her back from where the man had taken the tube of oil and made those lines on her, her skin so smooth and glazed with sweat and oil a man would want to bite into it, feel against his teeth the salt surface of her like she was meat. All that ahead of her, Ray thought, for some man . . . but not him. He would never feel those things more than once and he'd had the feelings once, he'd had them already. He'd used them all up in longing and sex, all the feelings you could have for a woman collected up in him to use and use and Francie had had them all, every other woman or skinny girl only ever a reminder to him of her, of how he must find her, only her, and this time keep hold of her wrists, his fingers circling them in bracelets, cuffs, that would hold.

Looking at Mary Susan now reminded Ray of all the years, how young he and Francie had been then, she probably around the same age as this girl was now, but nothing like Mary Susan in Francie's words and body, in her long naked-ness lying out on the flat white stones, river all over her skin. Laughing, like the light coming out from between leaves – that was Francie, not like this other poor kid, skinny and quiet, like she wouldn't say a word; no, Francie would be all laughing and kissing him, and bringing him down to her where she lay on the flat stone, long and wet along the side of his still dry body, making herself like a beautiful eel moving up next to him, flattening her smooth surfaces against his surface, like a beautiful moving eel her sex for him, her shining skin, her silent wet tongue.

*Francie . . .*

Ray pressed in his arms to himself.

*Francie . . .*

And harder he pressed them, against his body, as if to stop his heart.

This morning, down in the Reserve, the feeling of her had been more powerful for him than ever. She was something, Francie. No one else could ever come close. The way she used to talk, all her plans and ideas . . . No wonder she couldn't hold herself to this one small town. How many years ago it was since she had left it, with not a word of warning, yet it seemed to Ray like yesterday. So often he went down to the river to remember . . . certain days, celebrations – their little anniversaries of a year spent together, a month, a birthday maybe, end of term when she made As on all her papers, and it was like the time that had passed since then and now was nothing, it was nothing to him, it did not exist. He remembered when he gave her a piece of jewellery to wear, like an engagement, the light chain with the little pearl that hung from it like a tear.

'I love you,' she had said. 'I always want to stay with you,' but the twig she twisted in her hand snapped as she spoke, and he should have known then his fastening the light chain around her neck wouldn't keep her. He said he'd go to the city with her, that he'd get a job if the farm wasn't enough to pay, that he'd buy out his brothers and have all the land, if that was what she wanted, or none at all. He'd go south, north, wherever she wanted, if she didn't want to stay. Hell, they could go to India, to China, any faraway place that she could be happy in if that's what she wanted, for him to be with her.

'I love you,' she kept saying. 'I want to stay with you,' but she had not stayed.

The sun was waning in the last pale blue of the sky. Slowly, as the small group of people had been standing around on Main Street talking, Ray became aware it had begun to drop, and now, quite quickly was drawing down into the ridge of mountains that lay along the horizon line. It would be fine again tomorrow. The melted orange of the last piece of light made the mountains seem like paper, transparent almost they seemed, like thin, lovely, cut shapes laid out behind the hills, the far edge of land. All the acreage in the world, Ray thought, all the miles. All the farmland and high pasture, all the wilderness of burnt bush and dried grasses. All the blackened arms of felled trees that lay across paths no longer used, all the high, bare, shallow lakes no one ever saw, all the rivers edged with scree, bleached skulls of sheep, animals, sharp pieces of rock . . . all this dear country so known to him, so dear, but only an image, a print in his mind, not enough.

For even as they had lain together there had been the little damaged seeds; they were scattered around them. In the bush where they trod, damage, on the flat stones, tiny soft husks split. Even when they had slept, in the heat of the day finding shadow, even then they had had to break twigs, snap boughs to find their sleeping place, they had ground their feet into the dry earth and pulled roots to make a bed. Yet how he would love her, with the split twigs, and the brokenness and the little lost seeds, how he would love her though the separation was between them from the beginning, like a branch rent in two and him the piece that showed where it was torn, the green. She'd cried out and the little seeds scattered from pods the twigs held, falling nowhere, like beads or tiny links in a chain that could not be planted. How he would still love her, with the split twigs and the seeds that fell with no issue, how he would love her for ever.

Yet there had always been this thing about her that meant he couldn't keep her, that he couldn't have changed, that no one could have changed. It wasn't just that she was restless, that the town was too small, but that there was a kind of loneliness there, bred in from the start. It was from her mother, a woman who'd always lived alone, with only a daughter for company and the old simple brother down the road with his armfuls of flowers . . . Not enough of a family for a girl to stay in, and too quiet Ray thought, the way old Nona kept her daughter in. Sometimes he used to imagine just turning up at the house, knocking on the door and letting Francie invite him in to sit with her, and with Nona and Sonny if he was there. He'd just sit, Ray would, inside the house, maybe get offered something to eat, tap at Francie's feet under the table. He'd smile at her when the others weren't looking, maybe . . . But nothing like a visit ever happened. Instead, what occurred, out of need and frustration, and anger even, with desire, with not being able to get into where she lived, was that Ray could find himself at Francie's mother's house at night, late, when everyone was in bed, he'd find himself on the lawn by Francie's window, he'd look in on her sleeping. How he longed then to tap the glass to free her, so she'd wake, open the window and come out into the night with him. He never did it. He would just stand there a while until he felt the dark grass cold through his shoes . . . and then he'd go back down the garden, down the path to the road, along the road to where he'd left his truck parked . . . Then home.

All this was so long ago, and Francie had left; he was the one who didn't leave. Though all they'd had together were those times down at the Reserve, at dawn, or later, at noon, skipping school with the shadows of sun on their melded skin, still he'd known the landscape of her to be the only place where he could live. There could be nowhere else. Feeling out the cool rinsed inside of her mouth, like a lazy bather his tongue there, tasting river on her, from their swim, and smelling his own salty odour in the tangle of her wet hair. All the countries of the world he'd had with one woman, all the secret places when he was just a kid, when they were both just kids, and now she was back having waited for all this time no longer felt to Ray like weakness. Now it was something in him like power, the past, like something he could taste and smell and use.

He might be here, standing with the women in the road, these people he'd known all his life, standing with them and Mickey with his poor rolling eyes, all these people, all these things so deep in, yet none of them were connected. He might seem to be there with the others, look interested when someone asked attention of him. He might say the odd word, but all the time he was folding his arms hard in front of him only to keep his body in all its pieces together, only to keep his own loud heart in.

'Guess what?'

The girl, Renee's girl, was coming running over the road towards them.

'Guess what?' she said to Ray. 'There's someone come to town,' she said, 'and I never seen her before . . .'

Ray looked at her, and Renee, and Evelyn and the poor boy; they all looked at Mary Susan that moment, they seemed to wait, all of them, Ray thought, at that moment, as though their waiting inhabited all the moments of time. The light that had been fading was going out and a long shadow had formed in the road. Blue and grey were the colours of the air about them, the high sky touched with a faint mark of the last of the day, of gold.

'You sure?' Ray said, but he didn't have to ask.

He knew.

She was out there now, close. She was watching him this second, just round the corner, behind one of the trees that were planted along the street. Or she was on a swing in the playground, or sipping a milkshake in a paper cup, sitting on the steps of the library. Maybe she was down at the river, by the dark water, but she was close. He would wait for a while, with these people, he would stand with them a little longer, talking with them a little longer. He would let some time elapse, go home maybe, wait . . . and then he would find her. Mary Susan had already seen her. Ray would see her.

He lifted his bare arms right up over his head and stretched, and if at that moment a lorry had come rumbling down the street, the driver in the cab would have seen a man, no longer young, with his arms up and his head thrown back, like a man crying for something, calling for something, his arms stretched high above him like this man in the road was trying to pull the last of the light down from the sky.

# FIVE

You know that time of day. The light is fading, but not gone. The sky is still violet and clear, it is still high above your head and pale like shell along the horizon, yet you know it will be dark soon.

How is it to be outdoors then, in that half-light, in all that air? To be there in the road with the end of the day deepening into itself, minute by minute, second by second finding its own darkness, when the things you see are obscured by shadow, long strips of blue that form exits in the road where driveways used to be, turnings in places where you could see before?

Only strange. There may be the last of the sun's light in a streak of pale gold behind the mountains, fine lines of pale gold on ridges of the far hills. There may be warmth in the air still, held from the sun, three stars are out in the sky and you're here, right now, yet still you can't quite believe it. You don't really know, any more than you know the hour, or the kind of light that's forming around you, where you are, why you've chosen to be here. It's like the way you see some things very clearly at this time and others not at all. The branch of a tree you may see against the sky, or the bicycle leaning upon a low wall, but it's seeing as though you could read the pages of a book you were holding but even so not recognise the person waving to you from across the street . . . You are part of this time. You are here in the midst, caught in this half-light, and it's as if you're weightless now. As if, with the warm open air all around you, your own body has no density, no substance or form or bone to hold it to the earth but only hangs to the air like a paper shape. That's the time, then, when you hear your own breath against the paper, that you know that you've arrived here. You may have pulled the car up at this kerb, parked right here outside the post office which is closed for the day, but still there are a group of people standing outside the post office talking.

You've stopped, and you're just sitting, and these are people who live here, at this place where you are a visitor . . . Yet with the windows of the car wound down so you can smell the sweetness of the air, with the familiarity of the voices . . . you can feel that there are some things you already know.

'What do you think of that, Ray?'

The voices. Their voices.

'I don't know what she's telling everyone . . .'

That's how far you've come.

Stay.

## SIX

Harland had no thought of himself, only the building. Was its wood clean enough, were the rows of hard seating straight? Would the cracked backs hold good for another year, the lintel hold? Every Sunday he felt parts of the structure creak and bend beneath him when he walked about, moving down the aisle, testing the weight of the decorative cross. Even when he stepped up into the pulpit he could could feel it, the shift beneath his weight as though he were aboard a tiny, rotted boat on cold water and himself the only passenger.

The pen was in his hand, but these his thoughts, not the words he was writing. Though with word after word he had covered the page, elected the psalm, turned open the hymn book to find those verses that were most familiar . . .

*Thee we would be always praising*
*Pure, unbounded Love Thou art.*

There was no feeling there.

He had written: *Refer: Romans 1, verse 17 . . . Note: Here is revealed God's way in faith . . .* He had written: *See: Acts/mid-section . . .*
   Yet all the time, all through his working long hours at his desk, there were no thoughts for the phrases and lines that would fit, but only for the building that encased him. Only its walls, its black cross. Only it, this place.

This was where Harland kept most of his time now, no longer moving between church and home, bedroom and pulpit. He no longer visited his parish as he used to, most people too busy during the day anyhow, to stop and talk about devotion and love. It was a duty to them, the church where he kept himself apart, a duty that he himself used to attend with reverence and hope. Then, there had been the glories of trust, faith, the pen in his hand and ink running easily from the nib . . .

'Truly my heart waits silently for God,' said the psalm, and truly he did believe then, in the vine that was the Father, and the fruit of the Son. There had been for him Galatians, and James 3 and 4, the power and understanding in the messages of Matthew and John and in Luke. There were the prophets, the great songs of Jeremiah and the mighty thirty-eighth chapter of Job – 'Who is this, said God, whose ignorant words cloud my design in darkness?'

In those days he could believe, could remember all the passages of verse like they were the passages and channels of his own blood and breath coursing through his body . . . 'Brace yourself and stand up like a man, said the Lord; Where were you when I laid the earth's foundations? When the morning stars sang together who watched over the birth of the sea?'

Now Harland wrote:

*As Scripture says, 'He shall gain life who is justified through faith . . . '*

Then paused, rolling the pen between his thumb and forefinger. Faith. He rolled the pen between his fingers, backwards and forwards, backwards and forwards, as though rolling a cigarette freshly made, or rolling between his fingers the tiny fabric hem of a girl's dress . . . What faith? There was nothing for him in the words he'd written, just empty thoughts; he had no thoughts. The church was the only thing now, its white painted sides, the steeple fixed secure to the roof's green tile. He'd even helped Johnny Carmichael take down the entire spire last spring. Together then they had galvanised the long spine of metal at some foundry Johnny knew, straightening the backbone that had weakened and buckled over the years, making good the paintwork, using acid to get rid of the rust. And what was that thing Johnny had said to him then, when they'd been at work with the rust-eater, looking at him with those pale blue eyes? *Father?* That thing, that word, looking at him with those pale blue, drinking, loving eyes? *Father,* he'd called him, causing Harland's cool, pale skin to feel flushed, with God or tenderness or some strange sensation outside the bounds of his usual closed emotion. *Father,* he'd said. *Father, I'd know you to be the kind would want your church to be a fine thing, standing there against the hill for us all to see it, its lovely cross against the sky, Father. Father?*

And Harland had had to look away.

That had been last spring and the steeple now certain in its place, but Harland was as much a betrayer now as then. No more, no less. Nothing had altered since with his thin faith. *Faith.* Just to write the word seemed wrong, when it was a word that was itself the exact shape of the void one would have to have inside oneself for the word to fill, and he did not even have that shape carved out within him. He had nothing. Harland had nothing. He could not serve. He had nothing to give, no need within him to give from. He saw his own white, bony fingers taking up the pen to work it again across the page . . .

*Paul writes to the Romans not about necessity of belief, but about the necessities of faith . . .*

He saw the cotton cuff of his shirt, the sections on the paper marked out . . . *Ref. Acts/chapter 13, verses 47 to 50. Hymns 32, 17 . . .*

Words.

*Thanksgiving as Faith . . .*

*As Belief . . .*

Words, words, words. He had written all over the page with words, but no meaning in anything he had written, for what was any of it but words? . . . Like the word for faith, or for his heart. A word for something that was not present within him, to be named.

Harland laid down the pen, pushed back his chair. If these were his thoughts, if there was nothing for himself inside himself, then what temple? What God? He put back his head, closed his eyes to pray but saw only whiteness, like an empty page. Even the word of the hymn – *Praise* – would not sing in his whitened mind . . .

He didn't know how long he'd been sitting. There was the pen laid down, the stack of books and paper on the desk . . . It was getting dark.

*My God . . .*

Once again he had nothing to write for this Sunday. Not for any Sunday by now.

*My God . . .* Harland tried to pray again, and at that moment, outside the open window, something moved, he thought he heard it. Perhaps it was a branch snapping, or a twig underfoot. A quick breeze amongst the trees causing something to scrape against the white sides of the church, some small girlish breeze . . .

*Awake*, it said.

The breeze shifted, turned. Harland felt it pass through the window, across his arms, his shirt.

*Awake, north wind and come, south wind;*
*blow upon my garden that its perfumes may pour forth,*
*that my beloved may come in . . .*

He looked, and the air seemed to move in the room, as though the breeze were moving through the room, touching the room . . .

*While the day is cool,*
*and the shadows are dispersing,* whispered the breeze,
*turn, my beloved, and show yourself . . .*

Harland could feel everything. The touch of air, his skin . . . his body beneath his shirt alive, and a pulse in his blood that began to beat . . .

Somewhere in his mind, in his body, a memory was coming alive.

Somewhere . . . in this soft pulse of blood, something he thought he'd forgotten but it was in him now, unfolding itself in him now, and the words of the memory coming back to him, sweet and whispering in the breeze as the words of a bridegroom to a bride.

*Arise,* said the words, and they were words he had loved once.
*Arise my love, my fair one,*
*Arise and come away . . .*

He looked out of the open window and it was like the night long ago when he had looked out of the same window and he had heard the Spirit of God moving in the garden . . .

*Come with me, my sister,*
*Come with me, my bride . . .*

There had been the dark sweetness of the air, the softness of the night, the mighty Spirit of God gentled in the shift of leaves, in the part and weave of the thin branches of trees and the stems of grasses rippling and closing as though they were seas. Harland looked out now as he had looked out then and there was the blue sky, darker now, nearly night . . .

But nothing there. Only the endless pale blue deepening into violet, into indigo, and the warm, dark air. Only the outline of trees in the church garden, only the smell of grass and damp undergrowth gathering moisture for the coming night. Nothing more.

After all this time, how could there be anything more? For a dry minister to pray for and believe? How could there be fragrance in the air, a sweet stirring in the leaves? How anything at all to smell or touch or taste or feel? For a dry minister made of bone? It was a Friday evening and there would be another day to pass and another night before he would open his church up again to his congregation with nothing again to

48

fill it. The lovely sky itself couldn't fill it, nor the growth of
vines and trees, nor the smell of earth nor the run of river
beyond his window . . . Harland stood up to close it.
Something moved again. Across his face this time, like
breath.

'Katie?'

But he knew it wasn't his wife.

'Is it you?'

◇

Past the garden, past the high hedge that marked the garden,
the home Harland's wife had made stood strict and certain as
the church beside. It was a white house, square and clean-
sided, the kind of house with doors that would barely need to
be pushed and they would close to with a tiny click of lock.
The house had many doors, many rooms, but the people who
lived in the house would not use the rooms, Kate Harland
knew, for they were not a family to use them. She had heard
too many times the sound of that little click.

She listened for it now. Lying in the tepid water of her bath
as the light around darkened into dusk, into dark, she still
waited for the quiet sound of her husband returning as
though she were a bride. There would be the opening door
and the shut and silence behind it . . . Even after all this time
Kate waited for that sound as though it were something she
needed. The water cooled and closed around her body as she
lay, listening . . . for nothing. They would never be a family
here. How long, she thought, it had taken for her to confess
that fact to herself as truth. All the years she had spent, trying
to shape a home by her desires, choosing colour for these
bathroom walls, making curtains for the large windows that
were weighted at their hems with lead to hold them down in
a breeze . . . all the years . . . Even as she'd lined those same
curtains with dark felt to protect her rooms against the brightness of the sun as it fell in this part of the country, all the time,

everything she'd done had come to nothing. The bathroom was dark. The leaden hems of the curtains hung, and shaded were all the things within the rooms that Kate had ever bought or loved or made. The fireplaces were swept out and ready for use in the rooms she and her husband could never share.

She put back her head in the tepid water and closed her eyes.

*Nothing.*

Hard to imagine she had been that woman once. The woman who had tended and cared. Hard to imagine she had had passion, touch. She moved her head in the water and felt the weight of her hair moving with her, heavy like a hank of silk. Now she had only this, the wet of her own hair. She rose up again in the water and felt the weight of it painted down upon her shoulders and back. Such pride she used to have for her hair and her body, such feeling. She used to rise up like she rose up from the water now towards that man who was her husband . . . Hard to imagine it now. Now he was like a stranger, like someone she had never known . . . And yet, Kate had felt once, when he had brought her here as a girl, to this country town, that he was bringing her into all the world, as if she could have the world with the tall, young husband who had brought her, as if they could have oceans together, mountains, seas. She had thought she knew him then. She had thought, in those early years of their marriage, when she still felt new to him, that though they were miles from anywhere, from cities, or highways, from the high rolling hills . . . though they were miles and miles away, still she had everything she needed here, with him, everything to live and to have love here, in this place. Her feeling of the town then was like its name, a feeling of such disparate elements touching – like a feather drawn down Harland's cheek before she leaned down to kiss him, like her bare foot in his lap when he had taken a tiny stone out from her shoe and would feel along the fine bone of her foot with his finger, to touch the slightly blooded place where the stone may have hurt her. It was as if all the elements they could ever need would be contained within one marriage, all the elements she would need, he would need. She had turned towards him then, and how disparate were their surfaces when they touched, one from another, her bird breast feathering against him, against the lovely weight and edge of cut stone.

She put back her head so the ends of her hair would dip and pull again into the water . . . There, just to feel the weight of her hair she did it, to feel the slight tug and pull . . . there. She should know by now only this would be left, the swirl of her hair in this water, this dark. Even at the beginning of their marriage Harland would leave her, and she should have known then he would be someone who would always want to leave. Kate would still be lying in bed and he would get up, go into the hallway, down the stairs. She could hear him open the door, close it behind him as he left, to cross the grass with the shadow of the steeple upon it, to the church and his study there. Sometimes he wore only a loose gown around him when he left her, and she liked to imagine him sitting there in the study of his church, with just that fine piece of fabric to cover him, sitting there in the lee of the table with the wine and the bread, his body still warm from the bed and scented with her odours . . . She liked to think of him that way, imagining that as her husband worked he would be smelling her on his skin as she herself could still smell him on her. How in love they were, she had thought, how in love. He would stay there for hours in his room of books, to write, or to pray, and his gown would shift around his long, pale body as he sat there, dreaming about his God, and she would be lying in the bed where they had so recently been joined together, and she would be smiling with the thought of him, full of him inside her, dreaming herself about God who had been made to live in her, in the breathing, living idea of love: a family, the children that she and her husband would make together.

But that was long ago and now her faith was gone. Kate had felt it leave her, month by month, with every show of blood a little more gone, and a little more. The girl with the long hair had become this woman lying here in water and even to think of her marriage now was like thinking of something that had belonged to someone else. It came to be that on Sundays when she saw her husband standing tall and strong at the front of the church, she saw him more and more as a thing removed from her, like a strong, powerful bird that had been trapped, enclosed in stiff woven robes and held behind the carved bars of his wooden pulpit as though it were for him a cage.

'Let us praise God, let us sing!'

He would open his mouth to call the hymn, and she would open her mouth, to sing, but as Sunday went from Sunday, one month to the next, month after empty month, the words came to her but the tune was gone. Though he stood in his tall robes before her, she opened her mouth but something was lost in her body, drained away. Month after month after month, God leaving her body in red blood . . . So how could she, praise, or sing? How tell her husband, when he stood so tall and proud in his wooden cage before her, how tell him that there was no risen God, that his blood still flowed?

She was barren, dry. All the hours spent lying in warm water would not change it. Her house was dark and outside the house the garden she had made contained only grasses. No fruits were in the trees, no low flowers craved to open their petals wide against the soil. She would not let them. There would be no fragrance for this wife now, no light, no colour, no green.

◇

From where he stood at the window, Harland could see right out across the garden and he could smell in the sweetness of the air the river, like the scent of a woman's skin.

'Is it you?' he prayed again.

The dark trees sighed, *No*, the air moving like gauze through all their fine branches. No wife would come looking for him now, only a woman. Harland could sense her like she was a shadow, a woman insubstantial as a shadow, like the frail shadow that fell across Christ's back as he knelt that day in the sand, drawing pictures there.

'Is it you?' Christ had asked of the woman then, because in her shadow cast upon him was all God's love, and tenderness and shame.

'Is it you?'

And the shadow moved upon him, uncertain, and still Christ was kneeling there, not requiring from the woman's eyes the answer to his own frank gaze. And the answer came back from the shadow cast across him, in the dark across the corner of his vision:

'Master, it is I.'

The air rustled again outside the window, and again Harland had the sensation of someone so close, so close she could touch him, like he could feel her breath moving across his skin. He was stirred again, as he was before, stirred deep within him, by the touch, by the sensation of touch. The scent was still there in the air, close to him, watery, rivery, mingled with the scent of leaves and trees and grasses, the scent of a shadow, a thing too small and soft to ever be a wife.

Harland looked down at his hands in the darkness, the whiteness of his long fingers. He could not touch his wife. There were his hands, his fingers . . . and they were like an old man's hands and fingers, old and unused upon his wife's body. She would not come looking for him now. Not after all this time, all the years, all the nights . . . No wife could make him feel the way he felt now, with the pulse of blood within him the insisting beating pulse of the Divine. No wife, never a wife. Something in her had always made him want to turn away. From the moment on their wedding night when she'd unpinned a length of hair that she had kept away from him, tied up in some twist or plait at the back of her neck as disguise . . . He'd known, that moment when she'd let all her hair fall down her back into their bed . . . But by then they were married, and Harland could remember as he stood at the window in the sweetness of the evening, amidst the pulse of the warm, dark air, how he'd felt then . . . Nothing like a bridegroom.

He shivered, though it was not cold. He'd only been a young man when he married yet already there was nothing like that other, sacred love in the love he had for his wife, nothing like. Nothing like the spirit of love that could move through a man and change him, could come looking for Christ in the desert and find love there. That love was gone from him, his wife had taken it.

*My beloved*, she used to whisper to him, and he could feel the hiss of her breath against the back of his neck.

*Please . . .*

Harland shivered again, he would close the window now. The memory coming back to him would make him close it, close out the pleading of that whispering voice, the breath against his neck and the ghastly touch of her long, long hair . . . He would close the window always, if that's what memory meant, to bring something back to him only to show that it was gone.

*Please, please . . .* said the memory, and Harland felt a cry rise in him, like a sob, like he was a child, remembering, remembering, the sweet stirring of the air outside the open window like a caress, touching him, reminding him . . .

*Please . . .*

For he'd wanted love, always.

*Please . . .*

He'd wanted to be husband to his wife, to join with her in marriage as a man joined to a woman. He'd wanted to tell to his wife the words of the Spirit of God and believe in the words, in the sweet taste and fruit and milk, in the wine of the words.

He had prayed, *My God, My Father* . . .

The bridegroom had prayed . . .

But God never took up his body and made it flesh.

*Help me*, said the bridegroom, but there was no help.

◇

By now it was so dark in the bathroom Kate could barely make out the lines of her body in the water.

The summer had been too long. There had been no change or variation within it. The curtains in the drawing room had remained closed, blocking out the day, the endless bright of light and sunshine that persisted, day after day, every exact day the same. There was a hardness to the season like the hardness Kate felt on her face when she smiled, a smile that seemed to fix in the light when she came outside, when she had to be out in that harsh, hot air. On these occasions, when she had to go shopping in town, to get petrol for the car, she felt the light upon her, burning and fierce, and came to be more and more exhausted by every little thing she had to do. All the time she had to spend out there in the light with the wives of the town tired her, more and more she became tired and old. There would be these women standing next to her, all these women who were wives and mothers, who wanted her time for meetings, for talk . . . these women with their children in church every Sunday, wanting to plan and decide with Kate about harvest festivals, birthdays and baptisms . . . She felt herself to be only a shape beside them, a worn-out shape like an empty bag, while the women bore about them all the fruits of their motherhood, all the ambitions of their fertility that came to rest in the church pews each week. They would close in then around Kate, after the service –

'Come and see me this week, Katie . . .'

'Could you visit tomorrow?'

'Are you free any time after Tuesday?'

And Kate had no choice but to drive to the farm that was thirty miles out of town, or take the walk to the house with the washing billowing on the clothesline by the paddock.

'Of course,' she would say. 'Of course, of course, of course . . .'

And no one knew how hard it was, to be there in the women's houses, with her hard little smile. There were the boxes and toys piled up on the floor, the kitchen an overspill of ice cream and milk, glasses of orangeade . . . and always, there were the children. The gardens of these women were full of children, like the flowers that grew there, the flowers that seemed so bright they hurt Kate's eyes, the snapdragons and geraniums, the endless thick tangle of roses and marigolds and pinks, the endless, endless flowering. Often the children would be running around the gardens when Kate arrived in her ironed dress, they would be running and calling and singing out.

'Hello!'

'Hello!'

'Hello!'

Like bells the children's voices in the air, and as the children called out, their mothers would talk, pouring out cups of tea and rattling biscuits from a packet onto a plate . . .

'Have one of these . . .'

Pushing the strands of hair back from their faces, smiling . . .

'Lovely to see you, Katie . . .'

Not even noticing the running call of their bright children all around them, running in and out of the flowers, dirt on their hands, sticky faces, their melted ice creams . . . They never noticed.

Across the country lawns and flower beds, from the paddocks that edged the house where the horses were, or a few sheep . . . the children came. The children, the children.

'Hello, Mrs Harland!' they sang out from their games, and sometimes one would approach, Kate would feel the touch of a sticky hand patting her arm –

'Excuse me, excuse me . . .'

Or she would feel simply a presence, a small dampish body pressed up close against her clean dress –

'Excuse me . . .'

'Excuse me, Mrs Harland . . .'

'What is it, then?' she would ask, taking the small hand in her own, and it would be a cake or a glass of juice, or a promise they were after, always something that was the price of holding one of those tiny hands, always a price, something, to remind her that she could never hold the hand and keep it.

'Mrs Harland, can we have a Sunday school picnic this year?'

'Can we have a party?'

Always something.

'Can we do a Bible show?'

And no one ever noticed. How hard it was to be out there in the sunshine with them.

'Mrs Harland?'

'Mrs Harland?'

To be out there in the garden with its bright flowers and the sticky, dirty, dear, lovely little children . . . No one knew.

For Kate it sometimes felt as though all the children that could ever be born were there in the garden with her on those days. The tiny children, the babies. The toddlers, the crawling children, older children. Children who were nearly grown but still they gathered around her as if she could give them something, as if she could give them anything at all. The older girls wanted to talk about hairstyles or sewing or what kind of lipstick they should wear.

'Can you teach me, Mrs Harland?'

'Mum won't let me use the machine here because it's too old . . .'

'I have a pattern cut out.'

Kate remembered all of it, every single word the children formed, every laugh, every song, all the sentences of all the children, all the boys, the girls. It was like it was her fate to remember. There had been Robert Wilson last week wanting to set a date for a sports day, Karen Graham asking if she could join the choir. It was Renee Anderson's girl who had talked to her about the sewing.

'If you could teach me, I'd be so happy,' she had said, and she was such a pretty girl she would have all the boys and babies she would ever need, all the children she would ever want running after her amongst the flowers . . .

'Of course,' Kate had said, and how she'd felt her smile harden in the light that day, with the girl so full of life and the future beside her.

'Of course I'll teach you.'

She looked down upon her own body now, that darkened, empty shape. As if she could teach any girl anything. The summer had been too long, and she was old. Below her, the house with its curtains drawn waited for the night. It should be darker, cooler, but even now, at the end of the season there was still heat left in the day. Kate could feel it in the thickened air around her, and in the shadows. Her body seemed itself to be a shadow, all empty shadows across its surfaces, her belly and throat, the marks of her breasts shadows, between her legs a shadow's mark. That was who she was now, what she had become, this dark thing. Her husband with his white body was too bright for her, after all the dead years between them, too much light in him. Even if he were to give himself to her she couldn't use his hard brightness now when she herself had gone to dark.

◇

Outside, the garden, the lawns, the trees, folded into black. It was late. Harland was tired. The thoughts that he had needed for his sermon had not come, only other unwanted thoughts; he could not bear them. He went to close the window for a second time against the thoughts, against the feelings those thoughts had brought him . . . and stopped. The air was too sweet to close away, too gentle, too soft, darkening in the silent, lovely enclosure of grass and trees, too sweet and lovely. He breathed in the sweetness, he closed his eyes . . .

*While the day is cool and the shadows are dispersing,*
*I will go to the mountains of myrrh*
*and to the hills of frankincense.*

And with his eyes closed he thought of his wife.

*Come down from your hillside, my bride.*
*Come down with me from the hillside, hurry down . . .*

He thought of her as he had thought of her before she was his wife, and the words of the song were coming back to him now with his thoughts, the words fully formed within him, moving and turning and reaching out into the dark air around him.

*Your lips drop sweetness like the honeycomb, my bride,*
*syrup and milk are under your tongue,*
*and your dress has the scent of the hills.*

If he could just keep these words, if he could hold them, if he could go to his wife now with the words full in him, taking him up, bearing him up . . .

*Awake, north wind, and come.*
*Come south wind;*
*blow upon my garden that its perfumes may pour forth,*
*that my beloved may come to his garden*
*and enjoy its rare fruits . . .*

He felt himself to be so close, like a scent that has been stopped up and is now released like myrrh, like oils of spice. He was so close now, to God, to his divine love.

*I sleep,* love breathes to him, and her breath is warm against his face . . .
*I sleep but my heart is awake.*

Suddenly the heat in the room became unbearable. Harland felt as though he couldn't breathe. With a wrench he pulled down the window as though to pull it down against the heat, pulling it down against the words that were everywhere, in the air, in his mind, pulling it down, now, now, against the heat, against the sweet, fragrant heat of the air. He flicked on the light switch and the room sprang into relief, vivid in its outline. There was the pen he had been rolling between his fingers lying on the desk, the top still screwed on tight; no ink had touched the nib. This was real, this. This empty room. The empty page. Not words. He had written nothing, that was real. Those other words . . .
*My Beloved . . .*
*My Bride . . .*

They were not real, they couldn't be real. He would always close the window against those words, he would keep it closed against them.
*My love . . .*
*Please . . .*

For he could not bear them, he could not bear their touch.

With the light on Harland left the room. He walked, then ran across the garden to the house. It was completely dark now, the day was over. Only the light from the church was flung down as a yellow square upon the grass, before him the house was in shadow. Still Harland ran towards it. The door was open.
*Open to me, my sister, my dearest . .*

Everything inside was quiet. It was a house, but it was as if no one lived there.
*. . . my dove, my perfect one . . .*
No one.

He was so quiet as he came in. Kate was still upstairs, but the water was cold now against her skin. He was so quiet, yet she heard him moving inside.

*My beloved . . .*

She heard him come inside.

*I have stripped off my dress; must I put it on again?*
*I have washed my feet, must I soil them again?*

He was inside, in the hallway, by the door.

*When I arose to open for my beloved,*
*my hands dripped with myrhh . . .*

She heard him reach into the china bowl on the hall table for the keys.

*My beloved . . .*

Seconds later, she heard the car move off down the drive.

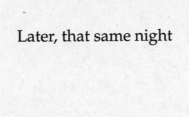

Later, that same night

# ONE

Johnny was thinking how by hell bright it was indoors. How it must be dark outside, he was thinking, or maybe he said it to Gaye. How dark, or bright. Couldn't be sure what he'd said really for the drink he'd been on, been on it some time now, since Margaret opened, and bright it was now, hell, and late.

'What time did we come here, love?' he said, but his wife didn't answer at first; she didn't hear him.

'Eh?'

He touched her at her elbow.

'Eh?' he said again, but she was talking probably, sitting there with him at the little table but not hearing, talking like everybody else was talking, and the lights so bright Margaret must have all the bulbs burning up at 100 watts apiece.

'Eh? Gaye?' Johnny said. 'What time . . .?'

Gaye turned to him then; she was laughing.

'What's that?'

The beauty. Just look at her, Johnny thought, laughing there, laughing at some damn thing, something somebody had said, something some other joker had said, to make her smile.

'What were you saying?' Gaye was asking him now, and she was still laughing, she was wiping the tears from her eyes.

'Ah, God . . .' she said. 'What's that you were saying, Johnny love?' She laughed again. 'You know,' she said, 'you should listen to this guy . . .' She nudged someone she was sitting next to. 'Johnny, he's got a story about builders, I tell you

65

. . . You'd love this. What was your name again, sir? I'd like you to meet my husband . . .'

Johnny looked beside her and he saw a skinny type of fellow sitting there, a skinny, bony type of fellow in a suit, someone passing through, one of Margaret's, taking an upstairs room.

'George Carstairs . . .'

The fellow put out his hand, and Johnny of course would take it.

'John Carmichael,' he said, straight up.

'My husband,' said Gaye. 'Now tell him, please, George, that thing you told me. Tell my Johnny about your builder, will you, Mr Carstairs? He'll laugh as much as I did myself and more, I know it, by God . . .' She shook her head, smiling, like she was saying *no, no, no*, but smiling at the same time, like she was a young girl. She took another look down at her shandy, then picked it up and sipped daintily from the glass.

'Ah, Johnny . . .' she said.

And *ah*, right back at her. For didn't he just love his wife then, at that very second of her lovely life, didn't he, Johnny? Didn't he just love her, with her smile and her laugh, and her coming to the pub with him on these nights, just so? Easy it was as much fun as having the boys here with him, and they were here too, somewhere, by God, in this bright room, somewhere, and the grandchildren, running about like little larrikins outside someplace, down the driveway, running around outside in the dark.

'Gaye, love . . .' Johnny said, and there was something right then in his thoughts, a thing that made him think he had something to say, a particular thing, something, but the drink was kicking in now good and proper, too much drink, but who cares? It was great to be here with his lovely girl, and the boys, and their little ones somewhere outside in the dark.

He tried again.

'What time we been here, love?'

But that wasn't the thing. It was something else, more important, like if it was time they should be getting home now, getting the kids home . . . or whether he was drunk by now, or just a bit tired, that was all, and the many glasses lined up along the table . . . Hell, it could be anything, anything to do with drink, and either way, he'd take another, if Gaye would. He would. She smiled at him again, shook her head, Johnny saw, laughing again at that same funny, skinny joker.

'Really, Johnny. You should hear this man . . .' she said, and she touched his arm, and maybe that was the thing, just there. For didn't he just love her again then, for the touch, for her gentle touch? For her hand that she laid upon his arm and the ring there she wore on her lovely hand, that he'd given her himself a long enough time ago now, if you added up the years, long enough ago, and he'd give her the ring again, if he could, over and over he'd like to give it, just to keep her smiling, the darling girl, just to keep her with him, here in the bright, with all the lights burning, and his friends here and the noise and the drink, and the laughter too, the joker's story, all of it, keep, for his wife's touch, for her lovely smile.

It was dark outside, there was the sound of children's voices. It was the grandchildren, through the open window Johnny could hear them, they were out there running around in the dark. It would be warm enough for them though, he thought, like it could be still summer for them, Rosemary and Kenny's kids, Robert's older two and the twins . . . It wasn't time, after all, made the nights go in. It was the season. The change, summer coming to an end but night still warm like a blanket, to wrap all the little ones in.

How old were they now? He was trying to think of their ages. Old enough anyway to come out with the funny stuff. They'd have him on, all right, always wanting something; money, that's what they'd been after before, when they'd come into the bar before and were crawling all over him.

'Hey, my grand-daddy, hey, hey, hey . . .'

That had been young Mikey and his sister, crawling all over him like a pair of little monkeys.

'Will you give us a something, Grand-daddy? Will you? Will you?'

Just as well Margaret didn't mind them. Just as well she wasn't bothered about kids coming into the pub the way a lot of people might be. Good for her. Good for Margaret. She ran a great place here.

'Can I take a bag of them peanuts, Johnny? Will you let me buy them?'

Not that a pub was a place for kids, of course he knew that, but still, wasn't it great, though? Margaret letting them all come in? The little ones? With that kind of hair children have and no one else has it. That kind of fine lovely hair, like the wee girl Marty had it, just like her mother with her fair hair, like her own granny's had been once, so fair.

'You can have anything you want, my darling,' Johnny had said to the wee girl, and she'd been there, sitting up like a fairy upon his knee.

'Have all my coins, my darling,' he'd said, and he'd stroked her lovely hair, and when was that now? When the children had come in? He was just trying to think of it, the time, but just as well anyway Margaret hadn't minded, that she hadn't minded a bit about the lovely children coming in.

The boys had done well, sure enough. Kenny and Robert. Four each, and that's what their mother always wanted. There was Craig still running around with the Carter girl, but it looked like they were going to marry and there'd be more babies there, soon enough, and John – well John was young yet, plenty of time for John. Sure, plenty. Johnny felt in his pockets for some money. Plenty, plenty. Plenty time enough, too, to get another round in, just anything at all. He was full up with it, he was, with the feeling of his family growing, his only family growing and filling up the town around him, and the little ones out there now in the dark, sucking on cans of pop and sweeties . . . He'd just get them all in now and buy them whatever they wanted, along with his whisky and beer, and Gaye's shandy, and her packet of salties. He put his arm around her –

'Can I be helping you to another drink, my love?' and right then, across the room, across the room full of his dear family and his friends, he called out, 'Margaret! When you get a minute, my darling, we're over here!'

◇

By the time he was walking towards the open door, in his arms a cardboard box of all the treaties for the children Margaret had put there, by the time he felt the warm, dark, outside air on his face . . . Johnny knew then it was late enough. Late enough, sure, late, late, even without a watch on, late. He wondered where John had got to. He'd seen Craig, and the older two, but where was John? It was usual they'd all be here together on a Friday night, all of them; they'd all meet up in the Railton on a Friday, so why not John? The drink in him by now was complete and he wanted all his darling sons here with him, that was just it, all of them, so.

He called out, 'Hey!' in the direction of where he'd heard before the little voices in the dark. He called out again, 'Hey there!'

'Hello! Hello!' came back to him, out of the darkness.

'I can see her!' Johnny heard.

He called again, 'Hey! Where are my Carmichaels?' and then there was a running and a calling out, and suddenly there they all were before him, all around him like chickens.

'We been playing,' Marty said. 'We found a lovely lady . . .'

69

She was hopping on one foot, then the other foot.

'We found her, we found her. We did.'

'Grand-daddy . . .'

Little Pat put his arms up then, to be picked up, but Johnny couldn't do it, not with the box in his own arms.

'Give me a minute, son,' he said, and he went to put the box down on the grass beside him. Carefully he leaned over with it, carefully to put it down, when he became aware of something, a figure out there in the driveway with him. He straightened up and took a step towards it, a tall kind of shape but hunched over, crouched over it was, on the grass at the edge of the driveway, no, it was sitting. Johnny's eyes could make it out more truly now, the shape of the figure, and it was a man, it was the minister's shape sitting there, his back resting up against a big stone that marked the edge of the driveway, the minister. Johnny took a couple more steps towards him, to be closer, and he saw bottles of beer on the grass all around the man, and glasses there.

'Hey,' Johnny said, but not to the children now.

'I saw her first!'

'I found her!' came their voices.

'It's Mr Harland,' Johnny said.

He was forlorn. Johnny could see, straight away, the man was deep in. The children were close by and Johnny knew they were there but he was not thinking of the children now.

'Grand-daddy! Grand-daddy!'

'We want to show you who we found!'

For now was not the time for treaties and games. Not with the man here at the side of the grass, the sad, forlorn man, Johnny thought. He thought the man might be drunk. He had these eyes, these hollow eyes, black eyes. Eyes that said: *What in God's name have I done?*

Johnny felt his heart skip a beat. Immediately his mind was back upon the grandchildren: where were they? Suddenly it seemed quiet all around him. Where were they that they had run from the man in terror? Johnny stirred himself, stumbled in the gravel. He knew he too was drunk, drunk that he could be down there himself against the stone with the minister, drunk and the glasses so scattered, he would break them against his foot. He would break them, do anything to protect the children, and where were the children now? Then there was a rush, a sound again of voices –

'I found her! I seen her!'

'I love her!'

– and there they were again, the one coming towards him now on the bicycle, and another two with the twins and the wee girl running beside.

'Is the box for us?'

'Can we take it away with us for to play?'

They were all around him again, like they'd been around him before, touching him, trying to reach out to the box he realised he was still holding in his arms.

'Here you are then,' he said to them. 'Wait . . .' and he started to take the bits from the container, the bottles of pop Margaret had put there, and the chocolate bars. He took them out like he was Santa Claus and one by one taking the things out from the box.

'For you,' he said. 'For you. For you.'

Of course the minister would not harm the babies. He loved God. He could never harm. He might have no children of his own to love, but even more so that would be why he would love the babies, he would baptise them. He would say the words of love to them, straight out from the Bible, and he would make prayers for them, and he would sing to them like Johnny himself had been sung to when he was a baby.

*The Lord bless thee and keep thee,*
*The Lord make His Face to shine upon thee,*
*and be gracious unto thee.*

Father, my father. He knew it. May the Lord be gracious. And mustn't he be drunk by now, though? To be thinking on the song for babies . . . drunk. The air informed him. Nothing like leaving a crowded bar to be so informed. In there, in the bright lights, with the noise going on all around he hadn't been noticing for true how the drink was taking place within him, hadn't been, but now . . . out here with the children and with the minister and with the air . . . Johnny felt sick suddenly, with the drink, like it had taken all his blood right out of him, given him back whisky instead, and beer.

The box empty of the treats, he threw it on the grass and sat down himself next to it, next to Mr Harland there on the grass. Just so. And what of it? The kids had their sweeties, he heard them running away.

'Where are you?' he heard them calling, calling to someone, who was it? He didn't know.

'Coming to find you!' they called, and he saw them running away and he saw them stopped, gathered together in a bit of light flung out by the open door of the bar.

'Thank you!' they called out to him then, from the light across the dark.

'Thank you too, my own grand-daddy,' called the littlest girl, and Johnny thought how her face would be covered with chocolate by now, and it would be down the front of her dress, and that would make her mother mad, wouldn't it though, it would make her cross.

'I'm going to give a sweetie to the lady!'

'All right, my darling,' he heard himself answer right back to her, across the night air, and just wanting now to close his eyes, just for a minute, to sleep . . . and what was that the wee one had said about the lady?

'Don't be giving anything away!' he called out, but didn't know anyone could hear, the children were gone, it was quiet.

Quiet, quiet. Quiet everywhere, only himself and the minister beside, slumped up against the stone. The poor man could do nothing, he could do nothing. He couldn't move. Johnny couldn't help him. There was just quietness and the dark, and anyone could think about sleeping now, sleeping like the man beside seemed to be sleeping, but then out of the quiet, out of the dark, came the sound of his voice and Johnny heard him begin to speak.

'What is love,' he said, 'if we cannot touch it or taste it, if we cannot feel it, like the sun upon our backs, if it fails to put its arms around us, then what is love? If it cannot give us, like a baby's cry may give us, a feeling of its own need, then what is love? Then nothing. It is nothing.'

The words stopped. Johnny listened, but it was quiet. There was no more sound. The man tried to turn, as though he was trying to turn away, but his body was too painful to move. Then Johnny saw him bring his hands up to his face and cover his face, like his hands were a cloth there, to cover, and he wanted to say something to the man, he wanted to help him, to say something, but he didn't know what to say. The empty glasses he'd been drinking from were all around him and Johnny went to shift some of them, for them to be away from the man's feet, but he couldn't do that, he couldn't move himself to help, he couldn't even do that. Sure none of it was right. None of it. To be here, and with the glasses. And what could he do anyway? What could Johnny say? It was an idea for fools for him to be trying to talk to a minister, when he was the man who had fixed the church roof scarce a year ago and having to stay sober too, for the time he did it. What could he say now, to a minister, when here he was drunk, and yet the minister was drunk too, Johnny was sure of it, so surely there was something he could say, for comfort.

'Mr Harland, sir . . .' he began.

'Father . . .'

Then he stopped. The man had uncovered his face. There were the dark, hollow eyes Johnny had seen before and looking at him, looking only at him.

73

'I don't know . . .' Johnny said, 'I wouldn't know, but I would say your wife loves you, sir.'

He shifted on the grass a little, towards the man. If he could just speak something, say something.

'I would say she loves you, Father,' he said, and still the man didn't move and there were just these eyes on him, eyes empty like the man would never speak again, but then he did move, he edged himself across the grass, and when he was close enough that he could put his skinny hand on Johnny's hand and close his hand over . . . he spoke then.

'Your wife loves you,' he said. 'You have love.'

The hand clawed on Johnny's hand, like it wasn't a man's hand.

'You', the minister said, 'have love. You have its body. You have its heart.'

Hell though but it was cold then, though it was warm. Cold, hell. Like ice. Johnny could feel the man so close to him like a coldness, with the words, cold, and the grip of the man's hand on him.

'She's gone,' he heard one of his children cry.

'She's gone and I can't find her.'

Johnny could feel the man's grip tighten upon him.

'You . . .' he said.

'I can't find her!' came the child's voice again.

'I can't see where she's gone!'

'You . . . have love.'

Johnny felt a great shiver go down him, like he was cold but it wasn't cold. Still he shivered like he'd been brought out of ice-water for it was true, the minister's words, how he did love his wife, how he loved her, he loved her. He loved her as she would be now, standing there in the bar, or sitting, as she had been sitting before, beside him. How he loved her, her warm touch on him, and her lovely face. Her soft hair tied back, and how Johnny wanted now, this minute, to be with her now, away from this man here and this feeling of cold,

74

and the man's hand and the lost cry of the children. How he wanted to be away from it all, the night, and with Gaye now, so he could place his hand there at the back of her neck, where her lovely soft hair was tied with a band, to lean over and kiss her there. He'd be getting into the truck, and he would have given her the keys so she could drive, sitting there beside him, driving them both home . . .

Home. The sweetness of that word. All the sweetness in the word, in the boys and the children and the boys' lovely wives . . . all of them. Home. And the poor man here with his empty glasses, what did he know about home, the poor man? What did he know that Johnny could give him from his own richness, something for the man's desert that would allow a flower there to grow? He had his family, his wife, his sons, he had his four boys . . . and nothing but richness in his home, in his boys. Robert. Kenny. Craig. John. The sons borne to him by the woman Johnny would keep and keep and keep safe for ever. There Robert. Kenny. There Craig. There John. John.

At that moment, as if the angels had brought him clean out of the air, John appeared before his father in the darkness.

'Uncle John!' came the sound of the children's voices.

'Uncle John, come and play!'

'Daddy?'

John leaned down to greet his father.

'What you doing there on the ground, Daddy?' he said, and there, Johnny looked up towards him, for there it was again. Richness. There his lovely boy, there he was, large as life, and Sonny Johanssen with him, standing behind him, behind his boy, his favourite of all the boys, Johnny's Darling, he used to call him.

'Hey . . .' Johnny said to him now. And then, remembering, 'Say hello to the minister here . . .' He turned to Harland. 'Father,' he said, 'this is my boy . . .'

But Mr Harland did nothing. He sat with his head bowed.

'Father,' Johnny said again, and then he heard the sound, the quiet sound that he knew the man was weeping.

*Oh, God . . .*

Johnny could hear him.

*Oh, God, oh, God, oh, God . . .*

'Wait . . .'

Out from behind John stepped the old man, Sonny Johanssen.

'Let me . . .' he said, and he put his hand out towards the thin figure on the ground.

'There now,' he whispered to him, as though to a child, and he put his hand softly upon the child's head.

'There now . . .'

The act was small, Johnny saw, and yet such tenderness was in it. Tenderness . . . in the older man's touch towards the younger man, and in how the younger looked upon the older, how his eyes were turned up towards him . . . Johnny saw . . . He saw as though he were in a dream . . . the hand upon the head, the touch, and, at that moment, he didn't know, but something else too, something of movement in the air, like a woman's papery skirt catching on a warm breeze, and a beautiful scent was there, like pefume.

*The Lord Bless thee and keep thee,*
*The Lord make His face to shine upon thee.*

All these things, shifting, in Johnny's vision, he saw, all these things taking place before him in the dark night air full of things and gentle, gentle . . .

There was a cry: 'I see her!' then, 'Gone!'

The night was empty again. There was just the dark, and the stars. Just the light and smoke and the voices crowding out from the pub's open door . . . just the sounds of Johnny's own breathing, his heavy-drinking breathing, and the lovely airy sounds of his grandchildren playing, calling.

'Where are you?'
'Where are you?'

Yet through the sounds, through all the sounds of the dark and the barefooted playing in the dark, through the sound down the gravel driveway, like someone running lightly down the gravel driveway and away, Johnny heard the minister whisper 'Thank you' to Johanssen, and he heard the old man's sweet sigh. *Home*, Johnny thought then, as he closed his eyes.

## TWO

The bar was emptying out. Last rounds. Margaret had that deep tiredness from working but she was excited too. She could feel the ride of her underwear, the touch of it, of those little pieces of silk.

'When you get a minute . . .'

Ray Weldon put his whisky glass forward.

'I guess one more can't hurt me.'

He smiled, that was Ray. He'd been standing up at the bar for the last part of the evening, drinking hard, drinking whisky and watching her, Margaret liked to think, watching her like all the men were watching her tonight. The empty feeling she'd had before was gone and she felt shining now, and smooth all her surfaces, her beautiful silken surfaces.

'Sure, Ray,' she said, and she let her hand touch his, just briefly so he'd barely guess she'd done it.

'Anything at all,' she said, and she turned to pour the whisky so he could see the long curve of her back against the pattern of glasses and bottles on the shelf, so he could think about her, imagine just how she might be.

*Hey, Margaret . . .*

Ray Weldon. Ray.

*I just can't stop watching you . . .*

That was how she felt tonight, that the men couldn't help but watch her. She was wiping down the bar with a warm cloth, drying the bar, and her mood was high. She was going to finish up soon, start tidying and think about closing the place. Minute by minute people were leaving. The open door gaped into the dark night sky, and she could hear voices: 'Good-night!', 'See you!', Gaye Carmichael calling, 'Night, Mar-garet!' on her way out through the door.

'See you tomorrow, Gaye . . .'

Margaret reached up to a top shelf to replace a couple of glasses, and there it was again, the pull and fit of the tiny pieces of silk. There . . . and there.

'Night, Margaret!'

'Goodnight!'

She was feeling really good.

'Goodnight, sweetheart!'

'Goodnight!'

She hadn't thought before that she could feel this way but now the underwear was telling her, yes, that she was quite something, wasn't she, Margaret? She was quite a little piece. She was running a great place here, a great bar, and she could handle them all, all the men who came in. It didn't matter who they were, or what they said or did, she could handle anything, anyone. It was coming together and she was riding, she was really good . . . and the earlier thing, that thing with the girl – forget it, forget the girl, she was the girl. She looked at herself, there in the mirror, smoothing a strand of hair back behind her ears, smoothing down the front of her cranberry-coloured shirt, cranberry wine. Of course she was the girl. She was spe-cial, the one all the men liked to ask for, wiping their mouths after their first sip of beer with the backs of their hands.

'How are you tonight, Margaret?'

'How's business tonight?'

She could take them all on. The hours that had been ahead of her before, when she'd stood alone in an empty room, were dissolved now, disappeared into the smoky light and there was only the future left, unrolling like a gorgeous long ribbon of men and scent and cigarettes and whisky and Margaret's red, red lipstick smile.

*Beautiful.*

That's how she felt.

Late and tired and beautiful.

Now the place was emptying out, she could start to think about going upstairs. More and more Margaret could feel that something was going to go on upstairs. She looked down at herself, where she was standing, at the cranberry length of herself, and she could feel it in every single inch. Something. She smoothed her skirt and looked across to the table where the Carmichaels had been, and there he was, just sitting there like he'd been all night, like he was waiting for her. Margaret remembered him from last time, and yes, it was possible, she thought, with him, she could have him. Earlier that afternoon, when she'd checked him in to the hotel, she hadn't decided at all what she was going to do, she'd simply greeted him as someone she recognised. 'Nice to see you again,' she'd said, but she hadn't been special to him in any kind of way. He wasn't a particularly nice one, or good-looking, or with that washed soapy smell she liked. He could be funny, she remembered that from last time, he could make her laugh, but even so, she hadn't been sure how she was going to feel later, at that time when she'd checked him in, she hadn't been at all sure . . . and then there'd been that thing with Renee and the girl. It came back at her again, like a little knife. The girl's voice out in the open air, the cut and glint of her legs as she'd walked away . . .

*Thanks, Mum . . .*

*Shhh . . . she'll hear.*

*Don't care.*

A knife.

There, right then, Margaret decided. She looked over at the table, at Jim or George or Bill or whatever his name was, and decided right then, that it might as well be him. The image of the girl was in her like something that could cut, quickly, quickly, little cuts that could make her bleed. Do it now, went the little cuts. Quickly now, decide it now, now, before the image could cut her more. Now, with Jim or George or whatever his name was, whatever any of their names were . . . do it now, like she always did it, to stop the cut, to stop the bleed . . . now, always now. Do it with Jim or George, or when any of them had finished going out and selling their bits or bolts or books or whatever it was they had in their black bags to sell . . . Do it then, between the time when they went to their rooms for the night and the next morning when they left again, do it then, do it, do it.

Margaret took a breath, it was working.

*Yes.*

There was a staunch, calmness could come back in. She breathed in, deeply into herself. The emptiness could be filled. She could be filled.

*Yes.*

She breathed in again. The emptiness was gone and her plans for the hours ahead could unroll as a ribbon would unroll, through the contours of her body desire unrolling . . .

*Yes.*

*Yes.*

*Yes.*

Like one long, silken piece.

She looked across the room and *yes* again, and soon. The Walkers were still here, and Peter Graham with someone she didn't know, David Struthers was still here, and old Mr Struthers, and two of the Carmichael boys, but even they were on their way out the door now, Rosemary and Elizabeth had already left with Gaye.

'Goodnight, Margaret,' Craig called out now.

'See you tomorrow . . .'

Margaret checked the clock.

Tick-tick.

Soon.

'Goodnight, Margaret and thanks!' That was Peter Graham leaving, and the Struthers with him.

'Goodnight.'

'Goodnight.'

Tick-tick.

Margaret made the sounds of ticking with her fingernails on the wooden bar.

Tick-tick.

The same sound her fingernails would make – *It's me* – ticking on some unknown salesman's wooden door.

In the end, everything was the same. The people in the bar now, saying goodnight, they were the same, and the men passing through that she kept upstairs . . . they were all the same. They had different names, the men upstairs, but they all had their creased suits, their black bags. They all stayed for one night and then they left and she was pleased that they left, she was always pleased to see them go. There were the cars they drove away, and they were always the same kinds of cars, and the coats they sometimes left crumpled on the bed behind them, forgotten, always the same coat. The same, the same . . . travelling salesmen passing through town for the night. The whole thing was a joke.

Margaret looked around her and at that moment realised that Ray Weldon had gone. The room was suddenly a little emptier. He'd been there at the bar, standing so near her . . . and of all the men, of all of them . . . But that was a foolish way to think. Ray wasn't there for her to have. He was a taken man, nothing at all like the others. They were parts, those others, of love and sex, little soft parts that seemed enough at the time, in the upstairs room, but were just parts, after all, in the end, little portions like she might eat little portions on toast.

Tick-tick.

Ray was different . . .

But no point in thinking about that now. Little portions would have to do. Margaret felt the pull again of her underwear and looked across the room again to the one she'd chosen. Someone like him would always be there. She waited, her gaze fixed upon him until he looked up, because she knew he would look up – and there, now. She caught his eye and he smiled. It was a quick, rabbity kind of smile, and of course he would be nervous, with Margaret looking at him the way she was, just looking at him, this woman in her blood-red shirt who might have anything in the world she wanted. She mouthed the word 'You . . .' and the ribbon that was coiled throughout her body unfurled, rolled across the room towards him and spun around him so she could pull him in.

◇

Jesus, look at her though. She was on and Carstairs couldn't believe his luck. Last time . . . well that had been last time, but here he was again and here she was, and she'd made it perfectly clear she was on. Look at her, standing there, looking at him that way. Of course she was on. He smiled at her, drained his glass. Jesus, she was scary though. She'd got him all worked up. He could remember vividly the last time he was here. Jesus again. Nine months ago and he was still recovering. He thought of how she'd come to his room that night, and he'd had no idea then, like he had the idea now, that she was on. He'd had no idea she was even interested when she'd come scratching at his door in the dark like a little cat.

'Let me in . . .'

It was all he could do to pretend he wanted it, to be in control, but she'd been scary all right, like she was scary now, making him jump in his pants.

He could do with another drink. Tonight would be no different, he could tell. It was like the nine months between then and now had never passed. He'd been drinking and that had helped him, and the stories, he knew that always made him feel good, to hear the sound of people's laughter . . . but he needed another drink, all the same. He needed one now. Up until now he'd been fine, the evening just fine, with a comfortable woman at his side who'd laughed at everything he said, an older woman, like a mother, and her husband with her, a nice enough guy . . . But it seemed a long time ago now, that he'd had that kind of fun and even then there'd been a part of his mind that couldn't stop thinking about what was to come, it was in the back of his mind, even though he was trying not to think about it, there it was, the sex that would inevitably come, like sickness rising, unstoppable, like sickness, sex, his thick clothes on him reminding him of the way she'd pulled at his clothes last time, at the way her painted lips were upon him, the way they left a mark.

When he could, George took another glance at Margaret. It was like he was a little boy looking at a lady. Was she pretty? Was she? He couldn't tell. She was queer, he knew that, in the way her face was so pale and she'd painted that mouth on dark as blood. Queer too, he remembered, about the way, when she was working on him last time, she showed her little teeth, like she was a little dog, a sleek and clever little bitch winding around his legs. He really did need another drink. It was too early anyhow to go upstairs. Margaret looked at him and he just nodded, Yeah, another, thanks, and in a couple of moments, although she seemed to have plenty of other things to attend to, she had laid down before him his gin and tonic, her fingers just long enough touching his hand as she passed the glass.

'OK?' she said, and he was a grown man but he could only nod his head, couldn't get his breath there for a second, couldn't draw breath even, for the catch he felt, in his throat, that caught him when he tried to talk back at her.

'You sure?' Margaret said, and there was that feeling of the touch of her fingers on his hand, like a graze. She held his eyes for a second longer, looked at him, looking right at him, the dog, the little bitch. It was like she was winding around him then, her tongue already inside his pants.

'You sure?'

And he nodded again, grinned. Like an idiot, for godsake. The thing should be fun and here he was acting like some kid, like he was going to lose all his blood to her upstairs, like all his blood was going to drain clean away under the workings of the bitch's tongue, and with her feeling in his mouth with those long fingers of hers, handling him like he was fruit, unpeeled, and she could taste all the way through him to the seed, to the very pit, the little dark stone.

He took up his drink and drained it in one go. He would have to go upstairs now, and wait for her. That's what she meant for him to do, her look had told him clear enough. *Now*. The stone was there in his groin like something he'd swallowed. *Now*. He would have to. He had no choice. He rummaged in his pockets for notes and change and left a handful on the little table as payment, though she didn't see him do it. He weighted the notes with his empty glass, the rim and inside still wet with the sweet beer she'd served him, and the tumbler for the gin he'd been drinking alongside. He took the lemon rind from it to suck on for comfort. Even so, his mouth was dry. He looked around the crowded bar for no one he knew, and his eyes felt dry too, just looking in that bright smoky room had made them feel that way, rubbed and sore; yet his eyes would be wetted soon, when she would come to him, when she would put her fingers in the corners of his eyes as he would kneel there before her on the thin carpet . . .

*Goodnight, goodnight, don't leave me.*

. . . Her fingers wiping out the beads of wet that had formed in his eyes, stroking out from him long tears, and *Don't leave me*, he would be thinking. *Stay. With your fingers and your tongue and your pocketful of keys.*

85

Margaret didn't notice him go, but she saw, easy as though he were the only one left in the room, Ray Weldon come back in. She thought he'd left a while ago and yet there he was standing in the open doorway, framed by the blackness of the night around him. His hair was damp as though he'd just washed it and he had a fresh shirt on, like he was going on somewhere. The bar still wasn't empty, but right then he was the only one there. Margaret could see every detail in him, the slight curl in his hair from where he'd combed it, the softness of his shirt and the way it was buttoned on him, opening at the hollow at the base of his throat where there beat a tiny pulse.

Ray.
Ray.
Ray.

Margaret felt a glut, of the things she saw in Ray, too much. She made herself turn away. He was still there in the reflection of the mirror, she saw him make his way across the room, but even so she remained turned from him, with a little cloth she found some work to do. She had to, had to make herself pretend she wasn't someone who would always want to watch him, want to follow him all the time with her eyes as he moved easily through the room, stopping, talking to greet someone he knew, Johnny Carmichael's son just come in the door, and Sonny Johanssen with him.

'Hey, Son . . .'
'Good to see you, Ray.'
'What are you doing here this late? It's late for you . . .'
'John brought me; I came with you, didn't I, John?'
Yet it was like a small hunger in her, to want to watch him, to be watching him now.
She saw him touch Sonny's arm, smile.
'Well?' he said, and the old man nodded, 'Oh, sure . . .'
Why was he here, anyway? What was he doing returning to the bar at this time? Margaret saw him smile again, that lazy smile, lean in and whisper something into Johanssen's

ear. It was strange to see him do it. Strange too, now she came to think of it, in the way he'd been drinking so long at the bar and yet was sober, but something different in him, Margaret hadn't seen it before, but there it was, in the way he held himself, kept himself held in: excitement.

Sonny laughed then, John with him. Margaret saw Ray put his arm around Sonny's shoulder, whisper again in his ear. The three men laughed together and then Ray broke from them and came across the room as though towards her. For a minute that's what she could believe, that he was just come back to the bar to see her, Margaret, as though he only wanted to come to the place where she was standing. Couldn't he want that? Please couldn't he just want that? To come to the bar, to lay his brown arms on the bar, to say to Margaret, Hello, how are you? it's a warm night, or it's a cold night, or it's dark or whatever the night was, for what did it matter what the night was? because he wouldn't even be looking at her, of course not, what was she thinking? he would never notice her because he was someone in love with ghosts only, everyone in town knew, and his heart might as well have been cut right out of him and thrown into the river for all the difference Margaret's little thoughts could make, no matter what he said, no matter what kind of night it was.

'None of us should be here,' she heard him turn back and call out to Sonny now, and laugh. He was the one who shouldn't be here. Just when Margaret had everything planned, he was coming back dressed in clean clothes to spoil it. What right did he have? To come back in that way, present himself in that way, as though he had something better to do? What right to be here at all when he was a man so taken up by memory nothing else would do? She was a girl, that was all, that thing in his mind, another girl like all of them were girls once, like she'd been a girl herself, yet Ray had made it that only the memory of this one girl could serve him. Only her upturned face, the straight of her back like a green-gold reed that would come to flower . . . only her. No one else could have him.

Margaret closed her eyes, and there, within her in the dark, her own memory. She remembered the sound of its voice, the outline of its lips when she'd drawn the lipstick on . . .

*Look at you . . .*

There was the sweet face turned up to her, turned up as a daughter's face may be turned up towards a mother's face, and Margaret had looked down into the face as though into a mirror . . .

*Look at you . . .* she'd said, and in the memory they were one face, one body.

Her and her.

But she had to forget the memory now. She had to open her eyes. There was no girl, the voice down the drive that afternoon had been the end of it.

*Thanks, Mum . . .*

*Shhh . . . she'll hear.*

Now she had only this, herself, her own body. It was the only thing left that she could use. Margaret saw Ray move forward, nod, Hi, to some farmer, Giles McCready, Robbie Monaghan . . . She saw him call back over his shoulder at one of them, 'Yeah, that's right,' because he could be saying anything, because he was just moving through, just moving through . . . and then suddenly he was there, before her, looking at her, smiling at her. Suddenly out of all Margaret's thoughts, his face in front of her, his smile. Margaret put down the cloth she'd been using, made herself wait a beat before she said the simple words.

'Hi, again.'

The minute she spoke, though, though the words were easy enough, casual enough, she couldn't do it. In that second of speaking she was suddenly tired. It was as if all the effort she had made through the evening was gone, her smiles and looks and touches, and only an old woman was left, the kind who has no daughters, who takes the money and lets the old men pay.

'What's brought you back here so late?' she heard herself say and she could feel the tiredness of those words like all the words –

What can I get you?

What would you like?

What can I do?

– all words, too many and none of them right. It was late. She wanted to close up. She wanted Ray to leave now, go do whatever it was he wanted to do without her, but he just stood there, looking at her, with his pale eyes, and there was something in the way the pupils of his eyes were dilated, excited, because they could see something no one else could see, that made Margaret think that she had been a fool ever once to believe she could compete, ever, with that.

'What can I get you?' she said, and in the brightness of the smoky light, she knew how she would appear to be to him then: that Margaret, that thing stooped over by long hours of serving and smelling of beer and liquor. She was the woman who ran the bar, that was all, here tonight like every night for the men who came in to lay their piles of dirty change on the table, who held their empty glasses out to be filled, their cigarettes up to be lit and Margaret would light them, using her own fingers to strike the match that were themselves stained yellow from all the cigarettes she had smoked through her long life, all the way down to the butt, to the stub.

'All right, Margaret?'

'All right, sweetheart?'

She would strike the match because she was her, that woman with the yellow hands, with fingernails ridged and cracked by detergent and beer and no amount of dark red polish could make them pretty again.

*Look at you.*

Margaret closed her eyes, she never wanted to look, she

couldn't bear to look. Tighter, tighter, she closed her eyes, for she could not cry, she must never cry.

*Look at you.*

*Look at you.*

'Any chance of a drink around here?' she heard Ray say, and she was turned from him but still she had to wait for a second or two before she could answer.

'Everything OK with you?' Ray said, and Margaret opened her eyes then, turned back again towards him.

She smiled. 'Of course,' she said. 'Everything is fine.'

He was nice enough with her, he spoke nicely enough to her, but it was too late now, everything she had gathered together for herself was gone.

'Sonny asked me to ask you something,' Ray was saying. 'He wanted to know if you've seen anyone new in town.'

He looked at her, his eyes fixed on her, wanting an answer, but there was nothing to say. What was there to say? What was he asking her? What was he doing here?

'Have you?' He was still looking at her.

Margaret shook her head.

'Sure?'

He just stood there, facing her at the bar, his clean, soft shirt buttoned through to his throat that was so close Margaret could have touched it.

He shook his head. 'Doesn't matter,' he said, and he smiled at her, and another day, another night, that smile might have meant something, Margaret could have made it mean something, but not now, no longer now.

'Just that Sonny thought . . .' Ray said.

She shook her head again.

*Look at me . . .*

The cloth was in her hand like it had been in her hand that day Mary Susan had come to her, and she'd put the cloth down, taken the girl's upturned face in her hands and looked down upon her as though into a mirror. That was how it had been then, the girl some kind of gift in the way she'd wanted of Margaret all the lovely things and Margaret could give them. She had learned that she could give to this girl like a mother might give to a daughter lovely things, nothing but lovely things, like the way a mother might take a sweet upturned face between her hands and say, 'I love you. How beautiful you are.' It had been months ago but for Margaret a time of such freshness, of flowering, and she would have given Mary Susan anything, over and over she would have given, the memory of being with her turning the cloth she held into petals, like Margaret held a flower, a full-bloomed kind of flower that was tearing into soft petals in her hand.

'It's too hot for me,' Margaret said then. 'In here, I mean. Even with the door open all night. I feel it airless sometimes. You know what it's like, between serving one drink and the next, I don't get the chance to get out there, out into the air –'

She stopped. What was happening to her? These words, not the right kinds of words? This talk about herself, about her feelings? She didn't do that, she never did that. She never wanted to talk on and on about herself, never – but something was opened up in her like it had started to open up before and it had cut then, but not like it was cutting now, making her want to tell everything, how she had nothing in her but regret, how her time had gone, how it had been wasted. How she had nothing in her life now, no youth to take up where her own age had left off, how all she wanted was to be the girl again who could want him, whom he would want, with her legs and her skin, to be her, to cover her, envelop her, their skins melding and blending, the white with the gold, the soft with the dry, melding, covering, being covered, endlessly, endlessly, mother, daughter, one girl, one woman.

'I feel . . .' – and she heard herself say these things, but couldn't stop herself – 'I can't express it,' she was saying, 'how airless it can be, and the men come in, and it's airless for me and I feel, I feel . . .'

Ray looked at her as she stood there, he looked at her, this strong, good-looking man with his smooth arms she wanted to touch, touch with her fingertip the golden fine hairs on his arms, touch him like a girl would touch him . . .

'C'mon . . .' the girl would say, teasing him. 'Let's go . . .'

And he would smile, the lazy smile, the smile that came from hours of lying endlessly by the river, the lazy smile coming back for the girl as she dipped her head down and began to nuzzle the soft blond hairs of his arms . . .

'Whoa!' Ray put his hand up.

Margaret started, like he'd grabbed her hard.

'You're shaking, sweetheart,' he said. 'You've been working here on your own too hard. It doesn't need to be your enemy, you know . . .' He gestured down at the cloth she was still holding, and Margaret looked at it, bruised and torn like it had suffered the work of a little knife.

'I must be going crazy,' she said, and she put the cloth down. What was she doing? What had happened to her?

'Anyone would,' she said, 'working here,' and she laughed. That was it, make it into a joke, laugh. It could be just that, like a little joke, Ray could think it was a joke.

'You wanted a beer?' She took up a glass, pulled back the lever of the pump to fill it and as the liquid filled Margaret could feel herself filling, like she could always make herself be filled again, like she could always make herself be herself again and the other thing nothing at all, just a silly joke.

'I'm going to be closing soon anyway,' she said, and by now she was almost back to how she always was. 'This will have to be your last,' she said.

Ray reached out his hand and she passed him his beer. It was as simple as that, it could be as simple as that. Her pouring him the beer she always poured him and passing it along the same, the same like he would never be anything different for

92

her than that, that same drink, that same time, just the same glass that she would hand to him and his head would be inclined forward, like that, to take the first sip from it.

'Looks good . . .' he would say, he would always say, and there would be nothing more than that, ever.

'Be quiet!'

There was a roar from the other side of the room, the last people left, were they playing cards maybe, or throwing darts at the board?

'What are you up to?'

'Get away!'

Nothing more than that.

Margaret turned away from Ray and saw in the mirror the brief reflection of a woman, with thick red hair tied back off her face, with a dark lipstick mouth. That was who she was. That woman. She would always be her. She turned back again to the bar and took up the money Ray had left as a pile of coins on the counter. It was the same, the same. All the men leaving the money the same and Ray was the same, she could make him be the same. Already he was gone. The amount would be there, in change, the exact amount. Always the same. The money all the men left, the drink and the money, the same, the same. The customer upstairs in his room waiting, the thin carpets under his bare feet . . . he was the same, the pale skin of him like a child when the old woman would come to lay him down. She could have him there, she could tend to him there, and only as she began would she slowly come to feel the mercy of her act, the grace, the change . . . The old woman become like a girl again, like a young girl as her underwear fell from her, like petals of used cloth, to the floor.

# THREE

He couldn't figure how long he'd been standing there. Couldn't figure time, hours, minutes, night or early morning. Couldn't figure what he'd been doing at all to find himself suddenly back in his own house, standing inside the front door, a queer place to be when usually the turns caught him in bed, or when he was dozing in a chair someplace, or in the garden stretched out along a flower bed, where no one could see, just sleeping.

It was a queer place right enough, to find himself now. Neither in nor out, the front door wide open as if it was day, but there was no day. He could see the dark violet of a night sky thickened in parts in shadows across the lawn, he could see the silver point of a star. Late then, to be so dark, for the one star to be so clear and sharp. He screwed up his eyes as though the silver light would prick him. What was it he'd been thinking about? Where had he been? He couldn't see. There had been the garden, the late afternoon . . . the slow loss of light, a voice . . .

Behind him, down the short hallway, Rhett lay like a dark mat. Johanssen could hear him breathing. The dog's eyes would be on him, even in the dark, watching Johanssen, waiting for him to move, but he could not move. He was standing there by the door and the dog's eyes would be like two shiny black marbles in the dark.

*The best kind.*

Dark marbles were rare, black the hardest to find. Other boys didn't have them, you had to buy them with money and be careful they didn't break.

*Always the best kind.*

He'd loved those marbles when he was a kid. All the colours, some of them green or orange, or red and shiny like jam. They were that pretty he used to suck them, sometimes, like sweets. The green like the clear green bits in fruit cake, and the orange like a boiled lolly, like something to eat. All the pretty sweet colours. Nona said he would have swallowed them if she hadn't made him spit them out.

*Let me have them . . .*

Sticking her fingers in his mouth to get them out, he'd crammed the colours in all at once. They were a mouthful of smooth round glass balls, but she'd made him spit them out.

*Let me . . .*

He must have been pretty much a baby still, to be up to that kind of nonsense with the marbles. Causing his sister to have to bring them out of him in that way, have them in a shiny pile in the palm of her hand.

'Don't do that again,' she tells him, over and over, but he will keep doing it.

That was Nona, him causing her to be a mother to him when she was just a kid herself. He could still hear her voice, years later, telling him things, how to do things, and both of them old by then: Nona with the gimp leg from where she'd fallen down the front steps that time; Nona with her hair soft and white and no longer brown like it had been when she was a girl.

'Don't be so damn silly . . .'

Him touching her white hair, when she lay in the hospital bed, stroking her hair that last time, when she didn't come out of the hospital again, for comfort. And her saying then, 'Don't be so damn silly,' but not meaning it, not really.

The night was dark around him, he could hear his dog. Hungry, he can't have fed him yet, but still Johanssen could not make his body move. The queer turn, the last of it, was still in him, he could figure, and it was that making him not able to move, keeping him here with Nona's voice telling him things like she always told him.

'You can't keep people, Sonny,' she was saying. 'It's not like they're animals, like if you feed them and care for them they will stay. Don't be unhappy, don't cry. She's a girl, she's only going away. It's only so many miles. We can see her any time we like, make a visit on the train. We can call her on the telephone.'

It was there, the whole thing, Nona talking to him, telling him everything would be all right, and the silly damn tears just popping out of his eyes and he couldn't stop them. Lucky it was dark with no one to see. Lucky only Rhett's breathing in the hall, not a person.

'Don't be unhappy, now . . .' Nona said, and he could hear her like she was there. Like she was still just a girl and could make him feel nothing had changed in all the years even though she was an old woman by then but still she could make him feel safe, that poor idiot kid who used to suck glass.

'Little boy . . .' she says. 'My little boy . . .'

He was crying now, good and proper. Queer quiet tears, though, not like the other crying kind. Secret tears, with him stroking Nona's soft hair, and Francie gone. And they never did call her on the telephone, and then, in time, Nona was gone, like she had left too, and the house up the road where she used to live dark all the time, no lights on when before he would look up the road to see the yellow lit windows in the dark.

He realised he had soiled himself from the crying.

'Silly damn fool . . .'

It was part of the turn, him not knowing what was happening and letting himself go, like he was a silly kid. It could be that way sometimes; he'd wake up, wet through and having to change his pyjamas.

*Don't go!*

He'd want to call out then.

*Don't go!*

But they had gone, lovely Francie gone, Nona gone. And now there was no family to stand with, only this doorway. Only dark up the road at the house where the lights used to be, but still he wanted to call out 'Don't go!' to Francie now.

It was the afternoon that had done it. The queer sun in his eyes, thinking he heard Francie's voice but not being able to see. That had made the turn come this time, it was in his mind in the glint of sun. There had been her voice, his looking up – and it had started then, in the garden, in the light. You couldn't bury these things, Johanssen knew. It wasn't like dug-up flowers and weeds you could get rid of, the past was there like fresh. Like sudden growth it came up. There was the child running down the road in her nightdress, midsummer, and the nightdress too big for her, flapping around her as she ran down the road from Nona's house to his own house.

'Uncle Sonny! Uncle Sonny!'

And of course it would come up fresh, that memory. Of course he would start again, remembering, when he would hear that voice.

'It's me!'

He could see her now, running towards him in her nightdress and him bending down to catch her in his arms.

'What is it, honey?'

And holding her so close, the little girl. There would be the evening meal at Nona's, the child in her thin things; he could carry her home. There were her little feet with grass on them and him brushing the grass off when he had her in his arms to carry.

'Come home now,' she tells him. 'Mum says it's time for tea.'

Johanssen turned.

'What was that?'

He heard his own voice.

'Where are you?'

He heard it again – but wasn't she just there?

'Uncle Sonny!'

Hadn't she been there before? Standing behind the hedge, calling out to him from behind the hedge, and he'd seen her, hadn't he seen her?

'Where are you?' he heard himself ask again, but it was only his own voice he could hear. He looked around him, looking for her like he'd looked before, but there was nothing. Only dark. He was alone. He'd have to go and change his trousers. He unbuttoned the front and let them drop, and his underpants, wet through.

'Uncle Sonny!'

Like a kid.

'Uncle Sonny!'

Like a dirty, silly kid.

Next thing, and was it now? or did it happen before? but John Carmichael was there. Hadn't heard him, not his car, not his footsteps up the path, his voice calling:

'Hey, Son!'

Not a thing. He was just suddenly there at the door.

'What's up with you?' he was saying. 'Have you lost your electrics or do you like hanging around in the dark with no clothes on?'

He was standing right in front of him on the front step, large as life.

'Just as well I came back, eh? To check up on you?'

He stepped towards Sonny, to the part of the doorway where he was standing, neither inside nor out. It was John all right. And hadn't he been with him before, sometime in the night? Hadn't he just been with him? He didn't mind, John often caught him like this, at strange times, when he wasn't expecting anyone to call. The young ones understood somehow, that you could find yourself acting a bit peculiar, sleeping funny times, standing like this in the dark and not being able to move. They probably put it down to liquor, and age, but Sonny didn't mind at all that it was his good friend John.

'You came back,' he said. 'Didn't you just bring me?'

John nodded, 'Sure did. From Margaret's, remember?' he stepped closer. 'We saw Dad, and Ray, and the minister was there . . .'

*The minister . . .*

'Remember?'

*Yes . . .*

Sonny did remember.

There had been the weeping man.

He had been weeping and he was cold to the touch. Sonny had touched him and felt him cold, rigid through his body like in church on Sunday mornings, like the cloths the man wore then, stiff from the stuff they put in the cloths to make them solemn.

*Yes . . .*

He did remember.

And there was something about Francie, too . . . What was it he remembered? Not just her voice, but something more? He'd touched the minister and felt Francie was there, that was it. As if at that very minute she had been standing near them and watching . . .

*Yes . . .*

She'd seen it all. Francie. The weeping man who was cold through to the touch with lack of love and so different from the other man who'd put his arms around Sonny that night, inside, in the hot bar, and so close Sonny could feel his loud heart beat . . .

'She's home.'

It was Francie, for sure. Though the house up the road was dark, the feeling Sonny had had before, in the garden, in the light, was in him now and deep . . . She was here. Ray knew it, he knew it. She was right here; moving all amongst them. Watching over them all.

'You remember?' John was saying. 'We were outside, then we came inside, and then we went home?'

Sonny nodded. He was starting to remember more and more . . . the dark night, the yellow of the bar. The driveway and the man out there sitting in the driveway alone . . . It was all there, and something else, too . . . the flash of red hair reflected in the mirror . . . Margaret. She was there, in the mirror, Sonny could see her and she was weeping, and where had he been that he could see her? But there she was, it was her, and beside her another, this one surrounded by water and less known to him but he did know her, a quiet woman soaked by water, as if by tears . . .

*Yes* . . . These things, strange pictures . . . It was all there, all of the day was there. He'd looked up and thought, *I know you*. He'd pulled his hands out of the earth and looked up to see . . . and there before him now was the little girl who carried on her feet the stains of green, and another, also caught in gold with the last of the light, with golden slippers strapped on.

*Yes* . . .

*Yes* . . .

It was dark, but these things were in his mind and he could see now, when he could not see before. The minister, his wife. The woman at the bar, the girl, and somewhere too, Ray, with his loud heart, out there somewhere in the dark and roaming, restless, not able to sleep because Francie was home.

◇

John stepped closer, saw the old man's face glazed with tears, wet trousers on the floor.

'The secret life, eh?' he said.

Johanssen didn't say anything. John put his hand on the old man's thin shoulder, it was like he could feel bone right through the cloth of the jacket. He felt how Sonny was trembling. He'd found him before in this way, standing shock-still, his body kind of rigid and thin but with these trembles going through it like the bones would fly apart if he wasn't wearing clothes to hold himself together. It could be strange to come in upon, but the best thing to do was act normal. If he could get him to put the lights on maybe it would not seem so bad.

'It's hellish dark in here, you know, Son,' John said. 'Have you lost your electrics or you just don't want anybody to see you hanging around the place half naked with a bare bum . . . Are you in or out of the bath, or what?'

Sonny looked at him.

'John . . .'

Sonny wiped over his face with the back of his hand, but John could see there were still tears bright in his eyes.

'I've had a queer afternoon, John,' he said. 'I've been all over . . .'

Well, at least he was speaking. That was something, but, John thought, the old man was looking at him queer. The kind of look an old man might give a stranger, not someone he knew.

'I tell you,' Sonny continued, 'with young Frances coming by . . . it's started something, John. She'll be looking for Ray. I told him, I said, "Look out, boy!" I told him, I said, "How lovely she was . . ."'

He put his hand out to John to take his hand and John felt a little afraid at the way it seemed to be that Sonny was grasping at him, like a stranger in the street and not at all someone he knew. He drew his hand away. It was part of Sonny's fit, of course he understood that, but it made him feel peculiar, all the same, seeing his friend with his face wet, with that needy, grasping hand.

'Steady on, Son,' he said, to make it better for himself. 'Let's go inside. I've brought something to eat . . .'

But Johanssen was not listening.

'A queer light, and I didn't feel right about it,' he was saying. 'It started making me think I couldn't see things, but now I got it figured, it's easy. They are all here, that's the thing. Francie, Nona, too, I can hear her. She was telling me not to worry, because I do worry, sometimes, about the dark house, I miss them both so badly there, you see . . .' Sonny squinted up his eyes. 'You understand, don't you, John, how I always needed them there, and now . . .' Sonny turned towards the house. 'Ray's there now, and he shouldn't be there, John . . . The place is all closed up, it's dark . . .' His voice cracked. 'It's true, John, what I'm saying, and it makes me frightened when the spells come on, they're strong. Look at my trousers, look what I've done and I am ashamed. Nona would have me in a bath, I better run a bath. That's what she says, isn't it? That she'll always take care of me that way, and Francie too, that she'll see I'm OK?'

He ground at his eyes with the heel of his hand to dry them. Poor old bugger.

'Come on, now . . .' John took him by the arm.

'Shhh . . .'

Quietly he led him up the short hallway to the kitchen. He set down the beer and packet of fish and chips he'd brought on the kitchen table.

'Come on now, Sonny,' he said again. 'It's not that bad . . .'

He was glad he'd decided to stop back at the house. He'd had a feeling the evening had been too much for the old man. The drink and then Ray and the way Ray had been, the two of them on about the past like it was yesterday. And then, before that, the business with the minister and that was queer enough, the man out there on the driveway. Jesus. All in all, when you thought about it, maybe he should have just gone out with Craig in the first place, met that girlfriend of his and her friend and done something together, the four of them. But as it had turned out, probably just as well. It had turned out for the good he'd been able to stop by here and help sort things out.

'I thought I'd bring something over for us to eat,' John said now, and he thought about switching on the light, but decided against it.

'We don't need to bother just yet, but it's there for when we want it,' he said.

It was important not to rush Sonny out of the mood. John knew that. He became even more rigid, more stuck in the thing that had brought it on if someone was trying to push him out of it. He might as well sit down at the table and wait. It was just a matter of staying here for a bit, in the dark, maybe have a beer, let the lateness of the night wash over him and forget about getting too much sleep. He felt young, and strong, and it was Sonny, after all. Usually he would have no patience for old people, like old people hanging around a pub or someplace, with those stories about that was then, and was she married to such-and-such, and what was the year that . . .? All stuff from the past and dry, and old, old, like it could be dead. But something about Sonny's memories he could handle fine. The old boy crying and whatever – it was different. He was special, Sonny. Like he was here, but also somewhere else. Like he was from far away and travelling.

'Hey, Rhetty . . .'

John could see Sonny's dog had followed them in. He was a great dog, too, John had never known Sonny without him. He got up and walked a couple of paces over to the doorway to reach down to pet him.

'Hey, boy . . .'

He could see quite clearly in the dark by now. Johanssen's trousers and underpants soaking wet in a pile on the hallway floor. The old man still standing there.

'Maybe get yourself changed, eh?' said John. He said it while petting the dog, not looking up at all so it would be easier for Sonny to cover himself. It would give him time to gather up the wet clothes while John kept himself busy with stroking the dog's head. No one need know anything about

103

this, John thought, any of it. The old boy shivering there, with shiny eyes, with pee down his legs. No one need think there was something wrong with him, that he couldn't look after himself, that he was touched a bit, simple in the head. No one, John would make sure. He rubbed Rhett behind the ears.

'Just go ahead,' he said to Sonny. 'Don't bother about me. I'll sort out food and pour us a couple of beers. Don't worry waiting around, go ahead and get changed. You could knock on a light or two while you're at it . . .'

The light switched on at once. It was a shock, like a jump into brightness, and everything in the familiar kitchen strange, the colours a bit scary, but all right, Rhett was all right about it. He didn't move or start, just let himself be stroked between the ears. Sonny walked right past John, kind of like a ghost, that kind of walk like he was drunk. There was that smell, sure, that kind of sweetness, that always came off Sonny when he'd come out of one of these things. It was the sign of a fit, John had read that somewhere once, a smell of sweetness. Like Sonny really had been somewhere and had come back. John shivered. Like a body, fixed with sugar to keep it fresh, and then the body comes back to life . . .

'Hey, Rhett.'

John continued to pet the dog's head, the fine bones of the skull beneath his fingertips. It was a bit creepy to think about but not to worry. It would be all right. It was just a fit, it would be over soon.

'There you go,' he said to Rhett, and the dog's eyes were closed.

'Not so bad, eh?'

◇

But it would be all right, too. He could smell the food, that was a great sign, and John had said they would drink beer together, so he'd turned on the light. Now he would pick up his things from the floor and take them into the bathroom. He would get changed quickly and quietly there, no bother. He would have a quick wash and put on the trousers that were hanging over the bath, he could manage without the pants underneath. It would be easy. Then they'd sit down together like John had said.

John was a lovely boy. Of all the Carmichael sons, no wonder he was his father's favourite. He was always coming around, pretending for other things, but really, Johanssen knew, to just check up that he was quite OK. Bringing little bits of food, being gentle with Rhett there, like he was now, because Rhett loved a bit of attention from people like that, other people, not just him. He was starting to feel better, and that was all because of John. Just him being here had helped Sonny arrange things in his mind. The turns always left him confused but John had helped him. He could start to understand, see the sense in things that had happened. He could start putting them together in a pattern in his mind.

John was good for him in that way, making him be part of things and not living so, always in his thoughts, or in ideas from the past. John seemed to always have the time. Bringing beers so they could make a bit of an evening of it, or taking him to the pub, like he'd taken him tonight, doing that when he could be hanging around with other young fellows his own age, but no, he was coming with him, he said, staying with him. Making sure he got home OK, everything. He was feeling much better now, much better indeed. And all thanks to John.

'Mr Carmichael,' he called out, from the bathroom, and the hot water was running and everything was fine, everything would be just fine. 'I'll be with you in a blink. Get out the plates. Turn more lights on! Turn all the lights on!'

He was feeling great, just. There was no need to worry, not about thoughts . . . not about anything. Sonny used the washcloth and soap, dried himself off afterwards. It would all be fine. He pulled the pair of fresh trousers on, too big, with no belt. That would make John smile, Sonny thought. He started whistling, doing up the trouser buttons as he went through to the bedroom. Everything, everything . . . it would be fine. John here, Francie here –

Sonny stopped.
   Ray.
   Something wrong with Ray.

He was there, right now, he was at the dark house. Sonny could see him vivid. Ray up there at Nona's house, in the dark and looking through the windows and he shouldn't be there; Francie wouldn't be there, he shouldn't be there.

Ray.
Ray.
With his heart beating too loud.

'Take it easy, Ray,' Sonny wanted to tell him. 'Francie's home, but not in that way . . .'
   But how then? What did that mean?
   'You won't find her by looking for her there.'
   Sonny closed his eyes.
   *Not in that way.*
   Not as somebody to touch, to hold . . .
   'No.'
   Then how?
   Sonny saw Margaret's face again, for a second in the mirror, right there, her red hair.
   'I'll ask Margaret . . .'
   And, no, don't hurt her, boy. She loves you, can't you see that?
   Go easy, calm yourself . . .
   Ray.
   Ray.
   But it was too late, it was starting to turn, it was starting . . . There was the glint of light, a glint of gold on the strap of a shoe . . . and it was turning, all turning within Sonny again, and not again, please, not again, he couldn't take it again . . .

not now, but Nona was there, too, saying, 'It's all right, it's all right . . .'

Sonny sat down on the bed. It was like before, like standing in the doorway before when the fit came on him but different now than before because then there had been voices and pieces to see, but now much more was there and he was taking it right in. The people in the town he knew so well . . . They were there, in his mind, and turning, turning, their hands joining, one connected to the other, as though a dance were forming upon the green . . .

◇

John smiled, hearing Sonny's voice calling out to him, 'Turn all the lights on!' That made everything OK again, no worries now. One day he dreaded the spell that Sonny wouldn't come out of and he'd be there with that sweet body – but not tonight. He'd heard whistling from the bathroom, he started whistling himself, and then singing:
*Way down yonder in the bayou country*
*In dear old Louisianne . . .*

It would all be all right. He'd heard Sonny come out of the bathroom and go into his bedroom. He'd be combing down his hair to make it neat. John sang:
*That's where I met my Cajun baby,*
*The fairest woman in the land . . .*
He got out knives and cutlery from the drawer, laid them out on the table with the newspaper bundle of fish and chips, the flagon of beer set in the middle on the clean, wiped, blue plastic cloth. The little tin ashtray, too, was clean – the whole place, as usual, immaculate.

He knew a lot of people around town thought Sonny was a bit strange, never marrying, and the way he'd spent so much time with his sister, but John liked that, that he had such particular little ways. His house clean and neat, like kids always liked it because it was such a tidy little cottage with its fence out in the front, and maybe that was part of it, the tidiness, the way the place was so self-contained, somehow, like Sonny didn't need anything else. John felt that way. He may be nineteen, and the youngest – but still, he liked to think that he was a person with different ideas from most. He knew Sonny read a lot too, John was alert to that and he was interested that the old man was different in that way, looking out for fresh thoughts and curious little notions about things that John could understand.

'I'm lighting the stove in here,' he called out to the bedroom. 'You need to be warmer in here, you know all the windows are open . . .'

He busied himself lighting the range, shovelling a heap of coals inside the burner. Then he closed the two kitchen windows. Immediately the room seemed warmer, the light brighter. From the cupboard he took out glasses, salt and vinegar for the chips, the thick chipped blue-and-white plates. He knew everything as if it was his own, he could have lived here all the time he was so familiar. That's what his father and brothers didn't understand, that you had to observe people closely, be part of their lives like you were knit in. How else could you stop loneliness? Pop just drank all the time and Robert and Kenny and Craig all set to follow, even his mother couldn't stop them. They drove around town together, and his brothers might be married, with kids, and Craig had his girl . . . but that wasn't friendship. It wasn't finding the thing that could show you more about life – even if you weren't exactly sure what that thing was. All his family liked Sonny, everyone did, but they didn't want to look out for him, like John did. Care for him, like now, warming the place and that giving John real pleasure to do. He opened the range door and blew in a few times to get the flames up. Then he pulled out a crumpled pack of cigarettes from his shirt pocket, lit one.

'You all right?' he called out to the bedroom.

Better make sure the old man was dressed OK.

'Shall I come through and give you a hand?'

But when he went through to the bedroom, though the light was bright in there, Sonny just sat. Fully dressed, with his hair neatly combed, but just sitting on the side of the bed, his hands by his sides like a little boy.

'You all right, Son?'

John had thought everything was fixed, back to normal again but this was not normal. This was bad as before, the far-off look in Sonny's eyes, worse than before somehow, now he could see him so clearly under the electric bulb, worse.

'You all right?'

Sonny just stared, not seeing.

'Sonny?'

But he could hear fine, he knew John was there. In the kitchen the fish and chips steamed in the newspaper packets on the table, the flagon of beer beside unopened. He could see it all, the crack on the hall ceiling, the untied shoelace on John's shoe . . . He could see everything he needed to see, the things in Sonny now, like all voices, people, flaying around in his head, still Sonny could feel his mind gathering them all up into a kind of a pattern and he could make sense of the pattern. It was within him like a perfect shape, the circle, something forming like a circle, a shape drawn around empty grass that would bring all the people together. He couldn't yet know why they were there, these people who lived in the town he'd lived in for all of his life, he couldn't know why those hands were joining to form the shape there, in his mind, of a dance, but they were there, all of them . . . He put his arms up to be part of it, to be gathered in –

There!

And there!

He could see them! These people he knew, his neighbours, his friends, all of them together in a circle and there in the centre, the two who were gone, the shape of his sister's love on the empty grass, and her dear child.

John walked over to Sonny and realised that his friend was sitting, eyes wide open, but asleep. Quietly he removed his shoes, his socks. Pulled off the clean trousers, and eased the old man gently into bed. Rhett came into the room and settled himself down on the floor. John pulled up the bed covers, listened for a moment to the old man's steady breathing, then he turned out the light, went up the hallway and turned out the kitchen light, and left.

Saturday

# ONE

In the very early morning there is stillness. A pale grey light is the colour of the sky and the shapes of hills and trees are marked against it. There are no sounds, no colours. The streets are empty and in the fields and paddocks animals are sleeping. The river is dark.

To be outside at this time is to be the only person in the world. There is a scent of water, a fine transparent mineral that freshens the air and picks out the spike of the church steeple against the sky. Around the church, to the north and west, the houses of Featherstone are scattered upon the gentle incline of the land like dice. It is a while yet until the day will begin. In the garden of the Railton Hotel the dark hedge that separates the lawn from the gravel driveway seems wary of the wakeful hours ahead. It crouches there at the edge of the grass, not a hedge at all but some kind of spruce or yew or pine, a fierce little tree that has been made to grow low against the ground for protection. Its wiry twigs and stiff leaves shatter water to the touch: last night's dew that still soaks the paddocks and glazes the flowers in planted gardens. It will evaporate soon. Heat is already banked up behind the pale sky as a force of blue that will burn off the moisture that now makes the air so frail, gives to the trees such a fine delicacy of outline you might think the branches would snap. Everything is made, formed, given, to be broken; nothing can be kept, and yet, right now, it seems you hold all the wide earth and the sky in your arms. Right now you can believe all the love you ever received or gave or came upon by chance is yours, in this pale and early unbruised morning, to keep. Nothing can take it away.

This is what the empty streets say, the far hills. This is what the miles of pasture and high country sing: *Nothing can hurt me*. The land stretches out around the little town empty and untouched all the way to the mountains, to the sea. *Nothing can hurt me*, the beautiful land sings in the early morning. *I will be at peace.*

Down the long wooden corridors of the Railton Hotel, the doors are shut fast against the coming day, only the sash window at the far end wall is open. The faded rugs on the floor and the dusty light fittings suggest no one occupies these rooms that are available at nightly and weekly rates, six in all, arranged along the back and side portions of the first floor. You know the kind of thing: big square rooms with a washbasin in the corner, shared bathroom down the hall. You may even have stayed in one the same. It could have been last night you experienced the sort of old-fashioned sleep people enjoy in beds of a size no one makes any more, with huge creaking frames and wooden headboards and a mattress that is soft and yielding when you lie down. Everyone in the hotel is comfortable in this way, asleep. In her own sheets, Margaret is sleeping.

While inside, night is still caught within the bedrooms, outdoors, slowly, imperceptibly, the light is changing. The colour of water is fading from the sky and another kind of light replaces it, drier, softer. It shades the little vine that grows through the twisting stair of the hotel's fire escape, touches the wooden sides of the building and smooths them. In Main Street, the same light makes the shops and bank and post office look as though they have been drawn there, outlined and filled in with a great grey crayon that marks as easily as it can be erased.

All the houses of Featherstone are quiet now. It is still not yet dawn and, like the residents of the hotel, everyone is sleeping. In farm houses, rural houses, sleeping, in houses behind garden walls, down the ends of tracks marked 'no exit'. They sleep, the covers drawn up around them, in houses that sit side by side in the new cul-de-sac on the eastern side of town, and in other houses that are alone and abandoned-looking in overgrown fields on the southern road. More and more, as you move through the quiet streets, you see there is such variety in the way people live here, in the way they have made their homes speak for them in the silence of the landscape. There are houses of two rooms, three, large houses with wide verandahs, and, up in the high country, the gracious homesteads of big estates that have their own outlying cabins and huts for the shearing gangs and work parties, for the shepherds and fruit-pickers and term croppers. Back in town there are cottages out by the railway station, little bunks behind the shops, near the hotel, and there are the rented houses near the playing fields where nobody stays long. There are houses with peeling paint and a tractor parked outside, with parts of old machinery littered through the yard, and there are houses freshly cleaned, with shaded porches and gardens that are sometimes so filled with fruit trees you could not imagine how it would be possible, in spring, to bear the sight of so much blossom. So many houses for one small town, it is hard to think of any of them without walking around and seeing. Here is one little tin-roof villa with a single tree planted outside, a string for washing stretched from a branch to a hook nailed in at the side of a window. Sheets and T-shirts hang quietly from the string like they are waiting for something. The people who live inside the houses seem to be waiting, they lie so quietly in their beds, their windows opened with expectation into the air.

You can really see now how the light is changing. The grey lightens, whitens, as the last of the water is leached from it. The sky no longer appears as a thing of itself, placed behind the town or above it, but is now melded through the contours and shapes of the land . . . this beautiful place. This little town with its flowers, its church and steeple. The hills around are quiet, and the mountains. There is nothing but distance here, no minutes, no hours. Time has not started yet, in this early morning, it is too early for time. At the playing field, at the showground, the bleachers set up in the pretty wooden and glass amphitheatre are empty, the churned-up turf is still. A fleck of paper sits on one of the long benches next to an old penny. Like the people of Featherstone quiet in their beds, all these things, these objects, seem to be in waiting. In the field behind the showground, the meadowgrass waits and the tiny purple flowers that grow amongst it. The trees wait, the thick stand of macrocarpas bunched together at the edge of the road leading out of town, and the railway station yards wait, and the quiet railway line. Nothing moves, and still, inch by inch, the light continues to lift.

Down Main Street you can see it, in the shop windows, above the sidewalk, in the broad road with its wires and tele-graph poles, the light is there. And on the hills now, at the mountain edge . . . slowly dawn is staining the sky. The whiteness is going and there are marks of pale yellow, rose and geranium and gold – the colours rub and smudge. Along the back of the bush ridge down at the Reserve, above the river, dawn is feeling its way, it is brushing its fingertips across the sky, pressing against the soft rounds of the land, wanting day to begin.

In the fields the animals are waking. There is a chink of bird-song in the silence, coming through leaves. In the children's playground the swings hang lank, the smooth slip of the slide dull silver, a soft worn metal to the touch and warm now in the first of the sun. At the part of the park beside the swings, past the flower beds and trees, the little stream seems set upon its stones like glass, not at all like a living thing that has come out of the bush and will go back there again, to the river. As we watch it, though, the water breaks and changes in the growing light so that bit by bit the stream takes on the colour of that place where it belongs, the colour of earth, of stones, moss and brown. Bit by bit everything begins to take on a colour.

There is the colour of blue, small at first, but it widens, deepens. There is the sun rising in the sky. Now there is the sound of a farmhouse door opening. Inside, someone puts on water for tea. At the Weldons' high country estate a thin wind passes over the tops of the hills, disturbs the willows that grow by the river at the back of the garden. A horse shifts in the near paddock, whinnies. In town, in the room above the milk bar, Kath Keeley shifts in her sleep. There's a light smell of sugar in the air around her from yesterday's baking: yellow sponge cakes, jam tarts, all laid out on sheets of waxed paper in the shop below. You can see a little cat has let herself in through the gap in the window. She lands lightly on the bed and starts kneading the covers where Kath sleeps. At that moment the roses in Johanssen's garden ruffle, as though someone has breathed across them. They shake their soft pink and yellow heads and the scent is sweet there too, like the cakes, vanilla, cream. In the Carmichaels' lumber yard, of course, there are no flowers, only bunches of sawn-off timber stacked up beside Johnny's machinery, his woodsaw and massive clamp and chain. There is sawdust thick across the ground within the dark shelter of the lean-to shed where he stores most of his tools, his work stuff. It is Saturday, no one's coming in. Over at Bob Alexander's garage it's the same. No one will put their car in today, so the oily slicks on the concrete can just sit there, undisturbed by fresh spill, and there's the old hulk of the Viscount Bob's been working on, off and on, in his spare time for the last few years, starting a paint job and then deciding the colour didn't suit, rubbing it down and starting again.

The morning is truly beginning. In the Carmichaels' house some distance away from the yard, in the sun-filled front bedroom Gaye opens her eyes and takes in the fact that she's not in her usual room. Johnny has finally started the work papering in there, a pretty flower pattern Gaye picked out at Dalgety's a year ago. Johnny's told her he's going to do all the woodwork too, in a nice fresh white, and the bedroom will be just lovely then. Gaye looks forward to it, when she and Johnny can move back into the big old double bed they've shared all their married life. She looks over at him now, his mouth open, snoring, his lovely curly hair that's still dark from the stuff he puts into it sticking up all over the pillow. Her lovely man. She smiles and quietly slips out of bed, pulls on her housecoat and goes down the hall to the kitchen to make her first-of-the-morning cup of tea.

Neil McIndoe, who does the milk round for the local dairy company, has just delivered, Gaye can see from the window the bottles out by the mailbox. He's earlier than usual because of this weather, and just starting the round now at the Carmichaels'. The van's been working well since Bob had it in for a service last month and Neil likes the feeling of being the only vehicle out and about on the road this Saturday morning. He whistles through his teeth as he puts out the orders of milk and juice and cream. It's a great job this, for a retired man. He'll finish up here, do the new houses on the other side and then come back down Main Street for the shops and the hotel. The hotel will take a big order as usual, doesn't matter how many people Margaret has in. They'll all be asleep there now, but round the corner from the hotel, at the Grahams', Maureen is up and putting on the bacon for the morning rolls. They've someone staying with them at the moment, some old friend of Peter's he was out at the bar with last night, and she wants to do a proper breakfast for him. She fires up the grill and gets the coffee beans out of the fridge ready to grind. The minute the bacon is under the heat, the old black Labrador who's been sleeping heavily in his basket opens his eyes and slowly heaves himself up and goes over to the bench where

Maureen is standing. In time, she will pull a piece of bacon out from the grill before it is cooked crisp and leave it on the side to cool. That will be for Frank, that piece not too well done. He stands beside her now, waiting, fully awake now for an old dog, but down the road, stretched out at the foot of his master's bed, his good friend Rhett is still asleep. Thurson Johanssen is asleep, sleeping deeply the sleep of an old man and full of dreams. He feels he never wants to wake from them, his eyes just busy catching sight of all the lovely colours, so bright and clear Sonny wants to open his mouth and cry out, 'Yes!' to keep them, like he might cry out, 'Hello! I'm here!' and stay there in the bright colours for ever.

Outside his window, the sky is becoming blue and shining as a china bowl. This is the final colour of the day, this blue, this bright steadiness with no cloud, no haze, only the polished yellow of the sun in the midst of it. Already it is very warm. Sonny has the sash window drawn up and there, the tall heads of his stocks seem to be peeping in at him, into his shadowy bedroom that is filled with their fragrance. He planted them for Nona, she always loved stocks and that's why they look in on him now, taking care of him like she used to. The sun rises higher and higher in the sky and still Sonny sleeps and dreams the lovely dreams of Nona and her flowers, seems lately he can't stop dreaming and hearing her voice; and there's something else Sonny can hear now too, there, behind the garden there comes the sound of a sheep bleating, then another. It's the Weldons' flock of summer ewes in the sale yards waiting for the Northern Auction. Sonny stirs in his sleep, hearing again the sound of the little sheep in his mind. They will be gathered into close pens first thing Monday and sold off in lots of half a dozen, for wool mainly, next year's first shearing, and those that are left behind will get sent off to the works the same afternoon. Until then, though, all the sheep can graze here, on this warm late-summer morning, peaceful in the paddocks out behind

119

Johanssen's garden. He opens his eyes now to the gentle sound of them there. He enjoys it, to wake this way with the animals nearby, to hear them, to smell the smell of the farm. It reminds him of Ray.

# TWO

Ray wakes and the first thing he thinks of is her. The taste of her, the feel of her . . . nothing can stop the memory. She's moving in his mind, through him, across his body, doing that thing she used to do, using her fingers, pushing them whole into his mouth and getting him to suck.

*Jesus, Francie . . .*

He thought he'd be with her by now. In this airless room where he's slept since he was a boy, in this dark place enclosed within his family's home, he's a man who can do nothing but lie on his bed with the curtains drawn against the brightness of the day and there's this woman, this girl, and she's taken up all of his body and his mind so there's nothing in him but her. It's like even the sheets are a body, hers, twisted around him, under him, like he could have her now, make it now, make her be with him because he doesn't ever want to change it, doesn't ever want to wake at all if this is dream and not having her is the real.

But it's late, Ray knows, and he'll have to make himself get up. His mother will be wondering, and his father, though his father doesn't hold onto much in his mind any more, even so both of them will be thinking why it is that he's keeping to his room this hour, not following his normal routine. Still he can't make himself move, no way. Couldn't make himself find her last night, can't make the thought of her leave him now. He really did think he'd be with her by now but instead he's just here alone, a man in a boy's room and he can't leave it, with his parents out there somewhere in the big house, thinking about their son, what's wrong with their son, why he isn't out of bed when all the time it's getting later and later and the sun is risen high in the sky.

*Ray. Ray. Ray.*

What are you doing, boy? Stir yourself.

*Ray.*

There's the day before you, and all your inherited lovely land . . .

He turns over in the bed, twists the sheet. No good because there's just his blood rising, remembering, the pulse of his blood beginning to beat and no amount of cool pasture and high wind-combed hills can stop it, no amount of bright day. Francie should be with him. It's that simple. She should be here with him now, worked in beneath him and he could do anything he wanted if he wanted. He sees her face in his mind, close up to him, her beautiful face as he turns his own back into the pillow.

*Francie . . .*

He turns over again and imagines her there, feels her trace the outlines of his face and he succumbs to her touch like a child. She laughs. 'I'm so lazy,' she says, and she starts to kiss him, slowly, slowly . . . His eyes are closed and it's dark and he can't bear it, the pain at the centre of the sweetness. He can't speak at all, can't adjust himself for one fraction of a second, he's nothing with love for her, just this thing made for pleasure opening and she's the girl who wants to come in.

*Now, Francie.*

But no. The room is hot, and it must be near noon, with the heat of the day banked up behind the curtains, and he's naked, with just a sheet, and Francie's not here, it's only his own nakedness he feels. There's no softness, only dry stones. One stone, another stone . . .

He'd have to get up. He'd put off the moment as long as he could, but it was here, in the stench of his breath, foul taste in his mouth and his head raging like an animal. What had he done to himself last night to be like this? To find himself like this, what had he done?

'Ray?'

That is the call of his mother from the hallway; a sure sign something's wrong. Again she calls and she never does that, never calls him.

'Ray?'

'Yeah . . . I know . . .'

He closes his eyes tight, an attempt to waken. He can't go bringing the frailty of his mother's voice to his door. What was the matter with him anyhow? What time did he get in last night? Now he could hear the sound of footsteps retreating down the hall and it was all wrong, to get his mother worried up like that. Now she'd be going back into the little sitting room his father liked to use in the mornings.

'What's he doing in there so late?' she'd be saying to his father, and his father just sitting in his chair like a doll.

'What's he doing?' she'd say, while outside the window there'd be all this land, this wide, empty land with a house upon it where Ray's lived so long he's nearly forgotten how it's a place that was built for loneliness, standing out here by trees, high in the high country where no one ever comes, and there's only the sound of the wind, at night, sometimes, or early in the morning when it's still dark, only the sound of the wind when Ray drives home again in the dark, finally comes home again, returned to his little boy's bed.

'Ray?'

He drove back here last night. Now he's waking up he has to make himself remember.

'Ray?'

Has to. Think about what his plans are . . . because his mother never did that, stood just outside the door like that, and it's not his way to be unreliable. He should think about what it is he's going to tell her, then, what it is that he should do, and all he can think about instead is nothing about last night or what he should say, but only that green river smell of Francie close to him, that smell of water that would be on her when they were together at the river, her wet skin from swimming, water in her hair and the streaming water from her mouth when she came up again from the river for air, spilling water from her mouth onto him where he was dry.

*Jesus . . .*

He couldn't do anything with himself. What was it he'd been drinking anyway? Whisky? Beer? That was madness, however you looked at it, to go so bar-crazy like he'd gone last night, to go so bad that way, just on liquor.

*Jesus, though . . .*

He'd have to pull himself together.

*C'mon . . .*

First, to get up, get dressed. Then get to the bathroom, get some water for his face. He pulled on the pair of pants that were lying on the floor . . .

*C'mon.*

But it was cold in there, in the bathroom, like ice. He zipped himself up and he was shivering . . .

At the basin he splashed on water, in the mirror couldn't look at his face. God knows what they were thinking in town. He didn't know what he was doing himself any more. Down at the Reserve yesterday morning, all day feeling like a crazy man. Drinking and sleeping and drinking some more . . . that whole thing in the bar . . .

Just the thought of it made him have to go back and sit down again on the bed. He closed his eyes. There was the blood in his head pounding, the drink pounding there, mixed with the blood . . . God knows what was going on that he could get himself so worked up again about someone he knew years ago and she was just a woman, a girl.

*C'mon, Ray.*

He had to get himself together. Though he could picture his mother's face if he was to go through there now, into the little sitting room, tell her, 'Guess who I've just seen . . .' and the look on her face like the best present someone could give her. 'Guess who's come home and I've seen her . . .' Though he could imagine the whole scene –

'Guess who?'

He hadn't seen her. After all the liquor in the world, the lateness of the hour. After all the time yesterday spent waiting, last night all that time, waiting, watching . . . she was nowhere. There'd been only whisky and beer and him knowing there was some kind of madness in the way he'd been hitting it so hard and then driving all the way back to the farm, driving like a madman to do the distance in an hour – he'd come home to get changed, for godsake!

*Jesus.*

It was all coming back to him now. He'd run scalding water for a shower, stood there carefully combing his hair. He'd got all ready for her like he really was going to see her, like he was a kid, sixteen again the way he drove, holding the thought of her in the dark road ahead, in the white of the car headlights on the road . . .

*Francie . . .*

*Francie . . .*

There was that quiet sweat like he really was sixteen and driving his father's station wagon into town, taking off the edges of the road hard.

*Francie . . .*

*Francie . . .*

That quiet sweat when he was sixteen and he'd first asked her out and she'd nodded her head, *Yes* . . . Like that time, when he'd taken her by the elbow, steered her outside the school hall, and there was her body within the shape of the dress she was wearing, he could feel it, and he'd taken her outside and the minute they got there, into the hot night, with the soft dryness of the dark paddocks all around them, he'd known then, that second, she'd known – *yes* – and it was like a match set alight in the dry grass, the whole thing going up in a flame and all you can do is watch it burn.

Time to get yourself together, Ray. Yeah, but it's good here, with the past. Time to get on maybe, but even with his body feeling like it's in a vice, like someone has got hold of it and they're not going to let him go . . . It feels good here, and he just wants to stay.

Outside the window where he couldn't see, Ray knew it had to be well past noon by now. That thought should be enough to get him up and out the bedroom door. Should be. He'd acted crazy last night, like Mickey Parsons with his eye fixed to see only the thing that was right in front of him, getting all excited, that was him. Bit by bit, more of the night before was coming back into his mind. The drive home, then returning again to the bar – and what was that about, that thing at the bar, with Margaret? Hadn't there been something about Margaret? He'd been there, she'd been there . . .

But forget about Margaret. That was last night and this was now, it was different. He could start again. He'd fix some coffee, sober up. Give an account of himself to his parents and then begin again with the business of Francie. Just because he hadn't seen her yesterday didn't mean he wouldn't in the time ahead. There was the afternoon, there was the rest of the day . . .

Quickly he finished dressing, put on a shirt, found a belt for his pants. He drew apart the curtains to let in the bright day, and it was such a day, with the light all flung down across the hills and open and naked-looking. Of course he would find her today, out there in that immaculate light, no one could hide. He went over to the mirror and he could look at himself now. Easy. OK, so everything could be fine. He slipped into a pair of shoes, walked down the hallway to the room where he knew his parents would be and sure enough, when he pushed open the sitting-room door, there they both were, chairs over by the window and looking out at the same bright day, the same light cast through the glass and everywhere about them.

They both turned when they heard him come in.

'Hey,' Ray said.

But his mother didn't smile at him, say hello.

'Everything OK?'

Instead there was a second while she looked at him, not saying a word, just looking, and it was a strange look, as though she could not remember who he was, and was having trouble forming the thought to tell him so in her mind. Then she turned back to the window.

'I don't know . . .' came her voice. 'You could tell me, perhaps, if everything's OK.'

His father was sitting quietly in the way he always sat, but Ray saw that he too was regarding him in some close fashion, noting him, checking him. He had got used to the old man not talking any more, only *yes* or *no*, but suddenly his father opened his mouth and spoke.

'Your mother's worried,' he said, just like that, like he was back amongst them. 'Can't you tell?'

It was the first time in months he'd spoken this much, formed sentences.

'What's going on?' he said to Ray, and he leaned towards him, clear with his question, like a lucid man.

'Can you tell me', he said, 'what you've been up to these last couple of days?'

It was strange, the feeling, hearing his father talk again, like the stroke had never happened. Suddenly now there were these words coming out of the silence that for so long now had been carved within his inert body and for Ray it was like a question coming out of the deepest place, out of a void, and he didn't know how to answer, what to think, or do, or say.

'I don't know, Dad,' he said, and he found himself shutting his eyes tight against the question, against the answer. He found himself clenching his hands into neat fists.

'I don't know,' he said again, and he knew how foolish he

127

must look, just standing like this, with his eyes shut tight and his fingernails digging deep into the palms of his hands.

'I don't know,' he said for the third time. Then he opened his eyes and it was all black around him. For a second, he couldn't see, then his mother's voice came out of the air and the black pulse of blood that had obscured his vision cleared, and Ray saw that she'd turned back from the window to face him again.

'There's something wrong,' she said. 'It's none of my business, but there's something . . . What is it? What occurred last night, do you know about last night?'

She looked at him and her eyes were intent upon him.

'Do you even remember?' she said.

Remember?

Now it was Ray's turn to want to look away.

Remember? Sure he could remember. He'd gone back to the bar, and he'd really thought: This time, Francie. She'll come in. It will be her walking in through that door. So he'd waited . . . He'd stood there at the bar in his fancy clothes . . .

His head, his heart.

His heart, his body.

. . . Just stood there, waiting. He'd been drunk last night, but he'd had no choice.

'I had no choice,' he said to his mother. Then he said, 'There's something you should know. Yesterday, I found out . . . It's about Francie –'

'Francie!' His mother cut him off short.

'She's home, Elsa.'

'What?'

His mother stood up.

'What are you saying?' she said.

'She's here, she's come back. I know –'

His mother interrupted him: 'Listen to yourself!' She started coming towards him with her hand outstretched, but her eyes . . . Ray had never seen his mother's eyes like that, hard like

128

that, like she was angry with him or afraid of him, or both.

'What are you saying?' she cried out to him. 'After all this time it's Francie again!'

'I thought you'd be pleased,' Ray said. Surely, she should be. No matter what she was saying, how she was saying it, no matter that she was looking at him like she had a monster for a son, she should be pleased, should be, and his father, that Francie was home again. What was going on that they weren't happy for him now? Ray saw his father get up from the chair, slowly, using the chair to support him. The sentences from before were gone and he was shaking his head, 'no, no,' like an old man again, like he'd started shaking his head at the outset of the illness, 'no, no,' turned into a crazy old man in a hospital and 'no' the only word left in the world to say. He stood fully, then slumped back in his chair again.

'Now I understand why people have been talking,' Ray's mother said.

'One of the Carmichael boys told Gaye he'd seen your car out on the Reserve road yesterday morning. He thought you'd been fishing . . . Fishing!'

She put her hand up to her mouth. There was a silence, then she took her hand away. She started over towards him, made to reach out for him, but Ray backed off. None of this was right. His mother didn't understand.

But that didn't matter, because for his part, more and more he was coming to understanding. The memory of last night was forming more fully and he could start to see clearly what before had been a blur in his mind. Why, for example, he'd been talking to Margaret at the bar. It was because she was a woman who lived alone, she must know what it's like. So ignore his mother, the things she said . . . Think about what he was talking about to Margaret –

'I want you to listen to me, Ray.'

– but don't listen, think. Think about what was important. Had he been talking about Francie to Margaret? He would never normally do that – but now she was here, in town, that was different, wasn't it? So maybe he had talked to Margaret about Francie, asked her to help him? Asked her, made her? Had he spoken to her, or just grabbed her? 'You've got to come with me now, help me find her. You're a woman, you should know where women are . . .' Had he grabbed her like that, pushed her? 'You should know where the women are . . .' He was full of booze; he could have done anything, there was whisky all through him. He'd gone home, put a clean shirt on. He'd been all ready to see Francie, get her down to the river, all the old things.

'Ray?'

Anything. He could have done anything.

'Speak to me, answer me . . .'

But no, he won't speak, not yet, he has to think . . . He could have done anything. There was the way he'd been when he'd returned to the Railton and it was late by then, but Sonny was there. Of course, Sonny . . . *She's here.* That was it! Sonny knew it too . . . Ray remembered now, he wasn't the only one. Sonny knew Francie was here, he'd already seen her. She'd called out to him, he said, and Ray thought of the way Sonny was when he told him this, holding Ray by the hand, his eyes big and shining like a kid.

'She's back, Ray,' he'd said. 'I seen her. She'll be looking for you, boy, better watch yourself. Be careful, eh?'

Ray says now, to his mother, 'Sonny's already seen her.'

'What?'

'I'm not crazy, Elsa. It's not just me.'

He remembers how he felt something like an electric wire cut through him at the touch of the old man's hand upon his own, telling him. 'Be careful . . .' he'd said. That was Sonny, knowing the truth about things, the way the people you loved would come back for you. Ray would always listen to what the old man had to say.

'Sonny's seen her,' he says to his mother, and that should

count for something because everyone in town agreed there was a quality to the old man made you want to listen to him, just sitting around his kitchen table with a beer, like he and Francie used to do, stopping by his garden to watch him rake fallen leaves from the grass.

'Sonny knows she's here,' he says to his mother, and it's obvious he's going to have to explain it all to her, how it's not just him. He'll have to be clear with her, be rational. He'll have to be calm to make her calm because she is frightened now, he can see it, of him, her son.

He begins, 'I saw Sonny last night at the Railton and we talked about it. About Francie . . . He's seen her, he knows . . .'

He can hear the sound of his voice, there it was, telling his mother the whole story, slowly, so it could be understood.

'He saw her first, in the afternoon. That's when it began . . .'

But instead of listening Elsa just shook her head.

'That's a lie . . .' she said. 'You know it is. Listen to me . . .' She tried to reach out to him again, but Ray put up his hand to stop her.

'Francie's not here,' his mother went on. 'She would never be here, why would she be? After all this time, you have to realise it, accept it, Ray. Look at who you are, what you've become. You should be a man like your brothers, married and away from here. Not in this place. You should be away and not spending your life in wait. She's never coming back, Ray. Francie will never come home. She's gone. She went away and . . .'

'No, no . . .' his father was back to muttering to himself, over and over, 'No, no . . .' and his mother there talking on. 'You have to listen to me . . .' she was saying. 'Sonny doesn't know anything, it's in his mind. It's all in his mind, that's the way he is . . .'

Sonny.

'The way he gets things in his mind because he wants them to be true . . . That's how he is . . .'

Sonny, Ray thinks again.

He should have gone there, to Sonny's house, last night.

'Sonny doesn't know about anything . . .' Elsa's saying, but now the last part of the night before is back with Ray, in his mind, entire. Finally he remembers it all, the end of the night when he'd finished drinking at the bar . . . and he should have gone there, to Sonny's house, not up the road. He should have sat down in Sonny's kitchen, got himself sorted out.

'Ray?' his mother is saying, but ignore his mother.

Sonny always knew what was going on between him and Francie, he would understand . . .

'Ray?'

Only think about what he was doing last night, going right past Sonny's house the way he did, going right past him to go up the road at that hour, midnight, later than midnight probably, what was he doing?

'Ray?'

What was he doing?

'Ray?'

*I was doing what I thought was right.*

*I went to Nona's old house.*

*I thought Francie would be there.*

'It was late, dark . . .' he says to his mother now. 'But after everywhere I'd been that day, every place where I'd watched and waited, after all that time I finally realised . . . Francie would be at her mother's house. Why hadn't I thought about it before? That's why I finished drinking at the bar, said good-bye to Margaret and she said goodbye to me. There was her face, her sad face . . . She smiled at me standing there in my clean shirt and I guess she must have thought I looked like some kind of a fool. I was all dressed up. I was like a kid, but it was because of Francie, I wanted to go see her, at her mother's house . . .'

'A deserted house.'

*I was doing what I thought was right.*

'Listen to yourself! Listen!'

*I was doing what I would always do, go look for her, to bring her in. I remember exactly how I planned it, driving back to the farm and the lights still on in the sitting room but my own mother never even saw me. I came in, and I was stinking of whisky like petrol on my breath from having driven so hard to get home.*

'It makes no sense, Ray! Listen!'

*For you, sweetheart.*

'Listen to me!'

*I ran a shower and the water of the shower was scalding. I stood before the mirror and I combed my hair.*

'You can't believe any of this is true! You can't stop your life waiting for this one thing to happen. She's gone! She's gone!'

*For you.*

'She's never coming back!'

*Without my mother hearing, my sleeping father hearing, without my parents having to know they have a crazy man for the only son that's stayed behind to work their land . . . I was there, I was gone. Before they knew anything about me at all I was back down the gravel driveway, and onto the dirt track . . .*

*I knew exactly what I was going to do.*

*All my life I've known it, since you left, Francie, I've known it more. You're coming home. You're coming home and it's to my country you're coming. You're here because you belong, and I'm keeping you this time, I'm never going to let you go. I'll keep you so hard, I'll put my body against you as protection. You'll be able to listen to my heart.*

*Francie.*

*Listen to me, to my heart. It says: I'm never going to let you go.*

The telephone started to ring then, this loud, insistent, terrifying sound coming from such a small instrument sitting on the little table in the room. Elsa turned to answer it, to stop the awful sound, and in that instant Ray had left.

'Yes?'

It was Sonny.

Immediately Elsa turned but Ray wasn't there.

'Elsa?'

'He's gone,' she said. 'He was just here but –'

'Don't let him go,' said Sonny.

'Something bad, I can feel it. Keep him with you, Elsa . . .'

The old woman dropped the phone and ran from the room.

'Please!' she called out.

'Ray!'

But her voice came back empty in the empty house. Only in the sitting room the endless *no, no* of her husband, shaking his head like something was caught in his head and he was trying to dislodge it, *no, no,* the only sound, and Sonny's voice caught in the black receiver of the telephone that lay half-broken and swinging between the little table and the floor.

'Hello?' said the broken voice. 'Hello? Are you there?'

## THREE

You come in upon a person's house, you see the quietest things. Renee Anderson standing at the kitchen bench finishing the last of the washing-up, dishcloth in her hand, turned to face out towards the open window . . .

Thinking about her daughter.

What was it about her daughter? Renee couldn't get to the bottom of it. Some niggling little thought she couldn't push away, but it was there, like a pin might be in the carpet and you wouldn't see it but you knew that it was there.

Mary Susan.

Mary Susan, all right.

That girl had such ideas about herself, she got so fixed with them, Renee couldn't shake her loose. For instance, this business with the clothes all the time and wanting to be so grown up. Once there'd been this child and Renee had known her, brushed her hair before she went to school, given her a kiss goodnight . . . and now . . .

Renee looked down at the sudsy water and whirled the cloth like she was doing something, but she wasn't. It was a different situation altogether now with the girl. With her outfits, the way all the pocket money went on those kinds of things, and bracelets and bits of toiletries. It all seemed to have happened too fast, in a rush no one could be ready for. And she'd seen the way Mary Susan had looked at Ray Weldon yesterday. The girl couldn't take her eyes off the man.

Renee swirled the water again. She'd seen, all right . . . her daughter pirouetting there in front of a grown man like she was something in a circus – what would he have thought, but more, what was the girl thinking? Renee felt annoyed at the memory, the way she couldn't fix it. She couldn't believe how often she wasted time these days, like wasting it now, standing doing nothing with a cloth and odd thoughts from nowhere just filling up her head and not connecting. It made her mad. Like this worry now, about yesterday afternoon, Mary Susan running over with those legs of hers all over the place, pirouetting and spinning in front of Ray, and Ray must have noticed. Too polite to show it, of course, that was Ray, all the Weldon family like that, the brothers when they were still living on the estate, and, of course, old Mr and Mrs Weldon, reserved, with those sorts of quiet, lovely manners . . . It made it worse. Renee could see, plain as an egg, that her daughter had been acting up in front of the man, being a little woman for him.

She swished one of the lunch plates in the sudsy water. It was the modelling. That had to be the start of where you could lay the blame – like Mary Susan hadn't eaten a thing at lunchtime and all on account of some notion she had about her figure.

*Oh, Mum . . .*

Sighing like that, when Renee made her the wrong kinds of food.

*You know I can't eat that sort of thing.*

*Elena says . . .*

Elena rot. Renee swished the plate again, but she wasn't doing anything with it, she wasn't cleaning it, she just held it there, this thing in her hand, like she'd never seen a plate before. What was going on to get her so worked up? That little niggle she couldn't put her finger on, holding her up from getting the housework done, from acting in a clear line. It was as if she had an odd kind of a mood about everything today, not just Mary Susan, but that was touching everything else and making it odd, like the housework and not being able to do even a bit of a thing without thinking about her daughter, and something about the way the girl's body was changing . . .

*May I go now, Miss Farley?*

She remembered at the hotel yesterday, talking to Margaret, and Mary Susan out there in the driveway, and looking quite aware of herself, in the little skimpy clothes she had chosen, quite aware, in her top and in her legs . . .

Renee had been talking to Margaret, and yes, something in the mood had started then, with Mary Susan looking the way she did and how Margaret would have noticed, if she'd seen the girl, how she was dressed, how Margaret would notice things like that, and the way Renee would always feel uncomfortable around that woman.

What was the feeling? It came straight off Mary Susan but it was about Margaret, the way there was something in that woman's dealings with Mary Susan that made her seem hungry, as though Renee felt Margaret's eyes on her all the time with her daughter and they were these hungry eyes, waiting, watching . . . wanting to gobble something up.

Like Jim.

That was it, exactly. The way Jim was, how men could be who you'd fallen for. Something in thinking about Mary Susan with Margaret, the awareness the girl had of her shape, Margaret's awareness . . . it had all got Renee being reminded of Jim. She swished the silly plate again, saw her reddened hands in the dirty water. Seemed all she did these days in her life was dishes, tidying up. Even so, she'd never go back to that other dirty business. When she thought about the children's father now she could barely believe she'd ever been married. It was more like her husband had been someone she'd read about in a book, or seen in a film maybe, because he'd been a good-looking man. But not real. That's why she worked all the time, doing other people's work. Like for Margaret Farley and needing the money, because for sure there'd never been anyone else around who could have sent her some.

*Dear Renee . . .*

He used to write, and for a while there was money with the letters. Then the letters stopped.

Even so . . .

Renee ran her hands round and around in the hot water . . . It was five years they'd been together. They'd had the wedding, and the wedding party. She'd been a bride, hadn't she? And he'd acted so nicely with her in the early days, before Mary Susan came along, and she'd always known he wouldn't be the kind to stick around for ever. When you thought about it, Mary Susan was only just turned one and he'd started talking about business ventures and travel to do this or that, always the spare money going into plans for some electrics scheme, or land he knew about coming up for sale and worth a fortune but he could get it cheap. All in, it was a miracle Renee found herself pregnant the second time – that must have been one of his flying visits home right there.

But even so . . . five years.

*Do you take this man, this woman?*

*I do.*

*I do.*

And she'd liked the ring of that, well enough, the ceremony, the taking of a man's name to call her own . . .

*Renee Anderson.*

So that even though now she was far from the whole business of marriage and would never want any part of it, still she'd had something once, it was nestled within her, a little shocking and sweet feeling only she would ever know about, of what it had been like to be with a husband in those early years with nothing but chance all ahead of you and time, day upon day . . . To be a young woman and finding yourself caught unaware, held, tender in the care of another.

Tender.

That was it, the exact word.

And tenderness.

Like the way when you looked at Margaret Farley you

knew, even with all her smart clothes and such, that she'd never had that feeling once given to her, of someone's eyes looking down upon her with love.

Renee was standing quite still in the kitchen by now, not even moving her hands through the greasy, soapy water. That poor woman. Renee saw for the first time her loneliness, something gone wrong in her life and nobody around to put it right. How she must be ashamed, Renee thought, it was as though she had seen right through Margaret's appearance and manner and knew every little sad quality about her life. Who was there for her? Just nobody, that was all. Like Margaret would just have to make do with nobody and everyone knew that's exactly what she did.

Quickly, Renee fished around for another plate, something. Jiggery. She was in a queer mood all right. Everyone knew Margaret took men into her hotel and treated them like she knew them, everyone knew, but why be thinking about that now off the back of worrying about her daughter? Where were all the thoughts coming from that seemed to make no sense, have no connection? Where would the thoughts then go?

At that moment there was a great crash from the sitting room and Mary Susan's voice: 'That's it!'

'I didn't do anything!' Renee heard Eric shouting back. 'I didn't! I didn't!' and then Mary Susan again, 'I'm going to get you, you little monster!'

Renee smiled. Not so grown up after all that her little brother couldn't get the better of her with a bit of a tease. He came running into the kitchen now, a big grin all over his face.

'You should see her, Mum,' he said, and doubled over with laughter, holding his stomach like he'd told the most hilarious joke. 'She looks funny 'cause her clothes are all on all funny, and I made her fall, Mum. She was dancing on the table and I came up and I did this . . .'

Eric put his fingers out and did a little tickle on Renee's leg. 'See?'

Renee brushed him away. 'Don't be silly, Eric.'

She thought for a minute.

'On the table?' she said.

Eric started laughing again, hysterical and silly laughing.

'Be quiet,' Renee said.

What was going on?

Quickly, she pulled the plug on the sink, she'd never really been doing those dishes anyway, and went through to the next room to see . . . Nothing. The room was empty, no sign of a crash. The chairs were arranged around the table as always, and only a pile of clothing on the floor made things look different from how they were every other day. Renee went over and picked up the new top and the shoes Mary Susan had been using her pocket money and savings to buy. There was a scarf in the pile, too, she hadn't seen before, and the skirt with the ruffled edge that Kate Harland had helped Mary Susan sew on one of those afternoons at the church. The zip was pulled, like it might be broken, and bundled within it was some kind of bra thing, not really a bra because Mary Susan wouldn't be developed enough, would she, for a bra . . . would she?

*Developed.*

Now that was another word. Renee remembered the minister's wife had used it. She'd said, after one of the sewing sessions at the church: *She's quite developed now, Renee. She's a young woman, you know.*

It made Renee feel queer. The thought that another woman could tell her about something to do with her own daughter and really, it was none of her business. What could the minister's wife possibly know when she didn't even have a child of her own? Yet, for all that, the word was strong. It had some kind of a meaning in it, more important than it might sound, and caught in somehow to what she'd been thinking

140

about before, with Margaret, and, for that matter, with Jim
. . . It was sex. That was what it was. The Anderson blood in
Mary Susan after all, and the worry that it might make her, if
Renee didn't watch out carefully, someone like her father
had been.

She picked up another little T-shirt from the floor. It was
just a little girl's T-shirt but still it made Renee think about
how young she'd been when she was just married, how Jim
had said it was like starting all over again for him, with a
beginner. He knew it all, Jim. He'd shown her a thing or two.
Renee shivered. After all, at the end of the day, she'd had two
children with the man so she couldn't have been that much of
a beginner. It was the Anderson blood getting into her own
veins. Jim had been of a certain type, so who was to say her
daughter might not have a bit of the same in her too? Proud,
like Jim always had to have the light on when they, you know
– and Mary Susan could be a bit like that, always wanting to
show herself off to all and sundry.

'What was she doing up there on the table?'

Renee suddenly turned to Eric who had followed her into
the sitting room.

'Tell me! And what do all these clothes mean, that I found
here on the floor?'

Eric giggled, turned away.

'She's rude, Mum . . .'

'Shut up, you! Just shut up!'

Mary Susan's voice came through the wall.

'You're just stupid, you little tell-tale and I heard everything you said! Tell-tale! Baby!'

'Am not!'

'Are so! Baby!'

'Am not and I'm never playing with you again . . .'

Eric reached out to his mother. 'Mum . . .' He put his face
into Renee's skirt and for a minute she thought he was going
to cry.

'She's stupid, Mum, anyway . . .' Renee felt him nestling there against her. '. . . with her underpants. Isn't she?'

'Shhh . . .' Renee patted his head. He thought the world of Mary Susan, really. 'Stop it, both of you with your silly arguing . . .'

See? At the end of the day, they really were both just kids. Mary Susan still just a kid. A silly little girl.

Then Eric's comment came back into Renee's mind and this time it made her stop sharp.

'What do you mean?' she said.

She pushed the boy back away from her so she could see him.

'What did you just say?'

'Her,' said Eric. 'She was taking off all her clothes . . .'

'Shut up! Shut up!' came Mary Susan's voice through the wall, then she herself was running into the room wearing a dressing gown that she was holding together at the front.

'Don't listen to him, Mum! He's lying!'

'Am not!' yelled Eric at the top of his voice. 'You were taking off your clothes! She was, Mum!'

'I nearly broke my neck!' said Mary Susan. 'Because of you, you little baby!' Quickly she snatched up the bundle of clothing that Renee had moved to a chair and in the instant of her doing it Renee saw the flap of the dressing gown open and that underneath it her daughter was naked.

'She was, Mum!' Eric cried out again

Renee felt sick suddenly, in her stomach.

'What exactly', she said, 'has been going on in here?'

Mary Susan did not reply. She simply held the clothes close to her and looked away.

'I said . . .' Renee took the girl by the shoulder and turned her round to face her.

Mary Susan burst into tears and ran from the room.

Kate Harland had found herself in the garden early afternoon and now she was unable to leave it. She couldn't think what the day had held. Something had brought her here, to this strange planted place, not a garden at all, not really, yet something had brought her here. It was rare for her to come. She stood, and the feeling was something like a cooling breeze in hot summer, something strange and light in her body like held breath, standing in the bright day alone and quite still on the green grass that her husband kept shaved close and hard to the ground.

Why? Be here? She couldn't think of a reason. The unhappiness of the night before, her sleeplessness, the pills she took to stop the thoughts that had turned and turned within her ... all this had left her feeling empty. She had no more emotion left. Now there was just this garden. This bright afternoon sun. How simple everything seemed. There was grass, trees. Nothing more to concern herself with. She wasn't here, Harland wasn't here. There was just . . . nothing. It was so simple now to see it. Nothing at all she wanted to be doing, just to be here, in this strange garden, in the green.

She looked around the bright enclosure, within its hedge, and there the spike of the church steeple. It would be easy just to leave her husband now. Even the pills hadn't stopped her from hearing him come in last night and it was like something had broken through to her with his arrival. What was she doing in her long life? Still waiting? Why be waiting for him now, after all the years, why still be waiting? She'd heard Harland stumble, he was drunk. She'd heard how heavy he had been on the stair, but even then he wouldn't think of coming near her. How he must loathe her.

Kate plucked at a tiny leaf and held it between thumb and forefinger. This tiny thing. It had taken this long for her knowledge to break in. Her marriage was over, perhaps it had never been.

*I've always loathed you*, she could imagine Harland saying, out of his alcohol, or out of a prayer . . . Truth.

143

*I've never desired you . . .*

Kate held the tiny leaf and could not believe how simple it was, to understand. Could not believe it had taken her this long to see . . .

There was no reason for her to stay. Harland would remain here with his church, these people who lived in the town, the Johnny Carmichaels and all of their sons . . . These people he chose to spend time with, trying to understand them, minister to them . . . Let him. Margaret and Johnny and all of them, let him remain amongst them. She wouldn't come creeping in his way. The time was over for creeping, for laying her hand on his naked back. Instead, let herself stop pretending she'd ever been a wife who came in to serve his needs. Bringing a carafe of cold water to his bedside like she might have done in the past when he'd been out late the night before, making him something special on a tray . . . no need for any of that now. Just let him lie there, Kate thought, it was better, in his dark house. Lie there, he preferred it without her. The man of the people, holy man, lie there. Lie.

*And you can't help me*, Kate thought.

*And you know nothing about love.*

The knowledge had been like a calm since breaking, something for the first time in a long time that felt real. Seeing who her husband was, the absence of all hope in their marriage . . . it was a kind of peace, when you thought about it, perhaps the only kind. That's why she was standing in the garden with no thoughts, because it was like peace. To be here, on the grass, with no hope, no expectation . . . It was as if there was nothing that remained in the world for her to know. Kate Harland looked down at herself. She was fully dressed. She could go somewhere now, leave him now . . .

So perhaps she would.

She could take the car and drive way out of town. Pack a swimsuit in a tiny bag. She could drive to the coast if she wanted, why not? Arrive out there by the sea and stay, find some little beachside place. She'd spend hours lying out on the expanse of flat sand, baking in the sun. She'd be the only one. She wouldn't need to go anywhere, do anything. At night she'd just come in and put her swimsuit on the line to dry, and it would hang there under the night sky, like a little body, while she slept.

That's what she was thinking, these thoughts, what she might do. Her husband . . . She had no husband. Let him stay with his church. Let him go to the Railton every night if that's what his faith wanted. She couldn't wait any more for him to come home, waiting had made her thin. In her little dresses, standing at the back of the church . . . she'd become nobody, like Harland's God. Nobody everywhere he looked, in the pews and sky and steeple. Here she was, in the garden, and it was only herself, nobody. There was no husband asleep in the house, no other people anywhere in the world to disturb her, only nothing, nobody, in this mock garden, in this empty place. It could be as though there were no church building over the hedge, no account there she must keep. She could simply stand, feeling in the afternoon heat the huge silence around her. Silence of the green, silence of the steeple. The sky's endless blue. This glorious silence.

*Nothing.*
*Nothing.*

Like last night, alone in her bath's dark water, *nothing*, she was nothing – but better than last night because now the nothing was everywhere. It was the emptiness of the world's womb – teeming life already gone out to fill the creases and crevices of the earth and now nothing more to give. Nothing spent, used, nothing, every leaf was nothing, every blade of grass. Nothing was what was growing, giving life, nothing was all of life; nothing was everything.

She could get in the car, drive to the coast.

She could never come back.

Kate turned the ring on her finger. Her husband was asleep and she'd brought him no water, she'd not gone to sit by him at his bed. She turned the ring around and around and it turned easily on her thin finger. Who was he anyway, the minister? Only nothing. Why had she ever thought otherwise, turning the ring, and turning it . . .

*Nothing.*

Carefully Kate removed the gold circle from her finger and it came away easily, like a part of a shell. She placed it in the pocket of her cotton dress and she couldn't even feel it there, the little thing, little piece of her marriage gone and now she could take away all the other parts piece by piece. The house, another little part, the paper house, the garden . . . She surveyed it now, this enclosure with its empty flower beds grown over with grass so they looked like graves, a little graveyard the place where she'd tried to make a planting. It wasn't a garden at all. Not like other women's gardens. There were no flowers.

*Mrs Harland!*
*Mrs Harland!*
She would take the car now.
*Can I have a cake?*
*Can I have a cup of tea?*
It was easy.
*Can I?*
*Can I?*
She would go to a place that didn't even pretend a garden, that lovely, bare, empty place with its harsh, hot light, its grains of sand. Go there. Stay there. Turn herself in time into grains of sand.

In her other pocket, the one empty of a ring, there was a little bottle of pills. She fingered it, a tiny glass bottle but the seal was unbroken. It felt smooth and cool, and heavy, even for such a tiny thing, full.

Take the car.
  *Mrs Harland!*
  *Mrs Harland!*
  She could make it happen, it could be easy. One by one . . . little grains of sand. Emptying away, into air, into nothing . . . little grains of sand, and she could be gone.

◇

Inside the house, Harland's eyes were open. He'd just woken from a dream and Sonny Johanssen was in the dream. He'd put his hand upon Harland's head and Harland had felt it to be the hand of God.

  'Don't take your hand away,' Harland had woken up saying, and it was as though the words were still sounding around him in the room, like music, a psalm. He remembered Sonny in the dream had been surrounded by other people but he had placed his hand upon Harland's head and kept it there and Harland could not believe that this small physical thing could stay with him so strong.

  'There, now . . .' Sonny had said, and he'd stroked his hair.

  'There, now . . .' and there had been great comfort in the touch.

It was Scriptural, of course, Harland knew. Everywhere you looked Christ was in thick crowds, surrounded by people and always His hand outstretched. Why, you could argue, His whole ministry was a laying on of hands, not philosophy at all but a simple faith of touch, of palms, and fingertips, the hand placed upon the head to give the blessing:
*Awake, sleeper.*
*Rise from the dead.*
*And Christ will shine on you.*

147

Harland sat up, on his own bed. It had been no dream.

Sonny really had come to him last night . . . He placed his own hand upon his head now as though to remind himself . . . There, right there. Somebody had been close enough to him to do that, place the palm of his hand upon his head.

*Awake, sleeper.*

Harland had been blessed.

It gave him a small start, to think about it. That a simple touch could be something so much more . . . And yet, now the thought had come to him, there was no doubt in his mind that this was so, that the meaning of the gesture was benediction. Harland couldn't believe it. To think that he could find himself in the position now, after all his years in the church, of being available to a simple and straightforward act that in total represented some kind of conversion . . . it made no sense. Or rather, it made nothing but sense. That was what was unbelievable, Harland thought. That, in a strange way, sense was all he had. He remembered back to earlier in the same evening when he'd been at work in his study and the window had been open and there'd been a scent of perfume, a sweetness, in the air. Something had begun in him then, some sense of sense, the world around him presaged with a kind of foreshadowing, an under-knowledge . . . It was as though whatever was stirring in the garden, was stirring also within him. Remember? Of course he couldn't help but remember. The feeling had been like a pulse, a beat of breath, something so physical he'd had to close the window against it. God? He'd thought about God then, it was true, that strength of a presence . . . How could he not think of God? Yet wasn't the thing too rich in the way it had moved him, too human, sexual and powerful and full of fear . . .

*Awake, sleeper.*

Harland felt the beginning of a headache. He wasn't used to this, these kinds of thoughts. He didn't want them. Why should he, after all his years of contained belief, get caught up in fresh ideology now, some concept of physical rather than moral spirituality? It was madness for him, and what did it mean anyway, to make that kind of transcription, one form to another, what was that all about, in the Gospels: *the life of the body*? He didn't think in those terms. He was a craftsman, a shaper of words, not some simple-minded old man who went around the place having visions, touching people on the head, making them feel strange . . .

Acting like a god.

The thought fell whole into Harland's mind:
*For I have set ye down that ye may be all*
*Gods among me . . .*

That's exactly what Sonny had been doing.
*By their deeds shall ye know them.*

The headache was getting stronger – but there was no denying it, Sonny was fulfilling the Scripture, the life of the disciple. Harland couldn't bear it. The whole concept . . . it was so simple it had to be banal, embarrassing almost. He couldn't deal with this now. He was the one who shut the window, who turned away. He had the training of belief, not notion, and he wouldn't, couldn't, let himself be preyed upon . . . by that. Uncertainty. Not ever. By the sweet movement of air, night rustle of leaves . . .

*While the day is cool,*
*and the shadows are dispersing,*
*Turn, my beloved, and show yourself . . .*

He would always shut the window against that kind of thing. Again and again he would shut it. Keep his body safe. It was what he'd always done, mark out areas of definition, follow the mind's straight course. Not get caught up by the words of a Song come back for him now like it came in last night, insistent . . .

*Turn, my beloved . . .*
*Turn . . .*

For he hated it. The feeling. The softness of the song, the sense of it. His head was beating.

*Turn . . .*

It wasn't what he was used to. This soft, womanish opening up within him . . . What was occurring within his own understanding that would even allow it? It was as though he'd achieved nothing by going out and trying to lose himself in the company of others, to forget. He'd forgotten nothing. Here was the thing back at him again just the same, the same awful, soft, insistent words, Song of God's love but presented to the world in the gorgeous, the undealable, in the naked, messy reality of the body's touch.

Couldn't he write his sermon now? Better still, get Sonny Johanssen to write it. That's exactly what he should do, Harland thought, step aside, let someone who knew what he was talking about do the talking. After all, it was only ironic that the idea for the Sunday service should reveal itself to him just at the same time as he knew he was the last person in the world who could deliver it. He accepted that without question. He had no right. He was the fearful man, not one to start writing now about God as flesh. Not at this point in his career. It would make foolishness of every choice he'd made. Imagine, his choice of parish would become an act of disengagement, his celibate marriage an empty temple instead of a place of contemplation . . . He couldn't think about it. That all his choices might have been made in vain. That he'd taken a wife into a life of solitude in vain. *In vain.*

He put his hands to his head, for the ache was deep now, in the back of his skull, in his brain . . . To think he had ever thought he could come to an understanding of God's love through marriage . . . Johnny Carmichael would be a better man to preach about it. Johnny, Sonny . . . any of them could tell more about the life of God, of love, the real, living, breathing touching life, than he ever could.

*Turn, my beloved and show yourself . . .*

Yet still there were these words and Harland couldn't stop them, couldn't stop himself thinking about them. It was a kind of agony. Compared to this, yesterday's white page would be bliss, but already those other hours spent sitting in his study, unable to write, were like a lifetime away. He'd lived in a different world since then, been engaged in a different world, a junket of sensation where arousal and depression and drunkenness all jostled together with weeping in a hotel driveway, bowed over like a child when an old man came up to give him comfort.

'There, now . . .'

And did it really have to matter? Did he really have to think about any of this when all Harland wanted to do was not to think about it? He put his hand to his head, to the place where the headache was, only to touch the same place where was located that other, different feeling.

*Awake, sleeper.*

He'd been that close. That's what it came down to in the end. It had been a long time for Harland since he'd been with someone so near . . . And he'd forgotten. What people were like, how they felt when they were standing near you, pressed in close and wanting to hold you, he'd forgotten . . . The smell of their mouths, their hair, their sweet and salty skin . . .

*Awake, sleeper.*
*Turn . . .*

But he couldn't, wouldn't . . .

*Turn.*

He'd forgotten . . . All of that. He couldn't change now, it would be too late. For him, for his marriage. For the woman he had taken in vain.

*Turn.*

For that woman, his wife, his poor wife . . .

*Turn.*

It was as though he had killed her.

Suddenly Harland felt a thing like panic jump within him.

She was out there in the garden now. Alone. She was standing quite still. She was smiling.

*Kate.*

Harland wanted to call out to her, but she wouldn't hear.

'Kate!' he could call, but it was too late to call her, and *turn*, said his mind within him, within his body, *turn*, though it seemed too late and foolish still he wanted to call her and she just stood there, in the garden, she was fingering a tiny jar of pills.

'Kate!'

Harland leapt from his bed as though he was driven from behind and the word of her name the cry to drive him.

'Kate!'

He was up at the window, banging his fists against the glass, 'Kate!' he called out again – but the window was closed, she couldn't hear. Harland fumbled with the catch, the lock was caught fast, it wouldn't give.

He cried out again, 'Kate!' but his wife could not hear him, she just stood there below him on the grass and Harland brought both fists up to the glass, in one clean act smashed it through.

'Kate!'

The glass shattered like sugar. Light flooded the room. The huge sky was blue like a ceiling might be blue and Harland saw his own white hands, criss-cross with blood, stuck with pieces of fine glass against that colour.

'Kate!' he cried out to the figure below him who stood like a statue, on the grass.

Still, she remained unmoving. Tiny individual drops of red fell around her, onto the garden, onto the garden's green grass, her husband's blood falling in tiny drops, from him, like tiny drops of precious rain.

◇

Renee was back in the kitchen but couldn't think what to do. Like before she stood there, but worse than before, now she couldn't even think about finishing the washing-up, she could only just be there, in a queer state of sadness, shock.

Her daughter was going away. Renee knew it. That was the feeling she'd had before, deep down, the thing she couldn't name. It was her girl, growing up and leaving her, like all the daughters would have to leave, like she as a daughter had left, her mother before her. The time was coming for Mary Susan now. All the little farewells Renee had prepared herself for, all the tiny goodnights, good-lucks, goodbyes . . . they were all getting ready for this other, bigger leaving . . . It couldn't not happen. Her daughter was going to go.

From her bedroom, Renee could hear Mary Susan crying her eyes out like a little girl – but she was not a little girl. She'd had nothing on beneath that dressing gown, Renee had seen, her little girl was all grown-up. From now on Eric shouldn't tease her about it, Renee would have to talk to him about that. He should take some care with his big sister from now on and not do that thing – whatever it was he'd done, just now, to make her slip and fall. She'd have to give the situation her close attention, Renee had thought that yesterday. She'd have to take more notice of the girl.

*Thanks, Mum . . .*

She'd be grateful. No doubt about that, if Renee could make an effort to help her – like she'd helped with that business with Margaret yesterday. The girl was going to need another woman's influence now, someone with more time than Renee had, who knew about those sorts of pretty women's things. Someone, not Margaret. The more she thought about it, the more she thought how unsuitable that particular woman was, but there were always others. There were teachers at school, that silly woman who'd come about the modelling . . . and there was the minister's wife, that was a much better idea. Already she'd helped Mary Susan with the sewing and Mary Susan had loved it. Going along to those evenings at the church with the other girls, and the minister's wife showing her the bits and pieces, how to put the trimmings on . . .

*Kate Harland.*

She had a name.

*Kate.*

So why didn't Renee use it? In her mind? Why did she think of her always as the minister's wife instead of a woman with her own life and things to do?

It was probably because she had no children. Even so, whatever way you looked at it, no doubt that Kate Harland would be the person to ask about these matters over Mary Susan and her growth. Again, Renee had the flash of the gaping dressing gown in her mind, the look on her daughter's face when she saw that her mother saw. And there was another look, too, Renee remembered, the look on Mary Susan's face as she ran across the road yesterday afternoon, to where she and Evelyn and Mickey and Ray Weldon were standing . . .

Ray.

The warning feeling from before came up in Renee again: the way women were with men. The way she herself had been once . . . the warning. Remember how she used to be? With her new husband then? Remember how she would make herself available to him, always? Wanting to be ready for him whenever he wanted, waiting there for him so he could start?

Remember? The warning?

'I'm going to have a baby, Jim.'

There was no backing out once those feelings started, and he'd made it so easy, that man had, for her to be with him a certain way, easy.

'I'm going to have a baby.'

'Well isn't that fine, then?' he'd just said. 'Come over here and let me put my hand on your belly . . . Oh yes, sweetheart. I can feel it . . .'

Renee shuddered, but that was the way women were. The way men were. Those things, they were a warning of what girls could become, wanting to be touched and loved all the time, it was like a need. It gaped open inside you, opened you up, and just because women were formed differently from men didn't mean they didn't feel that physical thing as love too. It was terrifying. That need in people was too big. Renee felt the warning shiver all through her: her little girl.

She saw it clearly, now, what she'd been trying to figure out before. All the model nonsense, the clothes and the wanting to walk in a certain way, the gold shoes . . . everything . . . It was just Mary Susan's way of saying she was getting older, and wanting to be somebody different from who she was. None of it was doing any harm. It was as it would be, as would happen. It was Mary Susan getting ready to say goodbye.

Renee sat down on a chair, exhausted suddenly. Eric came running in.

'What's the matter, Mum?'

Renee shook her head.

'Go away, now, love. Later. I'm busy.'

'No you're not . . .' Eric came up next to her. 'You're sitting still, on that chair . . .' Renee felt him touch her face. 'You've got crying in your eyes, Mum . . .'

He dabbed at her cheeks with his little boy's fingers, so gentle, then put his face into the side of her neck so she could feel his breath there, his mouth forming words.

'You're not really busy, Mum,' he said. 'You've just got a bit of crying, but it's OK . . .'

Renee closed her eyes tight.

'I know . . .'

Then she put her arms around him, her little son, and she held him so close as if she would never let him go before he untangled himself from her and ran away.

◇

Anyhow, they were all stupid. Mum and Eric and the lot. She hated them all. The whole set-up was dumb, to be stuck here at home like she was some kind of a kid, and anyone could tell by looking she was turned into a woman now.

Mary Susan thought she couldn't bear it, the way she wanted so badly to be a woman. To have that tall manner – and what was that word Elena said? *Poise*. That was a word she liked to think about. Something that itself sounded like someone who was a model, some beautiful lady just sitting there, or walking into a really fancy restaurant somewhere and sitting down . . . *Poise*. Mary Susan could see how that kind of model would look, just know that the minute she stood up, people would pull back her chair, hold open the door for her as she would walk by. People would do that for a beautiful woman, no questions asked. Men would do it.

She wrapped the cotton front of her dressing gown around herself. It had been stupid to cry. It was just her sitting here, not her dumb brother, she was just here and she wasn't doing anything – what right did her mother have to treat her like a baby? She was just sitting on the bed and so what if she had no underwear on? It had been stupid to cry. She could do anything she wanted and no one could stop her. If she

wanted to wear nothing at all she would, she'd look at herself in the mirror with no clothes on, she could do that if she
wanted, just look, and she might have on just the shoes. So
what? Eric was only stupid, wanting to watch. He should
be lucky she let him, lucky she'd practise doing that kind of
show in front of him. He should be glad she let him, not
go stupid and make her trip. Not many little kids got to see
their sister that way . . . He was stupid. Anyhow, she didn't
care.

She had nothing on now and she didn't care about that
either. She was glad. She opened the front of her dressing
gown so that there was a strip of her body open to the air.

*There!*

*Look!*

They were all stupid not knowing. She wasn't a kid at all.

There was knocking on the door but Mary Susan did nothing.
She did nothing to cover herself either. Let them come in. Her
brother come in. Her mother. She'd show them what kind of
a person she was. She would rise up from the bed and her
dressing gown would fall away behind her . . . that would
show them, all right.

Still the knocking went on, and then Eric's silly little voice.

'Merry . . . Merry . . .'

'Let me in, Merry . . .'

'Let me –'

'Go away!'

Imagine. She could walk over, open the door to him, bare
as a buck. *Poise.* That was the thing. That would teach him,
and he should be so lucky to get to see nude shows like she'd
done that show for him before . . . he should be just so lucky.
Boys were lucky ones, men were. Getting to see, to look and
watch . . . what girls do.

'Merry!' Eric called out again.

'Go away!'

'You were being a rudie,' came his voice through the door,

and then the more distant voice of her mother, calling from the kitchen: 'Eric, stop bothering your sister. Come away and leave her alone.'

'Rudie! Rudie!'

He was yelling so loud, everyone could hear.

'I saw you!'

'Go away!' Mary Susan had to shout back at him, just to hear herself over the racket Eric was making out there. 'Go away! Go away!' She heard herself, and with every second the beautiful poise was falling away.

'Eric, what did I tell you!'

'Don't care, Mum.'

They'd ruined it all. Why couldn't they just leave her alone and let her do what she wanted in her own room? It was her place, her bed. Her underwear, dressing gown . . . They should let her alone to do exactly what she liked to do, in private. Only what she liked, no kids' stuff. She lay down on the bed. Only that.

Mary Susan sighed, felt every second. Outside it was another hot, blue day like every day in this dump town. It was like nothing ever changed here. And yet . . . something had become different, inside her, in her thoughts. Like a creeping idea that was moving through her and beginning to explore her . . . When she had first felt it, she hadn't known what it was, whether to be frightened, but it was stronger now. Mary Susan felt it as something that was making her into a new kind of person, forming out from within her, and she was getting stronger every day, the feeling of change getting stronger and all Mary Susan could do was sit by and watch it, enjoy it even – because it did feel good, like feeling lazy or full of the nicest food, like it could make her close her eyes . . .

*It's what I want.*

The sun beat in across her bed; again she opened out the front of her dressing gown.

*It's exactly what I want.*

Here in the room, now . . . to make the changing thing in her come, stay with her this time, make it stay . . .

But nothing was going to happen in this room. No way. Not in this place, this house. Not with her brother spying and her mother too close by and hearing everything. Her mother always seemed to know what was going on. Like there was that thing she was always saying, her favourite thing:

'Tell me why you've been acting up in front of your brother? Why tormenting him when he's only small? When he doesn't understand what your kinds of games mean?'

It was strange, Mary Susan thought, like her mother knew about everything. To come out with: *torment; your kinds of games.* It was like she thought Mary Susan might have some kind of a power, that's what it sounded like, and that she would use it over people – more than just her little brother. She wouldn't have chosen those sorts of words otherwise: *your kinds of games.* It was like her mother thought Mary Susan could have knowledge to use upon anyone, like she might show herself to someone and they might get excited about what they saw. That was an idea. Like her body could be some kind of a present that was kept within her clothes and she could let someone open the present. Like that person may want to keep the present, keep her.

Mary Susan decided that second she wasn't going to stay here any longer in her room. She'd had enough of the whole thing. Since yesterday, when that lady had been watching her, something had started in Mary Susan that was more than what was changing in her body, but was more like seeing herself whole. Like for the first time she saw herself as that lady might have seen her and she was just this girl, and she happened to live in this dumb town, but so what? Look at her. She was going to get out. That was the feeling, that lady's eyes upon her . . .

*Head up, shoulders back.*

. . . And it was nothing like the feeling of Margaret's eyes

159

upon her, it was a good feeling. Like that lady had really seen the kind of woman Mary Susan had become and had said to her, 'There you are, look at you. You're ready. Now off you go . . .'

She got up from the bed now, walked over to the mirror.

*Shoulders back*

She could feel the line of herself now, in the way she was standing. She bent down and carefully put on the shoes, stood up again and walked a few paces. The shoes felt right too, and not clunky like before. Now everything felt right. Mary Susan looked at herself. This way of standing . . . it was right. She turned and walked around the bed, back again. Definitely it was getting easier. The thin cotton dressing gown felt like a beautiful dress; she pulled it off her shoulders a little.

*There, like that . . .*

It felt really good. She looked really good. She put her head back.

*Click.*

That lady yesterday had thought she was beautiful.

Mary Susan felt much better now, thinking about these things, not stupid stuff. And her mother was probably only jealous anyway, and that's why she wanted to tell her off all the time. Just because she hadn't managed to be glamorous enough to make Mary Susan's father stay . . . no wonder. Wearing aprons all the time instead of nice things, coming back from work at Margaret's all hunched up with her cardigan on. Like yesterday, talking with Ray Weldon in the road and bent over like an old woman, she'd taken her cardigan off but she still looked like that, hunched and old and Mickey Parsons there with his googly eyes and her mother didn't even notice that he was that close.

*Yuk.*

She thought about the way Mickey had been looking at her, making eyes at her. He'd put his tongue out the side of his mouth and licked.

*Yuk, again.*

She hated that, Mickey Parsons looking at her that way and Ray Weldon not looking at all.

Did her mother ever notice that kind of stuff? She used those words: *taunt; torment* . . . yet she never seemed to know herself how she could look nicer, younger. She really didn't seem to care. Was it all because Mary Susan's father had run off and left her? Probably it wasn't fair to blame her mother, even so. Probably, Mary Susan thought, her father had never wanted to stay here, like she didn't want to stay and it wouldn't have made any difference what her mother dressed in. And it seemed to Mary Susan that maybe her mother had been different once, back then, when her father was still there. She'd only been little but couldn't she remember her mother had a necklace then, some dress made of thin green net stuff? . . . You had to dress nice if you wanted to try and keep a man. Though her mother had never told her so, this is what Mary Susan knew. It was like a memory inside her, and you had to be out there, the memory said, had to show yourself as willing. You had to get out of the house, not be like her mother, stuck inside while other people went off and away.

All right, so Mary Susan would go out herself, this minute. Even just to go somewhere in this town, still, she'd get out of this little pink-and-white girl's room, just go. Maybe she could see someone . . . anyone. Who cares? When she'd worked at the Railton she could have gone to see Margaret, that used to be fun. They could have talked, and Margaret would have given her make-up to try. She might do her hair in different styles, Margaret used to do that for her, like they were best friends. But then there was that last time when Mary Susan had gone in to work and Margaret had come up behind and held her. Mary Susan didn't turn around, didn't do anything, but that was the last time she'd go back to that hotel again and no regrets . . .

Still, she couldn't help but think it would be nice to call by the Railton now, see someone like Margaret. She could sit up at the bar, maybe, order a drink. She could stretch out her legs and look how pretty her shoes were, turning her feet this way and that.

'Have you seen that girl?' people could say.

'Of course I've seen her.'

Anyway, it was definite. She was going out. Not to the pub, that wasn't possible, but something. She could do something. She went over to the wardrobe and looked through the rack, but none of those clothes were any good . . . except . . . There was one dress. Elena said it was a good shape. It was fitted, with a print of tiny flowers and the back went down quite low . . . It was maybe a bit small on her now – but who cares? It would look good with the shoes.

*Look out for yourself* were the words that came into her head as she took it off its hanger, they were Elena's words. 'Little girl dresses,' she'd said. 'They're the most grown-up of all.'

Mary Susan pulled out fresh underpants from the drawer, and one of the new bras that would match. Like a bikini.

*Yeah.*

She started to make up a little song.

*Bikini, bikini.*

She hooked the bra at the back, and it felt nice, strapped around her, holding her in.

*I know you're a meanie.*

She stepped into the clean underwear, bent down to strap her shoes more securely.

*You're so very teeny,*

*That I'm messed up over you.*

Strange song, strange mood. Mary Susan felt tingly pulling the dress down over her, zipping it up at the back. It looked good though, she could see that. She picked up her purse from the dressing table, then went over and opened the bedroom door, let herself out of her room. Her brother was nowhere about. Down the hall she went, quietly, on tiptoes, but there was nobody there either. In the living room she heard the TV on, Eric watching cartoons. Her mother would be in the kitchen, she would always be – but not her. Not the daughter. The daughter was going out. It was Saturday, late afternoon, and she had money, she had the dress. She hadn't done a thing all day except think about herself and she was ready to do something now.

◇

Think about the time now. How the day is passing. How out in the country this time there's a fullness of light, such rumpled goldenness that it's as if the sun has come down and rolled like a puppy all through the fields and long grasses. The land could not be more golden. Has there been a time of unthinking fear or loneliness or joy or understanding? Today in Featherstone, after the various colours of the dawn, the light, which has not wavered in its intention, might seem to tell us that the answer only is to *hold*. Everything will come to harvest, don't look for answers. It may be enough just to let the grass ripen, pods give up their yellow grains. These days pass.

It's late afternoon now. Kate Harland, driving at low speed, is down one of those back roads leading away from the church, but she's without sense of direction, or of time. She doesn't need to know time or guess at it because it's like she can see time all around her: in the way the sun catches the broken tarmac of the little overgrown road, or flattens on the tin roof of a house, Renee Anderson's house. It's the same for Renee, sitting in her kitchen, drying her eyes. For her the light falls in a slab on the formica surface of her table top, the same light for Kate Harland, the same time . . . You know the kind of time it is. You come in upon a person's life, you see the quietest things.

After all, at the end of the day, come late afternoon, it's all the same, time gone, time left, in this high rural place of few houses, with few roads to travel down . . . only time. The sky is brushed blue. Late afternoon and still full of light but evening is there somewhere, you can feel it, contained deep within the shine the darkness, and Kate Harland can feel it, even with the sun flickering across her arms this minute, she knows the darkness is there, out on the coast of land, by the sea, it's coming in.

Time.

It moves, you move across the street, from rooms in the Railton Hòtel to the garden of an old man, to a minister in his room . . .
  Time.
  Let it. Come in. Pass by.
  Let it touch.

Kate Harland drives slowly by and you can see her within the glass and metal of the car, facing straight ahead. Is she leaving? There's a road that goes clean out of town due east, no turn-backs, all the way to the sea . . . but she's not headed that way yet. Right now she knows no more what she's doing than you or I can know what we might be doing waiting here, watching her car's slow procession. Like her we may have that curious emptied-out feeling of just sitting, moving through the minutes but not in them, disconnected from the round clock's slow tick.

That's how Renee Anderson feels. Sitting by her clean kitchen table, waiting, and there's nothing before her to mark time's passage now, no cake or glass of water or teacup with its milky stain . . . nothing. She's not even aware how long she's been here alone, there's just this . . . what? This dead, empty feeling. Renee knows she has come to the end . . . of some journey, the part of her life already past, and now doesn't know how she is to commence upon the rest. It's a feeling of being in the presence of something unknown, a future so

164

much bigger than the routine of her day and it's as though she's sitting here in order to prepare herself for that larger, more darkened absence of time, as though waiting on news of some terminal disease, or for someone you loved very much and who has booked their ticket already, to go. Second by second passes Renee in exactly that way – the enormity of what is to become filtering through the body by tiny degrees, drop by drop by drop to the bone.

So Kate Harland is occupying a time in her life that doesn't belong to her. She has pills in her pocket she could swallow, there's a road she could take . . . But instead she brings the car across the bridge to where the road forks to the playground, to the school. She pulls over, down into a dip at the side of the road, and stops there, by a ragged hedge thick with a blossoming of some kind of tiny spangled flower. There is no one about. The field behind the hedge is empty, and beyond it she can see the tops of the swings in the playground, a red-and-blue pole that the children use to spin from, and turn. It is perfectly secret where she is, the car down by the hedge and a tree with thick branches that leans over it, half-covering. Kate can sit here for a while, do nothing, or, if she decides, this could be a place where she could easily say goodbye.

Kate Harland.

The decision was first made, but now where is it in her mind? Here she is, pulled over in this tiny road not going anywhere, and it's hot in the car. She winds down the window and smells the green honey smell of the unkempt hedge, the smell of the tiny bloom. It's hard to leave. Bees drowse in the last of the sunshine. She's thirsty. She could do with something cold to drink.

That's what Mary Susan was thinking. Since leaving the house there had been a lot of hanging around, not doing anything but even so feeling the heat, and now it might be a nice idea to drink a little lemonade.

'I could do that,' she found herself saying out loud, surprised how loud her voice was in the stillness.

'I could go to the milk bar, get a lemonade,' she said, trying out her voice again in the open.

'Jesus it's hot,' she said, and, wow, that felt good! To say that swear word, to feel that grown-up because her mother never let her swear . . .

*My girl* . . . her mother would say if she heard her.

*Don't let me ever hear that kind of language* . . .

It was because of her mother being quite religious, going to the church on Sundays and always talking to the minister there.

*Not ever, my girl.*

*Not ever* . . .

Well, 'Jesus.'

There.

She'd said it again.

Mary Susan felt dangerous and adult thinking this way, and fully grown. Her body was snug in the little cotton dress and the perfume she was wearing had a hot kind of flowery stink coming off her, from the place where she'd put it, there between her breasts.

'Jesus, that feels good . . .'

She imagined what it might be like to be at Kath's Milk Bar, leaning over the counter and drinking the long cold drink.

'Jesus, yes . . .'

She'd been walking, that was all she'd been doing since she left the house, nothing fancy. Just out in the heat and it was mean kind of weather, this weather, when you had nowhere to go, it seemed sort of pointless. Even so, better than being stuck inside, that was worse, and though it felt like time wasn't really passing she only had to look at her watch to see it was getting later, and that was something, just getting through this dumb day. She'd come down the road from her house, past the other new houses with their little neat and silly gardens, out to the end of the cul-de-sac and onto the main road beyond it. There were daisies growing there, wild, on the grass verges. Mary Susan picked one and rolled the tiny petals along her cheek.

Behind her she could just make out the buzz of a radio, coming from one of the new houses near where she lived. She turned around to see which one and noticed that some-one had turned a sprinkler onto their lawn. It made her think again how hot she was, how much better it would be to go to Kath's and get a drink and then the sprinkler whirled and made that lovely fizzing sound and what Mary Susan really wanted to do right then was to take off her shoes and go running across the damp grass through that fine, sprinkly water . . .

Backwards and forwards . . .

. . . she could run and run . . .

. . . across the millions of blades of cool grass . . . run . . . and run and run . . .

But even with no one around to notice, she was too old for that sort of thing. Besides, she knew, if she took off her shoes for a second it would be hard to have to put them back on, and she had to keep them on.

OK, so she may as well go up Main Street now like she'd planned, to Kath's, maybe she'd find someone on the way. Anyone from school would do – Robbie Campbell, who still fancied her even though she wouldn't let him do anything . . . Better to see one person than nobody at all and Robbie might have his aunt's car so they could drive out of town to the High School swimming pool. That would be OK to do. At least it was something, even with a stupid boy from her stupid school, even though older men, in her opinion, were definitely better-looking.

Thinking that just made her think about Ray Weldon. Again.

If he knew the number of times . . . and yet he hadn't even looked at her yesterday, when he could have looked, could have thought *Yeah, all right then*, and then he could have reached out and brought her towards him and taken her in his arms, like in the movies, slowly, and then kissed her . . . Mary Susan imagined now the feeling of what it would be like to kiss Ray Weldon, and she felt a kind of a weakness inside. She was glad she was here where no one could see. Because she felt weak here, and thinned-out with wanting. Him. Ray Weldon. It wasn't fair. He was so quiet, too, you never knew what he was thinking . . . Mary Susan thought maybe he could have all kinds of secrets about her, wouldn't that be something? Like secrets of how he would behave with her, and he might tell her some of them, or maybe he would just do the things.

*Will you, Ray?*

She felt strange, a melted feeling, thinking about him.

*Will you?*

There was that way he'd stood in the road yesterday . . . and couldn't he have been looking at her, just once? Couldn't he have noticed her, thought maybe, just for a second, *She could be my girlfriend*?

She might as well start walking. Nothing was going to happen here. Might as well go off to the milk bar like she planned. Mary Susan started the walk down the road, and the shoes were hot all right, but she kept going, turned the corner round by the Railton on to the top of Main Street.

She looked at her watch: 4.20. OK. That was a great time to go to Kath's, and who knows, anyone could be there. She'd sit up at the bar, have a lemonade, and maybe she'd have a dish of ice cream. Strawberry. OK. So not so bad . . . and anything might happen. She walked along by the hedge of the hotel and the thought of cold lemonade got better and better. Some little kids were hanging around outside the toy shop but there was no need for Mary Susan to stop and talk.

'Nah! You fancy!' one of them yelled out to her as she walked by.

'Don't care, anyhow!' 'Don't care!' came the little voices behind her. They were just Eric's dumb friends from school.

Apart from those kids, though, there didn't seem anyone about. There were a couple of cars parked in the street, but no one's she recognised. Probably everybody was sitting up in the Railton, just drinking. Drink, drink. All those people, men from all over the place coming in. Imagine being Margaret and having to serve them. Margaret was queer.

Anyhow, who cares? She was going to have lemonade from a can and Kath would pour it into a tall glass with lots of ice. She was nearly there. She walked past Dalgety's and saw a cardboard notice in the window: 'Any Dress: Sale Price', and a lawnmower next to it.

*Jesus.*

What a place to live. Dresses next to lawnmowers in shop windows and everything on cheap sale price. She couldn't wait till she was old enough to leave . . .

At least the striped blue awning outside Kath's looked pretty as always. Here was at least one shop in town that you might want to actually go to. Mary Susan loved that awning. It reminded her of other towns, cities, there was a pink trim on the edging that made her think of places like Paris or London or New York. Mary Susan went inside, and it was cool and lovely as she'd thought, but quite empty, just two people she didn't know sitting towards the back; people who were passing through. They looked up when she came in, seemed to notice her . . . but maybe not. One was a woman who could have been that lady from yesterday, but she couldn't really remember what that lady had looked like – and it didn't seem to matter now anyhow. People were always just passing through this town and even though that lady had seemed important at the time, it wasn't who she was that counted. It was what she'd done. She had watched Mary Susan and it was

169

like she had really wanted to watch her, to see who she was, who she really was. What had made the lady special was that she'd made Mary Susan feel special, the kind of girl people might just want to look at sometimes and think, 'How nice,' to see her there and finished somehow, complete and whole.

'Hello there,' said Kath, from behind the counter. 'Hot enough out there for you?'

She reached across and fingered the fabric of Mary Susan's dress.

'What a nice pink, very pretty. Did Mum help you make it?'

Mary Susan shook her head. 'I made it myself. The minister's wife helped. She has sewing classes, at the church. I go most weeks . . .'

'Really?' said Kath. 'Well, isn't that lovely.'

'I guess . . .'

Mary Susan climbed onto a high stool and put her purse down on the shiny counter.

'Can I have an ice cream, please, Kath?' she said. 'In a dish, and a can of lemonade with a straw?'

'Anything you want,' said Kath. 'Hello, Mickey.'

Mary Susan turned and it was true, there he was, Mickey Parsons, right now, coming in the door. Anything worse couldn't happen.

'What are you doing anyway?' Kath was saying to her. 'A pretty girl going around on your own on a Saturday afternoon?' but Mary Susan couldn't concentrate. Mickey Parsons. Just when Mary Susan had started to think the afternoon hadn't turned out so bad, now the place that was supposed to be quiet and cool had turned into someplace creepy. Mickey Parsons, with his huge shorts hitched right up around his enormous crotch . . . it couldn't be worse than him.

'Yes, yes,' she heard him say, coming right inside, along the counter to the very place where she was sitting.

'It's Mickey, all right,' he said. 'Yes please.'

Mary Susan couldn't believe it, he was sitting down right next to her. The whole place empty and that's where he was choosing. There was nothing she could do.

'Old Mickey, eh?' he said, and though she was looking straight ahead he'd twisted himself around to face her. She couldn't believe this was happening. She thought about what her mother always said: *You should be nice to him, poor Mickey. He's like a boy, that's all he is. He could never hurt you.*

But there he was, and he was right next to her, next to Mary Susan, not next to her mother – and what did that mean anyhow, *hurt you*? He was sitting there, too close, and he was smiling at her, in quick little smiles, and squinting up his eyes.

'Eh, eh? Eh, eh?' he said.

Kath brought her over the dish of ice cream and the cold green can of lemonade. She reached behind her for a glass and a paper straw from the stand.

'There you go . . .'

'Thanks.'

Mary Susan could hear how quiet her voice sounded, still she poured her drink and unwrapped the straw in her usual careful way, just as though everything were normal. She could hear Mickey muttering beside her but she decided just to ignore him, that was probably the best thing to do, not even think about him, but then he suddenly leaned over to her and stuck his tongue out.

'Now, Mickey!'

Kath Keeley came straight over.

'Don't be so silly . . .'

But it was too late. He'd already done it. His horrible slimy tongue . . . it was still there.

'I want you to behave,' said Kath, but she was smiling as she said it, like it wasn't serious, and Mickey was still next to Mary Susan, doing that thing, and though she was trying not to notice, though she was trying just to get on and spoon up her ice cream . . . he was there, right there, and then he put out his hand and touched Mary Susan's leg. She jumped.

'Eh eh, eh?' Mickey started laughing. He was jigging up and down on his chair.

'Old Mickey, eh?' he said, and you could see he was getting himself all excited.

'What do you think of old Mickey now?'

Mary Susan felt like she was shaking. The touch hadn't lasted more than a second but it was like a big toad still sitting on her bare skin.

'I have to go,' she said. 'I'm sorry, I can't stay . . .'

Maybe Kath would think her rude, her mother, that she had to go but she had to. She got down from her stool just as Mickey was making another move towards her with his hand.

'Can I pay you next time?' she asked Kath. 'Truly, I'd forgotten – something. I have to go.'

'Mickey's frightened you away, has he?'

Kath was smiling. 'Never mind . . .'

Then she turned to Mickey and said, 'Now look what you've done. Do you think Mary Susan will ever want to be your girlfriend?' and she laughed then, like the whole thing was just a joke.

'My girlfriend!' Mickey shouted, but Mary Susan was already out the door. 'My girlfriend!' she heard him call out again, from inside, but she was gone.

God, she couldn't bear this place. Everybody was crazy.

*Go to hell*, she thought, and in her mind the words burned as she walked away, ran, away from Kath's, down the street, away. In her hand the can of lemonade still glistened cold in the heat, the paper straw caught in its lip.

*Go to hell, the lot of them*, she thought as she ran. She hated the place, all of it, all of them who lived there. All. All. All. All. All.

She was still running when she got to the end of Main Street and turned the corner, only then did she feel she could slow down, get her breath. She kept going, even so, still kind of running on, she couldn't believe she was crying.

*Baby.*
Sure, what a baby.
*Hate them all.*

She realised she was outside the children's playground. She stopped, wiped out her eyes. There was no way Mickey could have caught up with her by now, if that's what he'd been planning. She may as well go over and sit on one of the swings, drink her can of dumb lemonade, what a baby. The tears were coming again.

*Baby.*

She couldn't believe she was still crying. She may as well just drink her dumb drink and then go home. At least here there was no one to see her, it was much too late in the afternoon for little kids to come. Mary Susan swung open the squeaky, painted gate and closed it behind her, walked across the gravel, past the slide and roundabout to the row of empty swings. She sat down on the middle swing, and scuffed the gravel with the gold toe of her shoe. She'd just stay here, until she'd stopped crying, she'd finished her drink. The last of the sun slipped down behind the hills. Mary Susan wiped her eyes again, took a sip from the straw. The only sound was the creak-creak of the swing on its chain as the light grew darker and darker around her.

Creak-creak went the chain, with the swing, and the girl upon it.

Creak-creak.

Creak-creak.

Creak-creak.

◇

Renee paused, looked up.

'Is that you, love?'

But no, she thought she'd heard something but it was just a shadow at the corner of her eye, perhaps that branch of the

173

tree growing outside the kitchen window brushing against the glass.

All the same, when she started to think about it, where was Mary Susan by now?

'Eric?' she called out, but chances were the boy wouldn't know. He'd been stuck in with that television on all afternoon, so what could he know about what his sister was up to?

'Mary Susan?' she found herself saying, into the empty air. 'Love?'

Renee went through to the sitting room.

'Turn off that television or turn it down.'

Eric was there, sitting in front of the pictures flickering on the screen.

'Eric, did you hear what I just said?'

His head nodded, *yes*, but he continued looking at the screen, and suddenly Renee felt a surge of panic, fear. Did nothing she would say or do make any difference? To her children? To them, would nothing count? She went over and stood in front of the set.

'I'm talking to you,' she said.

'Oh, Mum . . .'

Eric craned his head so he could still see the picture around her.

'Mum . . .'

Renee turned the thing right off.

'Just listen to me, young man,' she was shouting, and that wasn't reasonable, she knew that. Still . . .

'Where's your sister?' she shouted at him.

Eric shook his head.

'I don't know that answer,' he said. 'I wanted to play, but she said go away. Can I have a biscuit now, Mum? Please.'

Renee stood, uncertain. She couldn't think about what to do. She was confused and with every second felt a gap beside her heart widening. Like a door wide open and black behind it.

'Mum?'

Where was her daughter?

'Mum?'

Where was she? What was she doing? It was getting late, suddenly Renee was fully aware of the time. The light of day would be gone soon, it would be dark.

'Mum?'

Renee would call some people, that was the thing to do. Ask if anyone had seen her.

'Mum?'

Her little girl, her daughter.

'Mum?'

That they could send her home.

# FOUR

'Leave that, Son,' Johnny said, for the old man had already cleared a space for him, free of twigs and mess, at the next tree.

'That's there now, thanks,' Johnny said. He didn't want Sonny anyway to be tidying up after him like that. He started stripping younger growth off the nearest branch with the blade of the new Rolliston cutting through the white bark easy. They were good trees, this lot, for burning.

'You've enough here to see you through the first part of next year,' Johnny said.

He finished on the low branches, turned the machine off and there was Sonny kneeling behind him, sweeping up the little bits like he hadn't heard.

'Leave that, now,' Johnny said again, but still there was no answer and Sonny just kept on trying to gather up in his hands the twigs and all the leafy scrim and a waste of time it was, to be doing that, and why was he anyhow?

Maybe it was the day. Because it had been warm enough this afternoon and you noticed it more, somehow, this late in the season, and maybe, too, Johnny thought, it was the work. They'd been here for a while now, down the back, and a fair load of young trees away. That could be a thing too much for someone Sonny's age, as simple as that, and Sonny not the type anyway who would ever want to just talk and talk . . . So there, nothing, probably, and don't go getting all worried up over it, Johnny Carmichael. Could be the man was just thirsty and could do with a drink, because Johnny sure could do with one, a cold beer right now and it would clear his head, too, after last night.

Johnny leaned down: 'Can I stand you a pint, Mr Johanssen, sir?'

But there, Sonny wasn't saying a word. He was just busy with the damn gathering up for no reason the little twigs, and his back was to Johnny, like before, he wasn't listening. There was the old jacket he always wore, and thin at the edges, and at the cuffs where his hands were brushing the earth off branches, and Johnny didn't like it, to see him troubling himself there with the bits of kindling, working away as though they were the most precious things and not just old sticks lying on hard ground.

'For God's sake, man,' Johnny said.

For it wasn't right, it was a Saturday, for God's sake. They should have finished up an hour ago, when the light was still good, when an old man might still have some energy for work. Now it was late. It was getting dark and a line of relaxation needed to be drawn. You couldn't have old people out all hours, in the twilight and not being able to see. Here was someone, right here, who had been working too hard, and it had affected him, of course it had, it had turned him in.

He leaned over to Sonny, to get his attention touched him, just so, gentle on the arm.

'Come on,' he said.

Sonny jumped.

'Eh?'

He turned around.

'Eh?'

He was looking all around him, at the trees and at Johnny, and Rhett beside him had started barking and usually that dog never made a sound.

◇

Sure, just looking around, you could see that the dark was starting. It was webbed in behind the trees, and black shadows were creeping underfoot. Look at his hands there, in front of him, Sonny thought, like spiders. Suddenly nothing in the twilight was how you saw it before. It had been grand having Johnny here for the afternoon, and nearly enough to stop the other darkness, those thoughts that were inside him, when Johnny was making him laugh before, and they'd done good work out here in the willows . . .

*But, Nona, see, there are ghosts all around us.*

*And this way I'm thinking, it's not just about you and me.*

It had only ever been Nona, Francie, coming to him in dreams or talking in his mind, and he always knew how they would be when they came up upon him in the night. But now . . . here were other people, they had started in as well, and he'd tried to put the thoughts away, all day, in the sun, while they'd been working here, but they were a presence, he couldn't stop thinking . . .

*Remember, Nona?*

There had been her house at the end of the street, and something wrong with it . . .

*Remember?*

. . . And the sense of something, forming in his mind . . . It was nothing like the usual dreaming spells, that the house was there for his comfort, like the comfort of having Nona close by to listen to her voice, or little Francie as a child calling . . .

*Remember?*

This time Ray was there.

*And nothing like you and me, Nona.*

*Nothing like.*

He looked around. It was getting darker, second by second. There was Rhett, he could see, beside him, he'd been barking before but was quiet now, and there was Johnny. Johnny. How long had he been there? Sonny had to make himself think. Was he waiting for him? Were they to do something together? He couldn't think. The trees were standing like a crowd of people, like they were waiting for him, but all Sonny knew was a bad feeling, all day he'd felt it growing and he'd tried to use the telephone against it, but the boy was away, Mrs Weldon said, and he was no boy, he was a man.

Sonny wanted to sit down. It was like a weight on him, this knowledge of Ray. Sonny had spoken into the telephone: 'Where is he?' but Elsa Weldon said Ray had gone. He'd left his room, he was out there now, in the thick air, forming, the thought of him getting heavier, being laid upon Sonny until he felt there to be something on his back, when he'd been working on the branches, its arms had been right around him, trying to strangle him. Johnny had been there, and lovely to have him, but the feeling of badness was there too, though the branches of the willow trees were beautiful and even though he loved Ray and would never want to call out against him . . .

Johnny was looking at him, the trees still gathered behind, waiting.

'I've been deep in my thoughts,' Sonny said. 'I'm sorry, but they're all around us here. I don't know what to do. I called Mrs Weldon, she was up in the big house . . . I had to tell her . . . It seemed strange, I know, but the right thing . . .'

Johnny looked at him, it was like he didn't understand what he was saying, but he had to make him understand. He had telephoned Elsa Weldon to warn her. *Warn her.*

'But it was too late,' Sonny said. 'Elsa told me Ray had already gone. He'd left the house, he's gone looking for her, you see . . . Francie . . . and I wanted to keep him in, I needed . . . I have to . . . tell him . . . She's not where he thinks she is. He won't find her in the places where he's looking.'

Sonny suddenly felt exhausted. He leaned into his friend and put his arm on Johnny's arm, the big man's safe and lovely arm. He could feel tears coming and he didn't want them.

'She's not here, you know, Johnny. Francie. I thought she was, I thought she came back to see us all but . . .

'. . . she was never here . . .'

That was it. Sonny knew. He'd woken this morning, in the

yellow morning, and he'd known, and in the night before, but he'd not yet understood: she'd been part of the dream. Francie. She was there, she was real – but not in that way you could reach out for her, to take in your arms and hold. She was deep in. Deep like a memory, and vivid, the feeling of her how it is to love someone no matter if they're there or gone, deep in and it never goes away.

Sonny slumped, it was too much for him. The thought was too big to contain, he could barely see where they were going, Johnny leading him somehow through the white trees. He knew now, that's what the vision had been about, Sonny could see it so clear. Francie had been there, she had been standing behind the hedge and Sonny had seen her, heard her calling to him . . . but that didn't mean, because she'd come to him like that, you could reach out and touch and keep her.

*Yes.*

That was it. Sonny knew it now.

*Home, but not in that way.*

She'd come there to him, from out of the light, to tell him –

*Uncle Sonny. It's me!*

– that he would have her always. That she was here, Francie, because she wasn't here. With him, like that, because she was gone. That's what he needed to tell Ray, all of them if they wanted to believe . . .

'She's here, Ray, you already have her.'

'Eh?'

It wasn't Ray he was talking to. It was Johnny standing there. It was late and it was Johnny – but it was Ray Sonny had let down. Last night Sonny had had him believing that Francie was there in the old way, as though he could find her again and this time keep . . .

'And I have to tell him,' Sonny said, 'Ray. That she's not here in the way he thinks, as possession. Make that not be the true thing, make that not be Francie . . .'

He'd stopped walking. He was cold but Johnny was beside him when he shivered, and he wrapped his own jersey around Sonny's shoulders.

'Let's go on up to the house, Son . . .' Johnny said.

'Yes . . .'

He started again, slowly through the trees. He had to find a way. To tell him, Ray . . . now, soon . . . before it was too late: Love them when they're gone, he wanted to say, the ones we love who've left us behind. Who don't need us any more, who have gone on or changed, who can't hold us, feed us, *love them.* Though we won't ever put our arms around them again or kiss, feel them next to us, their hand at the back of our neck when we are crying . . . It's what we learn on this earth from mortal love, to leave it, to let it go . . .

*Yes.*

Sonny is ready now . . .

To leave it all, the fitting and the starts – he doesn't need to see Nona's face again.

*Took you long enough*, she says, *to understand.*

Johnny was holding him. Sonny had Johnny's cardigan on. Johnny had his arms right around his shoulders, holding him and Sonny leaned in, felt the man's great kind body, felt his own yield to its strength. There. It was ease . . . there . . . Johnny's great warmth coming off him, next to him like an engine, and his arms around him, holding him.

'Let me take care of you now,' Johnny said, and then they were walking together through the thinned trees, back up towards the house, and all the time Johnny holding him, so he could feel the warmth of him, and he was steadying him with his great arms so that he did not fall.

◇

Johnny was worried, he wasn't going to pretend not. The old man had been quiet all afternoon, too damn quiet if you wanted to know the truth of it, and hell, he may as well admit it: something had been going on right from the beginning, from when Johnny had first arrived, that wasn't right.

He'd got to Sonny's house around four, and the plan was to help a bit doing some work down the back, clearing things out and it could be firewood at the same time. Sonny had been at the door when Johnny arrived, but not really like he was expecting him. He was standing there in a funny way, at a sort of a lean, like he was tired out from something and they hadn't even done a stroke of work. It had started then, all right, so it had. Johnny had thought how thin Sonny looked, when usually the old boy would be up and sprightly about the place, going from one thing to another, and he hadn't buttoned his shirt up right so Johnny could see a scrap of old man's chest. Something about that, seeing that little bit of thin and grey skin made you think how you could just blow on Sonny, a good strong breath, and he'd be knocked clean over onto the ground. It would be just like that. A little heap of a man left, like a bundle of clothes on the ground . . . Made Johnny feel queer. So he'd started in straight away with the talk, right then, and that had worked for a while, earlier in the piece, to make him think everything was just as it always was, but later, after they'd had a few laughs together, Sonny had fallen silent again, and then, just now, he'd started coming out with these scraps of things, about Ray, and some talk about old Mrs Weldon, and none of it was making any sense.

Johnny didn't know what to do. Only keep talking perhaps, the best thing.

'Didn't we put it away, though, last night, Mr Johanssen?' he said. 'And you were on crack form, yourself . . .'

He cast a quick look at Sonny now, as they were both making their way back up towards the house. Still looking awful, and his expression gone, but anything could look a bit off in this kind of half-light, end of the day. They'd feel better getting indoors and having a drink of something, that was the answer, before it got fully dark.

'All right?' he said to Sonny, but Sonny didn't say anything in return, the man. Then he spoke.

'The lights are on,' Sonny said.

Johnny looked up and sure enough there were lights on in Sonny's house, the back door was open.

'John,' Sonny said.

He was right, too. There, plain as day, when they took off their boots at the back door Johnny heard John's voice coming from within: 'Hey!' and when they went inside there he was sitting up at the kitchen table with the paper.

'Good to see you!' Johnny said, for sure it was lovely to see the boy there, just as he always was, relaxed and like everything was . . . well, normal, just that. His fine young son. The light was on, making the windows shine dark, maybe so, but it was bright, bright in every crevice of the room and John had the racing section out and he was reading from it.

'Red Banner came in second,' John said. 'So you lost money, too, Daddy, like me, and we could have been princes . . .'

Johnny laughed.

'Listen to you!'

It was a relief, thank God, everything normal now that John was here. Praise be. Johnny went over and took a cigarette from his son's packet.

'All or nothing, though,' he said. 'The only way to win and I've no regrets. You got to play as you mean it, Sonny will agree. Right, Son?'

But Sonny just said, 'We got to find him, boys.'

John looked up from his paper. Johnny saw he'd marked it all over with pencil. He must have been sitting there a while.

'Sonny?' John said.

Then he looked at his father, he put his finger to his lips, like *shhh*.

Then he said, just like Sonny hadn't spoken, 'Can I tell you about who's running tomorrow, at the afternoon meeting? Well, it's a good line-up, Sonny, kind of, that filly you talked about six months ago, from the Everton stable, she's running, she's a pretty-looking little thing, too . . .'

He looked quickly again at his father. *What'll we do here, now? I'm filling,* his eyes said, his voice all the time continuing: 'She's running against some kind of competition, though,' but his eyes saying, *We'd better watch him, Daddy, don't you think so? This is what I was telling you about, like last night, but can we help him, if we help him . . .?*

'The other favourites are outsiders,' he said, 'and older, but look, Sonny, there are some names here you'll know. I've a picture here too, it's in the paper, of that mare you had in mind for the steeplechase, and she looks fine, you can see her here, the Rose of Tralee.'

Sonny didn't do anything. Didn't move to look at the page John was holding up to show him, didn't say a word. He simply stood there, Rhett beside him, like neither Johnny nor his son were in the room with him, and then he went over to the window and looked out at the dark glass.

Then he said, 'It's the only thing we can do. We have to find him. He'll be bad, you know,' he said, 'with wanting her to be here and she's not here and he'll be wanting her all the more for that, and it might seem to you that he's changed, that there's bad in him because the wanting has gone bad within him but really, he's not a bad man, Ray, no more than any of us who want something and it's not there for us to have. He doesn't know that yet, the poor man, he's eaten up with want, and lost. We have to find him, John. I want you to go find him, take him to the minister's house. He'll know what to do.'

Sonny finished speaking, sat down.

'I'm tired out,' he said.

'That'll be the cutting,' Johnny said.

'No. You did all of that yourself, and you know it. It's not that, no, it's here' – Sonny tapped at his chest, that little chest, Johnny thought – 'here.'

'Come on, Sonny,' said John, and again Johnny felt how

glad he was that the boy was there with them, with his calmness, the way he folded up the paper now, just as if he knew
exactly what to do, and he went over to Sonny now.

'Nothing you're saying's making any sense,' said John. 'Let
me get you a glass of water.'

Sonny grabbed at him.

'Start at the river,' he said. 'When you look for him, start
there, where it's darkest, in the trees. You'll smell something,
like a rot, that's his fear, desire gone all wrong inside him.
Start there. It's where they used to go, don't you see, the pair
of them, and he'll go back, I know. It's where you'll find him,
and when you come upon him, John, he'll be scared. So take
him to the minister then, and after, bring him home to me.'

## FIVE

The situation is preordained. What he sees. How he'll see it. There is nothing unexpected, no strange turn to the events that will alter how things are to proceed, as they're marked out, written, in Ray's mind. He knows exactly what he's going to do. This man, he's not like a man, he's a boy, he's sixteen again and there's a girl he's crazy about, he can see her right now, there in the children's playground and she's waiting for him . . .

*Sweetheart, I'm waiting too.*

He goes up to the painted gate and he opens it. The only sound he can *hear* is his heart. Ray Weldon, hey. He's there, walking over the gravel towards this girl who's sitting on a creaky swing –

'I was really excited. I was acting casual, like I didn't even notice him, but all the time I was thinking: It's him. Over there, look, he's coming in. I don't believe it, I can't stand it. I'm here and he's here and . . . I was quite dressed up. Not all that fancy because what can you do around here? but it was Saturday night and I was wearing . . . I mean, it was like we could do something, you know? Like maybe he might ask me out, so maybe I should, you know, say something. I could –'

*No. Be quiet.*
*You don't need to say a word.*
*Really, I mean it. Just . . .*
*Shhh.*

*Let me just sit down on this cranky swing, OK?*
*Beside you,*
*what a crazy place.*
*What made you come here, I wonder, in the end, after all this time?*
*and it's late now, sweetheart. It's getting dark, but . . .*
*You don't care a bit, do you, about the time?*

'When he sat down next to me, on the swings, I still couldn't believe it was really him. It was like . . . some kind of story or like in a movie, when the girl is just sitting there and she's quite lonely and it's a Saturday night and she's doing nothing and then there's this man and she's always, you know, fancied him, but now here he is in real life and he comes over and sits down next to her like he's been wanting to for a long time, and he's just like, "Hi." Do you know what I mean? Like I'd dreamed about this happening for . . . so long. And then there he really was beside me. He put his hand out and made the swing stop. He was just looking at me. I felt kind of silly, sitting there and not doing anything and him just looking but then, this is what happened then . . . You know that place? At the bottom of your neck? Well, he used his fingers there, two fingers . . . and it felt nice, I mean . . . it was a really romantic thing to do. We hadn't even kissed, but then he did that thing and it was like we were together, like we were meant to be. I was wearing lipstick, I was being quite fancy, but with his thumb he just rubbed it off . . .'

*And the only sound –*

'And I liked that, the way he did that . . .'

*The only sound I can . . .*
*hear . . .*

'Like we really were together . . .'

*. . . is my heart.*

'And then he leaned down and really slowly he took off my

shoes. You know? My special shoes? They're still back there somewhere, in the playground I guess, I have to go and get them tomorrow . . . But anyhow, I suppose he just wanted me not to wear them tonight, you know? So he did that, he took them off and then, I don't know, it was kind of like a dream . . . he was doing this thing with the chain. Of the swing, I mean, with the chain of the swing, he was pulling it towards him. It was fun, kind of, the way he was doing it. How he was sitting on the swing next to me, and I was beside him, and he was swinging, just a bit, like he didn't really care, and pulling the chain of my swing towards him . . . right up close, he pulled the seat of my swing in that way . . . and do you see? How it happened? How it looked like an easy thing?'

*Like a spring.*
*That's how I manage this one.*
*The sound of my heart and the chain like a pulley to bring her in,*
*like pull the whole works over and get her in, that way.*
*Easy.*
*That's nice.*
*What a pretty dress.*
*Why not let me just . . .*
*Let me . . .*

'I mean it. It's kind of embarrassing to say, but –'

*Just . . .*

'It was really romantic.'

*Touch . . .*

'I used to think about that kind of stuff happening to me.'

*Your face . . .*
*Your pretty mouth . . .*

'It was –'

*Like touching . . .*

'I mean, I used to think about it with him all the time.'

*A bruise.*
*So go gently there,*
*with your sore mouth, be gentle with you . . .*
*Of course, I'm always gentle, it's you the one who likes to play*
*things, not me that way, but you . . .*
*Jesus, your mouth, your whole mouth . . . like . . . I don't know . . .*
*Like I'm going to crawl inside, make myself*
*so small,*
*you won't even know . . .*

'He started kissing me. It seemed to go on for ever.'

*What I've done.*

'I couldn't stand it. He was so good.'

*After all this time . . .*

'I couldn't not close my eyes. I couldn't not . . .'

*Sore little mouth and then it opens.*
*Little skinny arms, up around my neck and holding on.*

'I mean . . .'

*And hold on. Hold on.*

'It was kind of weird . . .'

*Let this be you who I'm kissing.*

' . . . I suppose. How he was doing it . . . because it wasn't like,
you know . . . He had the chain, it was bunched up in his
hands and I was right up to him, my arms were up around his
neck because I was holding on, and I said, "I love you",
because he was saying it. I said –'

*I need this by now. So . . .*
*Open your mouth. Wider, do it, wider. I've got to fit myself . . .*

'But I liked it. Don't make me say –'

*Inside.*

'I said, "Yes", I'm sure –'

*Open. Be
wider.*

'I said that . . . and it felt . . .'

*Wider.*

'Good, you know. I mean, all of you . . . it must have been the
same for you. Maybe a bit weird, kind of, but that's just
because he was older, and Dad was much older than you,
Mum, wasn't he, and Mr Harland's quite old? So you see
what I mean, like we used to talk about, Margaret, didn't we?
How it can be a really good thing? To be with someone . . .
who knows . . . Like it's more romantic, that way. You said
that to me too, Mum, once, remember when you told me?
That love could be a thing to make a person be whole, suddenly be quite different, in a way, inside.'

*This feels real, this is real, all right. You're real. You make it good
for me. I keep thinking I don't know who you are, but I do know,
don't I? Who you are? If I just keep on with you . . . like before, the
way you always wanted . . .
That's nice,
like that,
that's good, just let me . . .
There, like that, let me –
that's it, easy,
like that . . .*

'It changed me –'

*Easy.*

'And I said –'

*Easy.*

190

'I mean, I didn't say –'

*There.*

'I closed my eyes.'

*Because . . .*

'I –'

*You want it, you want this.*

'I –'

*Everything.*

'I –'

*You want.*

'I –'

*You're so open, you want.*

'I –'

*You.*

'I –'

*You.*

'And then . . .'

*Francie.*

'I mean, I said, "No" . . .'

*Francie.*

'I said . . . I tried to . . .'

*Francie.*

'No. Not like that.'

*Francie.*
*Let me . . .*

'Not like that!'

*Call you . . .*
*Francie, just like . . .*

'No!'

*Francie.*

'But he was still kissing me . . .'

*Like that, like*
*that . . .*
*Let me get . . .*

'And I couldn't . . . I mean, he still had the chain . . .'

*You.*

'But it wasn't like before, when it was nice . . .'

*You.*

'It wasn't like . . . He was using . . . his hands, he was . . . hard, with me. It was like he . . .'

*Shhh.*
*Easy.*

' . . . hated me!'

*Too late.*

'I mean . . .'

*Too late.*

'It was a Saturday night, and that's something, like this could have been a date, kind of, like we might have arranged it . . . You know what I mean, to be with someone you want to be with, how that feels, how it feels good and you want to be doing the things you're doing, you want to be there . . . I wanted to be there, but –'

*Sweetheart, I let go the chain.*
*You fly through the air, like a doll, thrown through the air, land, lit-tle girl, on the gravel, little stones, down there, on your gravel bed, my bed,*
*and I like it, the way you look, when I get to you. I can eat the tears, the dust and blood, they're painted on. Your dress comes apart in my fingers like wet paper, sweetheart, lying there, and don't say you don't want it, don't say –*
*Shhh.*
*Be quiet.*
*Be nice.*
*Make it nice, don't talk. I want you to be who you are . . . Freshwater tears, I want to eat them, your freshwater tears I want to hold them all.*

'This wasn't like that.'

*Shhh.*

'I wasn't saying . . .'

*Shhh.*

'A word . . .

'And it wasn't like before. When it was like he loved me, like when it started out and I wanted to be there, anyone would. I was wearing my dress, I was wearing my pretty shoes . . . Seems like such a long time ago now, like being in a film the way I was just sitting on the swing and he came over and he said "Hi", and I couldn't believe it, because I'd dreamed about this minute and I was ready . . . In many ways, I've been ready for so long. I've been doing nothing, just waiting here in this town for something to happen, something real, and this is what I have now, to keep. This happened to me, was done to me . . . and I thought I was special, I guess, like I had some ideas and I still have them, like plans, and ideas of what I want to do, but part of me's changed, it had to change, from what he's done, and he did it . . . He changed me. And what can you say to me now, all of you, about it, because you're sitting there? My name is still Mary Susan Anderson. I live in Featherstone. I'm still at school. Yet look at me, what he's done to me. And look, too, how beautiful I am.'

It was Margaret took the call; she could have left it. The bar was busier than usual for this time of evening and she was tired through with all the people who were there around her, wanting of her, demanding; she thought how they should go home now, how the place should be simply empty again. All Margaret wanted was to go to bed and close her eyes and to sleep . . . Still the call came in and the phone was there right behind the bar and she could hear it ringing, insistent, over the rage of voices, of conversation and storytelling and laughter, the mess of all that noise, so she may as well pick it up and it was Renee on the line, Renee. She was in some kind of fuss.

'I can't hear you,' Margaret said. She put her hand over one ear and pushed the receiver in closer to her head.

'What did you say?'

She had never before had Renee call her this way, at night, when she was working. The woman rarely phoned her.

'I can't hear you,' Margaret said again. 'You'll have to speak up, it's noisy here.'

Renee's voice came out in reply, something about her daughter, but high-pitched and all in a rush.

'Slow down,' Margaret said. 'What about Mary Susan?'

She couldn't find her, Renee said.

Mary Susan.

Mary Susan.

Of course, it would have to be about her.

'Young girls go off all the time, Renee,' Margaret said. 'Don't worry . . .'

What was the woman doing calling her at this time? She must know how busy she would be.

'What?'

Renee had said something else.

'I can't hear you. There's too much noise here . . .'

And who were all these people in the bar anyhow? Margaret didn't know them. A few of the regulars but a whole crowd she'd never seen before and some kind of rugby team or sports team just come in the door . . . Matching blazers and scrubbed-looking faces . . . more people to deal with . . . more people and Margaret only wanted to sleep.

'Renee?' she said into the phone. 'Don't worry, I'm sure there's no need . . .'

The girl was probably curled up in some car with a skinny boy somewhere, or slung up against the side of a building being kissed. Girls could do anything, of course they could, but you didn't tell their mothers that. Girls get anything they want and it doesn't make any difference in the end, but you don't say it. That they're still left some day, in some bar, ragged out and dirty in old clothes, that's all girls were, no matter how pretty they were to begin with . . .

'Renee?'

Margaret couldn't hear any kind of answer. It was as if, at the other end of the line, the phone just hung. Margaret had the impression the woman had simply run out the door.

'Renee?' she said again. 'Are you still there?'

But instead of the sound of breathing, all Margaret could hear was silence.

'Renee?'

How foolish she was being, Margaret thought, acting so about a silly thing. She hung up the phone and turned back to the thickened crowd, noisier than ever now the team of men who'd come in were jostling for places at the bar:

'What did you say you wanted?'

'What does she have?'

'Anyone not wanting beer?'

'You've got to be joking!'

The sound of men and voices, demanding, wanting, that was Margaret's life, not little girls and their ways. The years bring that on to you, she thought, even though you don't believe, when you're Mary Susan's age, curled up in a car, that anything will change. It's like there is a nimbus of light around you then, protecting, all the world offering itself to you and you can have any part of it. You open your eyes and people can't help looking.

It was the weekend that had done it, for Margaret, something altered in her mind to make things different from before. Starting with the girl, and then there'd been the man . . .

Ray.

Mary Susan.

Ray.

Mary Susan.

Those same two people, over and over, infecting her, getting into her thoughts, the same hopeless thoughts, all the things she didn't have come crowding in and the sex hadn't made it better this time, worse . . . Leaving early that narrow bed in No. 3, unwinding a damp sheet for herself to go back into her own room. 'Use yourself up on me,' she always said to men when she was with them, her legs wrapped around their back. 'Use yourself up,' and then at the end when they were used she had the man's trace within her but it was nothing because it was the wrong man . . . always the wrong man. She should be sick and tired of her behaviour by now . . .

She remembered how last night it began when Ray Weldon looked at her and smiled.

'Everything OK with you?'

And how could she have done that, last night, been so hopeful again? For him? And right after that thing with Renee talking about Mary Susan . . .

Ray.

197

How could she have shown herself so naked and he not even notice that she could be someone who would love him. No matter what. Love him.

Anyway, that was it. Between yesterday afternoon and standing behind the bar this minute, between closing and opening again for the evening trade . . . Something in this weekend had made it different from before, today not like any other day and it never would be again. After hours of dense sleep Margaret had barely been able to rise, and she'd never been like that before, barely able to find the time to dress, pick her clothes up from the floor and wear them . . . She was like a dead woman. She'd gone downstairs to open windows and doors in time for the lunchtime shift. She'd pulled herself through, heaved herself through those hours, tidied up in the afternoon perhaps, as usual, before the evening opening, but none of it was as usual. Usual was in the past. Instead there was only this other feeling, of change, of it occurring within her, curdling within her . . . Who cared? That's what she was thinking now. That who she'd become was a woman who says to herself: *Who cares?* There was even an odour coming off her, she could detect it, of stale clothes and sex and sweat, but she didn't care about that either. She couldn't be bothered, didn't have the energy – or perhaps, she thought, she even wanted it that way? To show herself as abject, let her crumpled skirt ride up, her blouse reveal itself in all its rumpled, dirtied creases? *Who cares?* she thought. *Who cares? Who cares? Who cares?*

She was engaged fully behind the bar now, glasses needing to be washed, and already the crowd that had been before her was replaced by another and any minute they'd want serving. And the thoughts of Margaret, all these thoughts . . . what she wanted for herself or not, what she intended or not . . . What were they? Just words next to this work. Her life was only here. She was a woman one hundred years old, two hundred . . . She may as well just do it all, do them all. This was what she was made for. Hands in hot beery water, ashtrays to be wiped out with her fingers in a cloth. This. Work. There was only this. This woman with working hands, who let herself have whisky poured into her glass and she would get down on the floor to drink it . . . This. Is who she is. Remember it. This.

'Another round, the same here, thanks, Margaret . . .'

Bob Alexander pushed a load of empty beer glasses towards her.

'All right?'

She nodded, 'Yourself?'

Anyway, she didn't care. She pulled the glasses down into the sink and replaced them on the bar with six that were clean. One by one she touched them to the tap and filled them.

'Everything as per usual, Margaret, A-OK,' said Bob, and Margaret just kept filling glasses, one after the other, until the order was done. She didn't care. All of them, Bob Alexander and the rest. Here every Saturday night, and some, like Bob from the beginning and others like the Struthers coming in later and staying the full duration. Nothing changed them. They moved in a mass, these kinds of people, they were always together.

She filled the last glass and pushed it over with the rest, waited for the money.

'All right?' Bob said again, and she counted it and said, 'All right,' back to him and she turned away. It was always like this on a Saturday night, too busy, weekends were always too busy . . . So again, Margaret thought, What had Renee Anderson been doing, calling her at this time? Why had she even begun to think Mary Susan would be here with her when Renee herself never worked Saturdays so why should her daughter be here instead? Why, the girl hadn't even come into the hotel herself to tell Margaret that she wouldn't work any more, only her mother had to do it for her. Then afterwards, how they both must have laughed. Mother and daughter sauntering down the road . . .

*Thanks, Mum . . .*

*Shhh. She'll hear.*

'Don't worry,' Margaret had said to Renee but now she was thinking she should have told her: Mary Susan would be kissing a schoolboy on the grass, some red-skinned boy who didn't know what to do with her and Margaret could have given, if she'd wanted it, Mary Susan, the world. She felt like doing that now, saying something cruel, because who did the woman think her daughter was, a child? It was Saturday night, for godsake, she felt like telling Renee so. Act like a mother, she wanted to say. Understand a few things about growing up and stop pestering me here. She plunged a dirty jug into hot water and swirled it around. Renee Anderson . . . what a strange woman she was. Margaret thought of her yesterday, huddled in the doorway, 'Miss Farley . . .' dressed once again in one of those shapeless cotton dresses of hers, 'Miss Farley, Miss Farley' . . . like she was terrified of Margaret. And yet . . . there she'd been on the phone, and it was curious for her to presume in that way. 'I thought she might be at the hotel with you,' she had said, and then she'd gone. She'd dashed off and let the phone just hang – and why? Margaret thought. Why would Renee, that nervous, shapeless woman, think, for even a moment, that her beautiful young daughter would be here, with Margaret, why here? Then Margaret looked up and Renee was standing right there in front of her at the bar.

Her face was in front of Margaret's face and her hair was down. She had no cardigan on, no jacket – so Margaret had been right: Renee had simply gone running out the door.

'Hey, Margaret!'

Some voice called out, some person leaning in.

'Margaret!'

But Margaret couldn't move to serve them.

'What are you doing here?' she said, and there was Renee, right there in front of her, with her soft brown hair down around her shoulders because she'd been running and she had not had time to brush it. Margaret had never seen her out of working hours before and without an apron on, her working shoes, and she looked younger, delicate somehow, as though she might be cold even with all these people around her, wearing nothing but a thin cotton dress and her skinny arms left bare.

'Why are you here, Renee?' Margaret said.

For the woman had just come running in.

'Why?'

And this was was someone who kept to corners, doorways . . . who never came fully in. Yet here she was now, and she put her naked arm out across the bar, with her naked hand she touched Margaret's hand.

'Miss Farley,' she said. 'Please help me.'

Something dropped in Margaret then, like a stone. She felt herself stumble. She looked at Renee and saw that her eyes were full of tears.

'I can't tell you how worried I am about her,' Renee was saying, and Margaret knew then that it was true, all of it true, and it was real, the fear for her daughter and her need for help, for Margaret's help, that she had no one else to ask and nowhere else to go but come to this busy, noisy, smoky place where Margaret was, to come here, because the girl was gone. Her own mother, in the deepest, most profound sense, did not know where she was.

'Renee.'

Margaret said the other woman's name.

'Renee.'

Again she said it.

And at that second, Margaret felt the empty passage of all she had ever wanted, gone, and understood that for Renee it was the same . . . As if the missing girl had come to represent to both of them all they didn't have and understand and know; and this was who they were now, this was all they were.

'Listen to me, Renee,' Margaret heard herself say. 'You must calm down . . .'

She'd have to find a way of telling her that she understood. That she felt the same way. That she'd lost something too.

'Girls go,' she said. 'They leave . . .'

And how strange it was, Margaret wondered even as she spoke the words, that this could be happening now. That she was even involved in this situation, with this person whom she barely knew and herself with so much she had to do and so little knowledge of what it was to worry about someone else, care for them. Here was this bar that she owned and ran and it seemed the place had never been so busy, that she herself had never been so least prepared and able to cope and deal and yet here she was . . .

'They leave,' Margaret said, and part of her wanted to run, even then as she was saying the words. For this was not what her life was. 'And we have to let them leave,' she was saying. 'We have to trust them, that they can be alone, all the daughters, that they do not really need us in the end, perhaps they've never needed us at all . . .' For why? She was thinking, Margaret was thinking, these words? She owed this woman nothing. Mary Susan nothing. She thought about the afternoon before, the girl's sly footsteps outside her window . . . She owed them nothing at all . . . and yet . . . There was this nothing within her too, this place within where she herself had been . . . And here was Renee now before her and the girl was gone, and she had to make Renee know that she understood: that even when Mary Susan came back she would still be gone.

'I really don't think –' Margaret began, but then Renee said again, 'Please,' and she closed her hand over Margaret's hand where Margaret's hand was, on the bar, a dirty glass beside it.

'You can help me,' Renee said, and for Margaret, some

202

unformed hunger she hadn't ever known before existed in her mind or in her heart or in her body leapt, something starving as though towards a source of food, reached out. And she found herself saying nothing, coming around the side of the bar and taking Renee's shoulder, putting her arm around that woman's skinny shoulder, and still without saying a word drawing her towards her in that busy place and holding her there, in her arms.

'Don't worry. We'll find her.' Margaret stroked Renee's hair. 'Don't worry,' she said again, for Renee had begun to weep. Quietly at first, her head against Margaret's shoulder, but then louder. Great wrenching sobs, tearing out of her, the heart in a spasm. Margaret stroked her hair: 'Don't worry,' she said again, but still the cries came out like great flocks of dark birds coming out, loss and love and grief and circling, circling, none of the dark-winged things knowing where to find their home.

A crowd had gathered. Gaye Carmichael came forward.

'Don't worry, Margaret. I can look after things here. Go with Renee, now. We'll be fine here. Go.'

A smoky, yellow place. A place where a crowd was gathered.

'Go,' Gaye said again.

That was how it began, a call, then Margaret had found herself saying, *I can help you*, and her arms now were still around Renee's arms and Margaret was thinking: *I am helping her now.*


Margaret led Renee out to the back of the bar, into the kitchen at the back where it was bright, too, like the bar was bright and all the lights on, but quiet and empty of noise and business, and she sat Renee down at the big table in the kitchen and it all happened so fast, the two women finding themselves in this way, alone, Renee thought, and together that their two bodies were close by and it had never been that way before, Renee thought, that way between them, that they could be two people and alone together, close by in one room. Margaret set a cup of tea in front of her, and there was a little glass, too, something stronger.

'Take it,' Margaret said. 'You need to calm yourself and the drink will help you . . .'

Renee took a sip. Brandy. Whisky, maybe.

'Drink it.'

She finished it down, like medicine, in three mouthfuls and it was like a bit of fire in her belly, and it was true she immediately felt better, the crying was gone, the awful wrenching of breath like she was a crazy woman gone.

'Miss Farley . . .'

'My name is Margaret,' came the reply. 'I'm Miss nothing. It's been a long time since I was a Miss. Call me Margaret. It's my name. You've known me long enough, Renee. You know who I am. I'm just the same as you.'

Kate Harland woke and it was dark. Something was all over her, like a blanket of breath, it was across her body and face . . . She'd been asleep, here in the car – when? For how long? What time was it? She went for her watch and with a horrible wrench remembered the pills in her pocket . . . But there, it was all right, she felt for the bottle and it was intact, the cap was still sealed. She hadn't opened those pills and used them after all. The sleep then . . . it was simply her own sleep that had overtaken her, not prescribed or chemical. She hadn't done anything to herself that would make the feeling of heaviness anything more than simply waking, cramped and dazed, in a small space that was not meant for sleeping.

She looked at her watch – nearly eight o'clock. It had been hours then, that she'd been here, just sitting, sleeping . . . She was going to have to consider what to do next. Waking just now in a panic that she'd taken the wrong kind of sleep . . . . What had she been thinking? That she would take her own life? That she would really do that? Then, she thought, she must have let herself entertain more of the wrong kinds of ideas about herself than even she would normally allow. For she was not that kind, was she, of woman? Who would be public in that way, do something that a wife of a minister would never do? And yet, even as Kate asked these questions of herself she also knew that her feelings were as real as the tiny bottle in her pocket described, that deep down, in the deepest part of her where there was no such thing as shame or foolishness or regret, this waking of hers now was not what she wanted, only circumstance and lack of decision at the time had made it so. The unchosen, delayed, sleep the outcome, what she'd ended up with, second-best.

In the distance, a car passed by, although it sounded much closer. Of course, Kate thought, the window was wound down – she'd done that before, when it was still afternoon. There'd been sunshine then, in the leaves and flowers of the hedge, but now the air was turned into a thick violet that seemed to smudge and change the shapes of the things around her. The hedge, for example, it seemed to have grown while she'd been sleeping, it was huge, and the tree by which she had parked had taken on a strange and twisted form, as though it had been built for the children's playground, a witch house, Kate thought, or some kind of a climbing frame that would be dangerous to play on. That was where she was, she remembered now, at the edge of the paddock that bordered the children's playground; she could just make out the tops of the swings and roundabout in the shadowy, uncertain air. Kate pinched her eyes closed with her fingers. She felt as though she hadn't properly woken. There seemed to be shadows everywhere, all these pieces of dark, and she felt disoriented, somehow, that she couldn't really see.

She should get out of the car. She should take a little walk down the lane, clear her head. Then, when she felt better, she would go home. That was an idea, go home. Harland would be wondering where she had been, even he would be thinking, *Where is she?* by now. It was time Kate started thinking about what she was going to tell him, acted like someone she knew instead of a strange, unhinged sort of person who would park herself down an empty lane where no one could find her. What, though, could she say? One by one the facts were presenting themselves like beads on a necklace you just wanted to throw down on the grass but there it was, hanging around your own neck. Herself. Harland. All the hours of the day . . . they just went on and on, the little beads, and they added up even though Kate didn't want them to add up to a thing yet there they were, facts, and she couldn't make them go away. It was as if she'd been a child, today, acting out for effect her emotions and desires, planning enormous leave-takings for herself when really she didn't have the nerve to do anything at all in the end. What would people think? Her husband? Anyone? The whole thing was like a dream.

Anyway, she didn't have the energy to think about any of it any more. The reasons for her behaviour would always be there, but kept tight swaddled, close within her. No one would ever see them. No one would hear them cry.

Kate opened the car door and stepped outside. The day was over. That was all the day meant. At least she hadn't seen anyone, no one had seen her . . . So the time could be described as simply passing, uneventful. The leaving, staying, going, not going . . . it didn't have to matter. She could be just someone who had allowed a few ideas to run through her mind in order to fill up some hours of the day, and though she might still have the responsibility of the next hours, and those that would follow, and the days . . . right now all she need think was that she'd fallen asleep in her husband's car, dozing like some harmless housewife . . .

Have a little nap, sweetie.

You were tired.

You go to sleep.

Actually, she was still tired – even now, out of the car – but Kate stretched, rolled her shoulders and that felt good. She put back her neck and stretched again. Even with fatigue it was better to be standing in the open air than stuck back in behind the wheel. That was how she should manage this situation, Kate thought: think about what was going on around her, trees and hedges, the calmness, deep colour, the stillness of light . . . The natural world, think about that. Make that . . . everything. The summer heat distilled to this deep-shadowed air, in winter, bareness, cold . . . Forget about whatever thoughts she had going on inside. Just be . . . here.

Leaving the car door open behind her, she started walking down the lane. It was only a few steps, but already Kate could feel herself affected by her own instruction. It was gorgeous to be out. The night felt ripe to her senses, as though loaded with the last extractions of summer fruits and they had all been harvested here, where she was. Kate walked on and as she walked the scent deepened, in the thickening air it seemed to thicken around her, a sweet perfume developing in intensity, second by second, pressing in. Kate found herself feeling heady with it, breathing the sweetness deep into her body and she had no control, it was filling her, dazing her into believing that the entire night could look after her now and keep her. How strange to feel this way, limpid in the air as though she had no thought about herself, only sensation. It was as though, as she was simply walking here, down the road, all the secrets of the world's garden were being made full to her, and to be tasted, like she might reach out and pluck fruit and flowers from a bough, like she might lie down. This was nature, it must be, the sensation of softness in the violet night, in the scent of flowers inviting . . . It was what people meant when they talked about that state of being at one with the world, natural and sensual and with a feeling of great ease. Yet as Kate walked it seemed like more than nature, too, and the further she walked, down the lane, further, into the shadowy violet light, with every step the lovelier it seemed, the ripeness, the air, the leaves and trees . . . Truly, she thought, this was the Gethsemane. It was there, wasn't it, in the scent of olives, the blue of grasses? Something greater than nature, wider and more knowing, a thing that might overwhelm her here, in this garden, this garden of gardens, a sense that she could be led on to go further, further . . . Christ's footsteps leading her further, and she would listen to where the footsteps would lead and she would follow . . .

Kate stopped, pressed the heel of her palm into her eyes. What was happening? A garden, where was a garden? She was walking in the middle of a country road for goodness' sake, and the footsteps . . . they were her own footsteps she could hear. So what was that just now, was she still half-asleep somehow? It might as well be as though she'd never even been outside, and worse than before, in the car, because the tiredness now was as though trying to rouse herself from a stupor, her whole body weighted in this air that had not woken her at all but only emptied her again into some deep dream, heavy and numb and deeply scented and it had been real . . . No! Not real! No more dreams, she couldn't go through all that again! She had to waken herself, not sleep. She had to keep going, make her way through the thick air . . . walk! One footstep, her own footstep, two footsteps . . . Stay awake! Walk! Make it . . . only simple, her life. Only walk. Think: she can stay with her husband or they can prepare for a separation. It's simple, it can be. No more strange dreams. There's a decision to be made – so walk! Choose. Make notes, start a list. Walk! Everything else was gestures, pretending to feelings that weren't real because they were nothing without words! So walk! Go back to Harland this evening and tell him, confess, knock on his door. Take him out of church if that's where he was to say to him:
'We need to talk now . . .'
'It's time, we have to decide . . .'
Either he wanted to be with her or he didn't; either she

wanted it or not. It was simple, make it so. Leave behind the great meanings loaded into silence, the poetry of scripture and prayer that had infected even the air around her and would take her and her husband not one inch further towards understanding. Leave it, walk! Only walk!

She'd come so far down the road by now, she must have been running more than walking. Her heart was racing. She stopped to catch her breath. This was what she needed, though, a brisk walk. It was so much better to have straightforward time to think. In a few minutes she would go back to the car, drive to Harland and tell him of her plans. She went on a few more yards. There again was a lovely scent in the air, but this time Kate knew that it was just the flowers that grew upon the hedge beside her, nothing more. She reached up to pluck off a spray to take home with her. It would be pleasant, she thought, to have it in a small vase by the window, to remind her, make her think about this afternoon and evening, the lessons she had learned. She would talk to Harland and tell him that she had realised in many ways she'd been lying to herself, that she'd realised there were many ways you could lie if you did not want to admit that the language you used about your life was not true.

'We have to talk clearly from now on,' she would say to him, 'about what has come between us. Not faith or loyalty or anything to do with your prayers, not the church. It's you and what you want to do with me that we need to discuss. It's not fancy. It's just you and me.'

She gripped the twig and pulled it, but it would not come away. How nice it would be to have, though, in the little vase . . . She pulled again. The twig held fast to the branch like wire and all that happened was that a whole flock of tiny white petals came off in her hands. She would have to leave it. That fitted her attitude about life exactly, she thought, and it would be part of her conversation this evening. How she looked at everything as she wanted it to be, as it seemed, seemed – but not really, as it was.

She looked around her now, with clarity, to be more certain. She'd been so deep in her thoughts, caught up with planning her new, well-intentioned programme about how to proceed with her husband and her marriage, that she hadn't even noticed where she'd been walking to. She'd been seeing the road itself, the hedge with its flowers, but now she looked around and took in her bearings. Half a mile or so away, behind a stand of trees, she could see the roof of a house, and another . . . the new homes built together at the edge of town. She could see dark shapes of cows in the paddocks between here and there, and there was the sound of cars, too, some traffic on the highway going out of town. The street lamps were coming on, late for this time of year. One clicked on now, just over Kate's head, and she saw that she was right outside the children's playground, she'd come that far, and she saw, too, something terrible was there.

At first, she could do nothing. Just stand, by the railings of the playground and look as though it were not possible for her to enter. She reached out for the gate and off it came the rank smell of metal and sweat, and Kate could see in the light of the street lamp, lying on the gravel near the swings . . . the orange of the sodium light had illuminated it . . . a shape, she must have run towards it for she was bending over it now, and it was a girl, Kate Harland could see her; although she had no memory of getting to her she was looking at her now, bending over her and she was a girl, she was only a girl in a dress that was torn and Kate Harland herself had helped make the dress and she knew the girl, she was Renee Anderson's child.

She felt something like a fist at her throat, heard herself cry out – because everything was wrong here! The dress, the girl – it wasn't supposed to be like this! Rage and fierce feeling and terror too hit and punched and fisted at Kate Harland's throat – not like this! The dress like this, the girl lying here like this . . . Kate kept hearing herself – No! – like it was her who was responsible, because she had helped somehow, with the dress, helping the girl make the dress, and she been there, all this time, a few yards away down the road, she had been there and she could have stopped this thing and now the dress was ripped, and could it be that the girl was not breathing, she was lying so still? Were her eyes open? Kate Harland thought, she thought. Would they open? She must touch, she must put out her hand.

She knelt down. She touched a piece of hair.

'Mary Susan?'

The girl opened her eyes. They were clear eyes.

'Mary Susan?' Kate said again.

For a few seconds there was no reply. The girl just lay there with her eyes wide open, these wide, clear eyes like she was waking from a dream. Then she said, 'Hello, Mrs Harland,' and she smiled.

Kate leaned in closer. 'I'm here,' she said.

Mary Susan closed her eyes. She was still smiling and it could have been as though she was drifting off into the most lovely sleep.

'I need you to listen to me,' Kate said, for she mustn't let the girl sleep. 'I need to know', she said, 'if you can move at all.'

With her eyes still closed, Mary Susan opened her hands, closed them again, opened them again.

'You're strong,' Kate said. 'That's good.'

The girl had been raped.

'Now I want you to tell me . . .'

She'd been raped.

'Do you think anything may be broken?' Kate Harland said.

Raped.

'Do you think,' she said, 'if I help you,' she said, 'you could manage to sit,' Kate said, Kate Harland said, 'if I help you, if I hold you . . . do you think?'

Mary Susan opened her eyes again. She looked at Kate and

she smiled again and Kate was looking back at her and thinking how calm she felt, how calm they both were, though she had found the girl and was trying to help her and who knows how badly hurt the girl was, how bad it was, yet here they were, looking at each other, and it seemed so calm, the girl left lying on the gravel in the dark, and there was blood on her and her underwear had been torn and the print of gravel was mashed into the side of her face like a pattern in the darkness, and still they were both looking at each other and they were both so calm.

'Do you think you could sit up?' Kate said and Mary Susan made a movement with her hands, not just opening them this time like she'd done before, but trying to help lever herself up.

'No –'

Kate heard her own voice and again she could not believe how calm she was, how measured her voice, like a nurse.

'Let me help,' she said, and she reached towards Mary Susan to lift her. She simply brought her up into her arms, and even then she was calm and not fearful, though everything about the situation could be fearful, she was not afraid and the girl was not afraid because both of them were strong.

Kate gathered Mary Susan up, felt how weightless she was, like a child . . . and she could do this . . . so easily . . . it was breathtaking . . . She had Mary Susan in her arms and she was standing up now, she was walking across the gravel, out of the children's playground, and through the open gate into the little road, she was walking down the little road . . . And to do this, have the girl like this to hold, to carry . . . it was easy, she could easily do it . . . have Mary Susan in her arms, carry her in her arms to the car, and when she got there, to the car, to lay her gently upon the back seat, smooth her hair away from her cut and bloody face, pull the fabric of the dress down over her, to cover . . . She could do it, all of it, it was easy for her to do.

*Put my hand out . . .*

*Stroke her hair . . .*

And as Mary Susan lay there on the back seat of Kate Harland's husband's car, then she could let her begin to cry, Kate could let her, and that was easy too, for the girl to cry, for Kate to say to her, 'Cry . . . Cry . . .' when Mary Susan began to cry because she should cry by now, it would be right to cry, let the tears come, Kate would feel them on her hands.

'Cry, sweetheart,' Kate said. 'Let it go. Cry. Don't be afraid, it's good to cry . . .'

And her husband, the cold church . . .

All that's in the day behind her, the night . . . Now there's only the girl, lying quite still while she is crying and Kate hearing her own warm, strong voice, 'Just cry,' and thinking, I'm not frightened here or alone, and I can do this, take care, this is easy for me to do . . .

'Only cry . . .'

And in this minute, here in the car, in the dark, after all this time, at last is the relief that Kate Harland's life has not until now afforded her . . . This. To breathe, after not breathing. To learn, after not knowing. To have, at last, someone else's care and needs be more important than her own, someone else's care and needs, and 'Cry,' she says. 'Cry and cry and cry . . .'

She settles the girl down more comfortably with a blanket that was in the back seat of the car. Then Kate comes round the front, gets in behind the wheel and starts the engine to take Mary Susan home to her mother. It only takes a couple of minutes, yet when they arrive at Renee's house all is dark, and Mary Susan's brother, sitting on the front doorstep calls out to them that his mother's gone somewhere, she's gone looking, he doesn't know why, what for.

'You stay there,' Kate calls back to him, from the car. 'Your sister's not well, I have her with me. We'll find your mother, and we'll come back here, so don't go anywhere. Just stay where you are and wait.'

'I been watching TV,' Eric calls out.

'Well, you can do that again,' Kate says. 'As long as you stay at the house . . .' And she drives on. But where? she thinks. Where would a mother go? To where people are, to ask them *Has anybody seen . . .?* So she turns the car away from the new houses back onto the main road into town and heads towards the hotel. She can ask Margaret there if she's seen Renee . . . It's the nearest place, and Margaret sees a lot of people, every day . . . The hotel is a good place to start, there it is in front of them now; she turns the car into the drive.

It's busy at the Railton. All the lights are on, and Kate can hear the noise of a crowd of people inside, all having a good time.

Mary Susan sits up.

'Don't worry about me,' she says. It's the first thing she's said since they've been in the car.

'Mrs Harland, don't worry about me please . . .'

'There's no need to be frightened,' Kate says. It's the noise, she thinks, after they've been so quiet together, and it's the lights of the Railton which are brightly lit up when they've been used to the dark.

'We're just here at the hotel,' she says. 'That's all. We just need to get you inside, help you bathe those cuts. We're right here now and Margaret will understand. She'll have some clothes we can borrow, we can call the doctor if we need to call the doctor, it might take some time for him to come in . . .'

'Please . . .'

'It's no trouble, sweetheart. You just relax. You'll be fine. We're looking after you here.'

Kate checks in the rear-view mirror. There's Mary Susan sitting straight up in the back seat looking at her. She seems very tired, Kate thinks, the side of her face swollen.

'Mum will be so mad,' she's saying now. 'It was getting dark and I didn't think I could move at all but look, I'll be OK. I'm worried that Mum might think, you know . . . I was out so late and I couldn't seem to move. I couldn't get out of that dumb playground, I don't know. I think I kind of, I don't know . . .'

'We're going to go inside here,' Kate says. 'But we'll drive around the back. No one will see us there.'

She knows Mary Susan is still looking at her in the rear-view mirror.

'I'll talk to Margaret,' Kate says. 'We'll get your mother. It'll be all right.'

'I know,' Mary Susan says. 'It's just Mum who'll be worried, but I'll tell her . . . I may have been sleeping, Mrs Harland, I'm not sure. I'm glad it was you who found me. You know, it was Ray Weldon who did it . . .'

The car stops at the back door of the hotel.

'But I don't know where he's gone.'

◇

Stop, now. Consider: why are the streets of Featherstone empty and quiet? The cars parked along Main Street dark and abandoned-looking, as though no one will ever come and drive them away? Why is it, if you wander down a side road you may see houses with all the lights turned on but nobody inside? A standard lamp throws its yellow glow over an arm-chair, a folded newspaper set down on its cushioned seat, a glass of water on the table beside – but the room itself has the desertion of a stage set, all the players gone, made their final exit for the night. Go into the kitchen and see for yourself how the surfaces are clean, the dog sleeps in his basket . . . but there is no one there. The only sounds are crickets in the dry grass, distant laughter coming from a television somewhere, and perhaps, in a bedroom, a little transistor radio is playing the news, or the shipping forecast where storms are predicted in rocky, icy waters far, far away.

Here, in warm late summer, we are protected from harsh weather, surrounded only by rolling seas of pasture and low hills. How beautiful the air is, how sweetly scented, with corn, clusters of dark fruit forming on branches and vines, and, this time of night, late-opening lilies which hold their petals full turned to the moon and exude such perfume it's as though there could be a woman here, moving quietly through the streets and back gardens of this town she grew up in, leaving it, returning, leaving again but always, always here.

Whoever said you can only come back to a place by first leaving? Or that the luxury of home is afforded only by time invested in one special part of the land? You can be a visitor while living somewhere your entire life, and you can also leave for ever, return, and again and again, and each time it's as though you've never been away. Visitors who come here, to Featherstone, even for a short while can't prevent ideas such as these becoming shaped and formed around them. Why she came here, that woman seen out of the corner of someone's eye, whose footsteps were heard running down an empty driveway, why you came . . . The only thing that need matter is that she made her return, her stay or her visit – whatever you call it, it's the same – and that for some hours this weekend, she has simply been here, and you have been here to watch, to listen. There can be meaning enough in that. In so many ways this woman could be anyone in town, Sonny or Margaret or Ray or Mary Susan . . . Her presence has become framed in the space these people inhabit, her fragrance in their inhalation of breath. She is there around them as a ripple of grasses on their empty lawns, a light breeze that ruffles the flowers and shifts the fine willow branches at the bottom of Sonny's garden. After a while, you have guessed it, you know exactly who she is, this stranger, familiar, she's dark air, the space between leaves, the pause you sometimes hear before speaking.

She could be here, now, where you are. This is a country town and anyone may expect quietness at any time, yet for you there is about the place at this hour such silence, a feeling

of loss and desolation that's hard to guess at or believe . . .
Only the windows of the Railton Hotel show the answer
because there, you can see where all the people are. Though
you're far away from where they're standing, you can see
them jostled there together in pairs and small groups, in the
brightly lit rooms which make up the bar. The sash frames of
the windows are lifted and, as you come closer, the sound of
conversation plays out into the night air like a summer party
you can hear . . . The door is open too as it always is when it's
warm outside and the voices and laughter pour out across the
hotel lawn now like waves upon a dark and gravelly shore . . .
on and on, the endless wash of people's lives, coming up
upon the sand in the darkness:

*Listen to me,*
*listen to me,*
and retreating again.

A couple of figures detach themselves from the crowd that
are pressed up close together by the corner window to go to
the front door – Robert Carmichael and his wife Geraldine,
stepped outside for a moment to check on the kids. Robert
says something and Geraldine nods, takes the cigarette her
husband's holding and has a couple of puffs, gives it back to
him. He says something else and she laughs. The sound of
children making the rat-a-tat of gunfire comes through the
dark air, and then you can hear one of them, little Robert,
yelling out at the others, 'Got him! Now tie him up and tor-
ture him!' It'll be cowboys and Indians again, Geraldine
thinks, hopes they're not being too rough. 'Is Marty there
with you? Are you looking after her?' she calls out, across the
lawn, and a great whooping sound comes back in reply. The
Indians are on the warpath. Robert puts his arm around his
wife's shoulder: 'They'll be all right,' and the two of them go
back inside.

Time is passing. These minutes into hours, and the houses,
the hills and land and fields . . . In part, there is something

217

about the emptiness you are becoming used to by now. The way you trust it, that it will reveal things to you from out of the deep shadows. The way a simple row of street lights may show the form of a girl. Or the moon may shift aside from the clouds to show a man's face behind a pattern of leaves. Featherstone. What, within yourself, little town, do you want to keep? The world? In your streets and soft, trampled paddocks, in the patches of dense woodland at the foothills of your high pasture . . . in the pale green hedgerows that grow up around quiet lanes, strings of wire from telegraph poles, Featherstone, Featherstone, what secrets? What can you do with these things you hold, the people you possess? One man stands alone now in the dark trees – and Featherstone, can you help him? Can you bring him back, to the streets, to the rooms where lights burn and the people are? Little feather . . . stone . . . Can you show the way? Bring him back from the dark place where he is standing?

It's getting late. Most people have chosen by now what to do with this night, but around the back of the Railton Hotel a car has only just arrived. It's an old car, the family-style model that's designed for dogs and children and boxes of their clothes and bags and toys, Harland's first car he bought when he was still a student. Kate Harland's face is white behind its dark windscreen – but she herself seems composed and calm sitting there with the engine turned off, as though she might stay for some time. Mary Susan is in the back seat behind her and Kate is thinking that the girl's mother will be here, at the hotel, as she has hoped. She sits a few minutes longer, then gets out of the car, opens the back door and helps Mary Susan to edge herself off the seat, stand up. Kate wraps something soft around her – a blanket or shawl, something that Mary Susan's been using as a comforter – for shock, cold? Kate knows nothing about the girl's exact physical condition but she thinks: Her mother will know what to do.

'Ready?' she says.

Mary Susan nods. She looks young and very pale, but together, with Kate supporting her, the two of them make their way to the hotel's back door. They don't knock. They just go inside.

Although it seems as though the entire town of Featherstone is drinking at the Railton tonight, it's quiet this side of the building and Margaret doesn't even hear the noise coming through from the front. She is sitting in the kitchen with Renee Anderson and the laughter and voices are muffled through the walls, there is nothing to disturb the atmosphere in this peaceful room. The two women are seated at the kitchen table, facing each other, and they look up when the back door opens.

'Thank God!'

Renee starts, pushes back her chair and falls upon her daughter, caught, wrapped up in her blanket like a child.

'Thank God! Thank God!' says Renee over and over, and Mary Susan looks embarrassed; her mother's never behaved this way before. She turns away slightly from the embrace, from the kisses.

'It's all right, Mum. Please don't fuss.'

It's clear to Renee, though, and to Margaret, that nothing about this situation is all right. It's the opposite of all right. The girl is too small somehow, standing there beside the minister's wife, as if she's shrunk into herself, as if she can't hold herself up.

'Look at you!' cries Renee, for the relief of welcoming her daughter in has turned to fear. She sees the swollen face, the ripped dress. She sees the blood.

'What's happened to you?' she cries.

Margaret is with her, she's come to stand behind her and Renee can hear her saying, 'It's OK, she's here, Mary Susan's here, that's the main thing,' but still Renee can't help herself crying out, 'What's happened to you? What's happened?' to her daughter, crying out, 'You must tell me!' and Mary Susan doesn't say a word. She stands, with her blanket around her, very still. She doesn't look at her mother.

'What's happened to you?' Renee's voice cries out again, fills the air. 'You have to tell me!' it cries. 'What's happened, you have to! You have to!' and Renee knows she's being frightening, knows she's making it worse, but still she can't stop herself. 'You have to tell me!' and Margaret is saying, 'Renee, it's OK, it'll be OK,' but when Margaret looks across the back of Renee's head to Kate Harland, Kate shakes her head, looks down and Margaret suddenly knows. She's looking at Kate, and Kate knows, and Renee knows, she *knows*, and 'It's all right, Renee,' Margaret keeps saying, over and over, like a chant or a prayer, and then Mary Susan says, looking out of the window, 'I'm all right.' She says to them all, 'Please,' and then she starts to cry.

No one in the front of the hotel, of course, is aware of any of this. It's like there's never been such a crowd present. Gaye Carmichael can handle it – don't worry about that – but she is wondering how Margaret manages on her own, day in, day out. It must exhaust a woman.

Her boys are playing pool in the corner, Gaye can see them; not John, he's not in yet, at Sonny's, probably, Gaye thinks, but the others, Kenny and Robert and Craig . . . they're here as usual, and the kids outside running around like little savages in the dark . . .

Where's Johnny, though? Strange Gaye's not seen him. He was to be at Sonny's, but that was ages ago they would have been through there. It was only a few branches needed cutting, not the whole wood. Anyway, Gaye thinks, it doesn't matter. She'll see him soon enough, that man, and John with him, and it's not as though she has the time here anyway for talking. There's some crowd in, arrived off a coach, nice enough young men but they're keeping her busy.

'Another round of the same, thanks.'

'Got any money for the cigarette machine?'

'Can you give us a light, love?'

Sure it's smoky enough in here, too. Over by the pool table where her boys are playing, Gaye can see a wave of thick grey air hanging in the yellow light. It looks a bit, she thinks, like some kind of a film she may have seen once: her young fellows lounging with their sticks and smoking too, and old Mr Graham and some friend of his standing beside and looking on. She can see the Carters over there too, the sister-in-law and her second husband, farming thirty miles out of town but they always come in on Saturday night to see the family, and the Edmonds are here, pretty much all of them and that's a big family if you take in the two cousins that come in to help with the late-season shearing . . . That's the weekend for you, Gaye thinks. There will always be a number of folk make the extra effort this one night of the week. The Greys and the Monaghans and the Sutherlands . . . all of them in from the hill farms surrounding Featherstone, meeting up here for a drink and a good time. Busy, of course, but especially with the good weather . . . You've got to expect it.

Bob Alexander has been standing at the bar pretty much since opening. Good old Bob. He's having a fine time, so who cares that it's been a while, he's decided he's just going to stay. The chap he wanted to see hasn't turned up – George somebody, he remembers – but that doesn't matter. It's always the same with those travelling types: they make big promises on a Friday night, but come Saturday and they've turned tail and gone back to wherever it was they came from. Someone told Bob earlier he saw this particular specimen buying a pint of milk off Neil McIndoe's van first thing this morning. Drank it straight off, standing there in the street, and poorly-looking, this fellow said, too much of a big night the night before, couldn't keep up with the locals, eh? Never mind, Bob doesn't judge him for that, but he could've used the man's contacts in the vintage car game – classics, that's what you call them now. He's stuck and needs some help with getting a fender piece for the Viscount – he must ask Johnny. Where is Johnny, come to that? Hasn't seen him in tonight, and that's not like Johnny, and with Gaye here, too, working up at the bar. Is there anyone else he can have a word with then, about that fender?

'I don't care anyhow,' Gaye hears Bob Alexander say to her across the bar. Has he been talking to her all this time? She hasn't noticed.

'I can talk to your husband about the parts and there's a good mail order service I've been using. We'll figure something.'

He puts his glass out for a refill.

'I'm spending too much on that car, anyway,' he says. 'I should probably sell the damn thing while I'm ahead and start again . . .'

'That sounds fine,' Gaye replies. 'Another one here?' She puts the glass under the tap without waiting for the nod. Of course it's another one, that's the thing about working this kind of place. It may be busy, but if you know the people, you know exactly what they're going to want – that's why it's not as easy here for Margaret as it could be. There's no 'no thanks, love' about it.

'What are you doing back there, anyway, Gaye?' says Bob. 'Where's Margaret?'

'She just needs me to help out a bit while she's busy in the back . . .'

She thinks how it feels good to say it. *Helping out.* Maybe this will be the start of something. Give Margaret this little break now, and who knows where it will lead. To bigger breaks, nights off, perhaps, and she might let some nice man invite her out for a fancy tea, go to that restaurant out of town a way some people talk about. Candles on the table and so on. That was the right kind of place for someone like Margaret. And that's what she should be doing, too, having a nice time with a nice man who took care of her and Gaye could help her with that. It would be something she could give.

She hands Bob back his full glass and turns to the busy line that has formed down the end of the bar. All those young lads . . . a rugby team it turns out, in for the night from a dairy town down south somewhere. They're going to be taking on the Featherstone boys tomorrow. They played the Young Farmers' League out near the Weldons' estate this morning, one of them said, but they were only limbering up for tomorrow. That got a laugh.

'What, flexing your leg muscles, kind of thing?'

'That kind of thing.'

'Having a bit of a run around.'

'Having a bit of fun.'

Certainly, there's a party kind of atmosphere about the room, and perhaps it has got something to do with this weekend being the first of the season. The ground's too hard, of course, but as Peter Graham said just now to Bill Walker and John McFarlane, 'These young chaps won't mind a bit of hard. They're keen, that's why, and the droughty summer may have made for a tough bite underfoot, but the boys are ready to take a tumble. I'm looking forward to the game,' he says.

'We are, too . . .' One of the young men comes in closer so that he may properly join in with the conversation. A nice, spruced-up fellow, too, Peter Graham thinks. The whole team tidy and smart-looking, if it comes to that, with the kind of eager, expectant air you only see in groups of young sporting men. Having them here makes him think about his own youth – they used to have a bit of fun back then in those days. He feels like calling out now, 'All right?' like he used to, all those years ago, and a group of them, just standing at a bar drinking beer like he is drinking now, would be up and off into the night and start a game out there, easiest thing in the world . . .

Out there. What a sweet sound, those words.

'And it wasn't like before . . .'
Out there.
' . . . when it was like he loved me . . .'
Where it's only silence, and the sky.
' . . . when it started out and I wanted to be there.'
Only dark and warm and infinite, an infinite sky.
'And I felt so stupid, that I could have really thought . . .'
Out there.
'Because this was nothing like love.'
Dark leaves.
'Nothing like.'
And the sky.
'I know the difference now.'

It is Mary Susan talking. The contents of her sentences are awful to bear, words cannot bear them, the story she tells, no story, a girl's daydreams and sweet thoughts turned into something else no number of words could ever hold up into the air for the light to see. It happened, the event she describes, and not more than a few hours ago, and the marks on her face, on her body . . . they're all real . . . and yet, there is calmness here, in the room where she is talking. Her voice is calm, even with the contents of these sentences spilling out horribly into the minds of the three women who are listening, even so, she is calm, this girl, and composed about the things she is saying.

Mary Susan's mother is asking the questions but Mary Susan looks at each of the women in turn when she replies. To Margaret, who is seated further away from her than the others, it seems as though the sentences she is hearing occur minute by minute, with accurate detail, each word as though it were a tiny blow. At some point, she has to look away from the girl's damaged face. There is something too eerie in Mary Susan's composure, like she is old well beyond her years and full of some understanding Margaret herself can't comprehend. It's sexual, but much more, Margaret feels, than her own notions of men and women, and right now she cannot bear to be witness to it. She has no idea what it is.

She looks out of the window and she wishes she did know. There are things about this night that have begun for her to open up some kind of understanding within her, of wanting to understand, but she's frightened, too, of where the thoughts will lead. She knows only that their direction will be away from herself, from all that she is familiar with and certain of, and it's dark out there in the night, and anything could happen. She makes herself look back at Mary Susan, sitting quietly on her kitchen chair. What *is* it, the knowledge this girl seems to possess, so composed and settled in the mind? What does it mean? How can she be this way, after everything that's happened? It's as though the girl has awareness of a vanity that can exist, in a woman for a man, and yet also she knows, this young girl, about the foolishness of that vanity. Is that it? Still Margaret can't be completely sure, can't really understand, can she, the reason for the girl's calm? Even though, while she is looking at her, thinking that she wants to see, she also wants to turn away, asking questions she's not even sure she wants the answers for . . . Then Mary Susan catches Margaret's eye and smiles.

It is a beautiful, vivid smile, Margaret sees it – like a transmission, like light. A second, that's all, in time, and yet at this second it's as though everything that ever existed between her and the girl . . . What was it anyhow? That existed?

*Show me*, Mary Susan used to say.

But no. For there was nothing Margaret could have shown her. It's there, Margaret sees, in the girl's composure, in her smile. It's always been there, and Margaret should have known it from the beginning:

*I can't show you a thing.*

Mary Susan is still looking at her, and there's this closeness Margaret feels, this intimacy of feeling . . . and it's something that's been given from the girl to her, Margaret was never the one to give it. It would have been like giving something of herself away to be so exposed as this girl is exposed, and yet there she is, Margaret thinks, her calm stillness, knowledge there . . . It's as though everything life has to offer has been drawn within Mary Susan like breath, as though she's been standing outside in the open and breathing in great quantities of air while all the time Margaret has been closed off in empty rooms.

*Show me*, Mary Susan used to say.

Show nothing. In her short life this young woman has let herself know more than Margaret ever could. She has presented herself to the women here in this kitchen now and it's true, as she describes it, what can any of them say about what has happened to her? Every single second of the afternoon, this terrible afternoon, is hers, only hers, to keep. No one else can own it. To take it away, make it better, make it different from before . . . No one can protect her. It's as though all goodness and evil, boredom and experience . . . all the ravishing, terrifying, unaccountable experience of living in the world has been gathered up by this young girl and taken in as one. And not a thing to be controlled because you cannot control it. And because, in the end, you would not want it any other way.

When Mary Susan came into the kitchen with Kate Harland, Margaret sensed apprehension in her then, fear almost, perhaps to be expected at this time, from a girl for her mother, but up until now Margaret's part in this drama has been small. To provide this room, this table at which they are seated. To pour whisky into glasses, make tea. A small part, and not connected directly to Mary Susan's situation in the way the others are connected . . . Then there was the smile, a message somehow, and for this reason, despite the sadness that must attend this situation, of violence and misunderstanding and tragedy and loss . . . Margaret smiles back at Mary Susan. She does that. And then Mary Susan says to her, though there are three women in this room, and Margaret is not the one who will take care of her, the girl's mother, nor is she the one who found her, the minister's wife, though you could say Margaret in these circumstances is the woman with least reason, least cause, to be here at all, still Mary Susan is saying to her now, to Margaret Farley, to her, only her and no one else, 'I knew you'd understand.'

She has finished her story. She turns to her mother.

'See?' she says. 'It's what I thought. Margaret knows. Things don't need to go to bad. You don't have to think that way.'

Then she stands up, she comes over to Margaret, who is sitting on the other side of the table by the window.

'All that time,' she says, 'I thought I was so young, that nothing was ever going to work out the way I wanted . . . It was what you used to talk about, I guess, that stuff about all the clothes and how to dress. But that's not really it, is it?'

She pulls back the hair from her face to show the long cut and swelling marked there, shocking and discoloured, from the temple to the chin.

'Really,' she says to Margaret first, then to the others in the room. 'You need to know more than just about how you show yourself. I reckon most girls don't like to think that way. Because it might look stupid sometimes, like we wanted too much, like we might think we could get anything we wanted and then it would only make us look ugly and sad when we didn't get it in the end. But you know what? I don't care. I don't care if it looks dumb to hope. I'll always be that way. I'm not afraid, and I'm glad I'm not. Better that than to hide yourself away.'

She sits down then, exhausted looking, on the chair. How very, very tired by now, Margaret thinks, Mary Susan must be.

'You do understand,' she says to Margaret again. 'I knew you would.'

She looks at Margaret, and still there's this strong feeling between them, it's palpable, as though they're touching . . . *Yes*. They are present, they are standing in the room. Bravery and innocence and something exultant, triumphant here: *Nothing can take us away*. Mary Susan smiles again to Margaret, and Margaret thinks she does understand. Whatever it was that began with Renee's touch, when Renee put her hand upon Margaret's hand and Margaret was able to help her then, was able to feel what it was like to help her . . . this has grown now, lifted itself into something given and there's no need to be afraid. Of gesture or touch, the rawness of someone else's emotion . . . The damage, of course it's there, on Mary Susan's lovely face, as Mary Susan says, as she has shown Margaret up close to be completely real, the bruises and cuts are real, no denying what has happened to her this night . . . but something more, this understanding more powerful than anything that's happened. To know that we can learn to bear ourselves, hold up and let whatever happens come. That, though the scars and discoloration may be there, we can suffer them and not feel the spoil, know damage but not ourselves be damaged. Like a body is washed through with its own fluids, undoing and reforming, wasting and healing, let the shift and tide of its waters and bloods rise and fall, and in time the hurt be gone again, leaving no trace.

A mile and a half away, the minister stands up from a chair where he has been sitting for many hours to walk through the rooms of his empty house. His wife has left him, she took the car hours ago – and all Harland can think of is the river. Last night he could smell river in the air, and though he tried to stop it, the powerful sense of something coming for him in that clean, dark fragrance, though he tried to shut the window against it . . . he knows now that what had stirred him, moved him, was not some idea of God or scripture, arrived like a strange unknown woman from out of the dark . . . No. The scent was a familiar. The recognition at last of the one who for all these years would have him bear witness to himself, to his own body, to desire and need and love and hope and lack of pride and fear . . .

How empty the house is without her now. Harland walks from room to room, opening all the windows. If only she would come to him, to all his rooms and fill them with the same deep perfume . . . He would not shut her out again. If only she could be here, where he is, to move around his deserted house, to the corners and spaces, to kiss his fingertips, ruffle the hairs of his head . . . If only, he thinks, the river would return.

Return.

Where home is.

Sonny Johanssen sits at the window of his dark kitchen and looks out into the night.

'Have him return,' he says, also watching, also waiting.

'Find him now, John,' he says, 'and bring him in.'

There are so many parts of Featherstone where a man could go hiding, but where Ray stands now, far from the streets and rooms of town, is where he can always be found. The river bends, past the shallow beach into trees . . . and there's a dread about the place, about the trees and stones, and something else, it happened before . . . A girl, but not that girl. It wasn't Francie there waiting for Ray on the swing. Sonny can't figure it. He can't properly see. There's been no dream or way of knowing and he can't work things out exactly in his mind. Only that there's been danger this night, and worse perhaps to come. But what, worse? He stands at the window with Rhett beside him, waiting, watching as though the answer is going to come to him from out of the dark.

*Find him, John* – but already that time when he and John and Johnny were all sitting here together in the kitchen feels like too long ago, as if too much may have happened since then to change things and even now for Ray they may be too late. Sonny's tired. There's so much he can't see, in this deep night air he's like a blind man with no pictures in his mind, and John's gone off in his truck like Sonny asked him and Johnny Carmichael home himself, by now, to an empty house.

He doesn't know what he's doing there. Normally Johnny would be in the pub this time, and instead here he is wandering around, turning on lights, turning them off again, standing in the middle of rooms . . . Something's going on. He left Sonny in his kitchen, what, two hours ago? Must be, easy, by now, left him, and still he can't settle with thoughts of the old man sitting there by his window as if Ray Weldon was just going to step out of the willows, tap on the glass, hello. Ray Weldon. Jesus. Sonny had been obsessed with the man. It really was like he expected him to come walking out of the dark, the most normal thing in the world – but nothing normal about it. Sure the man was somewhere in town, God knows there'd been all that stuff Sonny was saying before . . . It gave him the creeps. Just better hope John finds him down at the Reserve like Sonny wanted. That John can see him all right down there in the bushes in the middle of the night, seems like a crazy idea to old Johnny Carmichael. Why would anyone want to hang around there? By that bit of the water, where it runs so cold? What would a man be thinking? On his own at that kind of a place, at this hour? What kind of a man?

Ray is not even thinking. He stands by a thin white tree that's like a bone. In his hand there's a sharp-edged stone he's been using, driving the cut edge deep into the palm of his other hand. Doesn't feel it. He digs the sharp edge in so it goes deeper each time, into the skin near the bone and forms a thick gash of blood. He wants to hurt himself, to damage himself so completely. He grinds the stone in, digging deep into the wound as though he could push it all the way through; it won't go through, so he takes it up and drives it down the side of his face, feels something like an agony there that's relief but not enough. Again he does it, deep into the same place of the cut and it's whole now, the wound, it's opened flesh and raging, and he wants worse for himself, to make everything he does to himself worse, and more than worse. Again he does it, and again, and again. He's an animal by the water, hidden by white trees of bone, and he'll tear his own limbs out of the trap he's caught in if he has to, anything to be finished with himself, to be free.

He looks at what he's holding, drives its edge down into his other hand, but like before it's not enough. He puts his hand up against the tree and mashes the stone into his palm there, over and over . . . The stone, break the stone. Against his own flesh break it, because his own flesh is stone that can never be broken.

Stone.

Use the stone.

Stay here in this place he's found to hide himself in, deform himself here, that's all he wants. His bare feet sliced through from running and broken, his hands a mess of blood . . .

Stone.

Just to stay here where no one need see . . . never see . . . the trap, this place . . .

Featherstone.

He can never go back to where people are.

That's what everybody would say. In houses and in rooms, in the shops and bank and post office . . . The judgement would be upon him, *He's no longer deserving.* And yet, little town, there are exits and passes within your boundaries and a man could use them who needs to turn his face away. Miles out from where the last farms are, past empty paddocks, tussock and heather, those parts of the hills where no one's walked for years because gullies drop away unexpectedly and a man can fall there and be lost for ever . . . Featherstone, from now on, are these the places where Ray must be? Or further inland, up towards the sides of the mountains where bush grows in a matted tangle so dense that deer and wild animals lose themselves and the sheep who wander that far are gone for ever, pieces of wool float and tangle in prickly branches like a sign but you'll never find them . . . Where even the plants that scrabble for life have no names, Featherstone, when he's finished with himself here, beneath his white tree, is that where you'll release him, with his gashed side, his bleeding hands and feet?

Featherstone.

The judgement is here, within you to decide.

Featherstone.

But hurry. For his time with you is running out.

Sonny knows it. Ray may be at the river now, but every minute that passes, every second . . . is time passing, too much time.

*Can you make it, John? To that exact part where he is standing?*
It's late, and the water there runs so deep.
*Can you find him? Are you able to see?*
Sonny rubs the heels of his hands into his eyes, peers again through the empty window, looking out into the darkness as though into his own mind . . .
*Where are you?*
He has to be able to see.
To make out a shape, some person he can understand in his mind . . .
And he looks out in the dark, and he closes his eyes tightly, and slowly . . . there is something there, someone . . . a man, but not Ray. Tighter he closes his eyes and now the image comes to him strong: the minister. It's Reverend Harland Sonny can see. His head is bowed, and he's praying, *Where are you?* Like Sonny, *Where are you?* but this man is praying for his wife. He wants to see her, find out where she is, but instead of seeing his wife it's the river shown to him, there in

the minister's mind, it's the river he can see. Sonny looks closer, closer . . . The man's bowed head, his darkened room . . . and more and more it comes to him, that the minister is seeing the river in his prayer and another figure, not his wife, standing by the river, by a tree . . .

*Do you know who he is?*

Another figure.

*Mr Harland? Do you know?*

And blood coming from him, from his hands and head and feet . . .

*Do you know?*

It's Ray there, Ray's blood Harland sees.

The vision is gone again but a wrench has gone through Sonny, something like a sobbing left, like a wanting to cry out . . . that he has to see these things . . . has to see them . . . and yet he has to stand aside.

*Featherstone.*

For there's nothing he can do. He lives here, in this place, in this small town, for all his long life he's been someone who's belonging, and yet he has only his own window now, the darkness of his garden, beyond it, a few houses, the street . . . The whole town so known to him, so dear, and yet he can't walk out into it and change things. He can't be the one. He may see, know, but he can't change this night, alter the course of people's lives within it . . .

*Featherstone.*

Only Mr Harland can help Ray now. Sonny has seen it. And all Sonny can do is hope. That the minister will understand, that he'll take Ray in. That he'll open his arms and hold him, and see in his face his own face when he holds him, a man, only a man.

Sonny's so tired by now. Is it possible anyone could find anyone at this hour? Where he's sent John is a section of the Reserve not many people go to any more – so will he be able even to remember, to find his way? It's overgrown with scrub and bush, and the river runs deep, with huge boulders that rise up quietly beneath the surface. No one goes swimming in that part. There are creepers and vines, too, Sonny knows, that have woven strange shapes to form patterns across the water, and they shift and change with every current, with every pull of the undertow and the weed. The little beach where Ray and Francie used to go has mostly been eaten up by water now and thick leaves collect in pools at the place where they would once lie together in the sun. How does Sonny know about all these things, about the river? but he does, about the boy and the girl who used to go there, Ray has told him the story so many times and he knows the rest by heart. How the girl was greatly loved by the boy, and Sonny loved her, and her mother, they all loved her, even after Francie had gone, and when her mother died, years ago they put her in the ground and Sonny went to the funeral and sat over the mound of earth wondering where Francie was then, that she hadn't come back to say goodbye . . . But none of that matters now. There's no sun at the river, only shadows, and the boy who used to come to the river with the girl finally knows . . . the end of the story. That she's not coming back. That it's finished for him there. He's never going to see Francie again.

Ray stumbles, drops. Only the side of the tree holds him up.

And how can he go anywhere from here? This is his place. There's no empty field to turn him out in. No mountainside. His exile is here, Featherstone, within you. Trodden down in your sodden earth, at your river's dark heart . . . as much as the flowers and the fruit and the houses, where Ray is now part of you. He may be finished with himself here, but there is nowhere else he can go. Nowhere else for any of us, we who are left. Too much time has passed by now for anyone to leave, after this silence, and this dark. Too much time and too deep.

Feather.

Stone.

It would be possible just to close your eyes . . .

Feather.
Stone.

Let Ray close his eyes . . .

And nobody would know.

Feather.
Stone.

Or see . . .

Feather.
Stone.
   Sleep drifting down through the dark air, like a feather . . .

Drifting down . . .
   Before your closed eyes . . .

A feather.
   Falling . . . falling . . .

To land on a tiny stone.

Featherstone.

The name of this town like that game children play.

Paper to scissors.

Feather to stone.

One put in place beside the other – and who wins? there are
no winners. No losers. It's a game but it's not a game, it's
chance. A stone to split the feather's tiny spine or the feather
can shadow the stone's harsh side.

Stone.
   Or feather.

Feather.
    Or stone.

It is a game, chance. Like children play – but not for winning.

Now the feather floats down before the eyes of Sonny
Johanssen, frail and white like a flake of snow. Slowly it falls
. . . slowly . . . Sonny closes his eyes.
    *Feather . . .*
    *Father.*
    *Forgive him.*
    It drifts, going down, drifting down . . . slowly . . . to the
earth . . . Stone . . .
    Stone.
    For your shoe.

Sonny starts. Ray the stone, biting him there. And he can't
sleep, mustn't . . . though he wants to sleep, Sonny needs to
sleep . . . It's late. The hotel is emptying out, people going
home. Everyone is tired now, everyone needs to sleep.
Children . . . animals are sleeping. In the bedrooms of the
Railton Hotel, in the houses and farms, brightly lit rooms that
were empty before, people are returning . . . In ones and twos,
they fold back the sheets of their waiting beds, turn off the
lights, to sleep, sleep . . . Everyone is sleeping. Look down the
long country roads all the way to the Weldons' estate, far out
in the hills and in the house there, in their beds, Elsa and
David Weldon are sleeping. They lie with their eyes closed
and far away from where their son is, no longer is he in their
minds. He's in a dark shadowy place and he's no one's son . . .
    *Hurry, John.*
    Already it might be too late.
    *Hurry.*
    Sonny looks out into the dark and there is the minister, he's
waiting, there's John driving hard down a narrow road . . .
    *Hurry.*
    And here the poor boy who doesn't belong to anyone, who

has only death in him, endings, a creature not deserving . . .

*Hurry.*

And maybe already it's too late. Maybe no one can help him. Maybe any second the minister will want to do what everybody else in town is doing, turn back the bed, slide in between the covers . . . Maybe John will turn off the rutted pathway, exhausted, cut the engine, close his eyes . . .

*Hurry, John.*

Sonny himself needs to close his eyes.

*Hurry.*

Needs to sleep, but he can't sleep.

*Hurry.*

Even though he's never been so tired.

Harland can't sleep. Something has come to him while sitting quietly here, an image, and not expected, of a man . . .

*Father.*

*Forgive him.*

A familiar man . . . and Harland has never had this before, meditation yielding up such a clear picture, to hold onto, to see . . . A man, a tree . . . and he's a familiar man . . .

*Forgive him.*

And the prayer, also there in his mind and he can hear it . . . a familiar prayer . . .

*Forgive him.*

But not the prayer he knows. So why then?

*Father.*

This other prayer? Where has it come from? This image, emblem, of another man for whom he prays? Is it from a dream, a part of something he has read to be so clear to him, as a memory might be clear, a recognition . . .

*Forgive him.*

For the prayer is the same as the prayer he knows but not the same . . . And yet, somehow . . .

The same.

*Forgive him.*

Who?
*Him.*

Himself? The other man? The man hanging there on the tree? *Forgive Him?*

But the man before him now is not . . . He's no one's son . . . and yet . . .

'The Son of Man has no place to rest His head . . .'

There are these words, prayers.

'My God, my God. Why hast thou forsaken me?'

There is the certainty of this image. Blood coming from His hands and head and feet.
*Take this cup away.*
Harland looks down at his own cut hand and blood is still there, he hasn't cleaned it.
*Take this cup away.*
And, of course, it can't be taken.

Of course he can't sleep. Harland must wait. Prepare himself somehow, for answer, instruction. He doesn't know what it is that he should do, or how it is that he should hold within himself a capability or any kind of understanding that he can give . . . Only that this man here before him, who's lived among them . . . has no place to rest his head. And that, in some way he can't fathom, he needs him, Harland, this man, to wait for him, to minister to him . . . to forgive him.

Forgive him, this one man. The one who's hanging by a tree . . .
Who's used himself . . .
Like stone.
Used her . . .
Like stone. Hurt her,
left her lying . . .
On hard stones.

Margaret Farley keeps Mary Susan in her gaze. There upon her are all the marks of the things Ray Weldon has done. What he's allowed himself to do, it's animal, worse than animal, an animal would not do what he has done. And yet . . . there she stands, this girl he left lying like a rag on the gravel . . . and the marks of him are all over her, and . . . Margaret feels calm. Like the girl is calm. Her understanding passed on to Margaret like a torch now bright burning within her, that what happened, whatever happens . . . The sin of thought and word and deed, the ugliness of fact and sadness of the world . . . It can be accepted in.

Margaret can't believe that she can see things this way, but it's true, all true, there's no rancour or remorse. She turns to the others in the room. 'I think I do understand what Mary Susan means,' she says, 'about what's happened to her. I don't know why, but I do.' She pauses, how to put this. With her mother here, and Kate Harland, the woman who brought her here, how to describe this feeling, acceptance, utter calm. 'She's here,' Margaret begins, 'and both of you are here, and she's needed both of you, her mother and, Kate, what would have happened if you hadn't found her . . . But there's something else too, Mary Susan is telling us . . . that, though we are here, our presence . . . and this perhaps is of some help . . . that, in a way, after all, there's nothing to help her with.' Margaret pauses again. After what has happened, these hours, this day, how can she even be saying these things? And yet she is, and continuing to say them. 'At the beginning, I didn't know what this night would bring,' she says now. 'For all of us, I think we didn't know. A night . . . how it would be. Yet here we all are, and there's been this act taken place, of violence and great shame, and yet from it . . . we can be different now. Something has changed us, all of us, tonight, if we allow it . . . For it's something in what has been terrible that has made the change. Though impossible it seems, to think, or to believe . . . Still, it can be true . . . We can make it be true . . . that comes . . . out of terrible, something . . . not terrible at all.'

Margaret looks at Renee, looks at Kate, at Mary Susan. *Yes.* And everything is calm here, in the kitchen, like night hasn't fallen, like we are standing in the holiest place. It's warm here and it's beautiful, softly lit. The noise comes in from the front of the hotel but as though from a great distance. Margaret nods at Renee: *Yes. We are going to come through.* Then she takes Mary Susan by the hand and leads her to the back door, opens it, and the two stand there together looking out into the deep night. The stars are thick, no moon, but the night like deep velvet with stars, everywhere they look up, everywhere. All of life is here, all of life in the darkness and the stars, all loveliness, all love, and only the one man who did what he has done is beyond the benediction of the night. Only he is beyond tenderness now and only tenderness will save him, Margaret thinks, only love.

For him, this man in Margaret's mind, the night is caught amongst trees' branches and with that darkness there can be no stars. He himself, his form, is part of the darkness, a shadow, like a reflection in water, a part of a tree. He's like something caught, held in place, stuck fast with a pin, a fine splinter piercing the heart. His face is blackened out with darkness, yet all the time, from his room that he hasn't left, where his own shattered hand shows traces of blood across the skin, Ray Weldon's minister is waiting for him. God has brought him this far and now he waits upon the final illumination . . . There . . . As Ray Weldon stands amongst the trees, Harland sees . . . Him.

He closes his eyes to pray and a feather, Sonny's feather, drifts softly down before him, settles . . .

'Father, forgive him.'

Harland hears his own words, gentle as the feather, settling, resting . . . Gentleness . . . over what is harsh . . . over what is stone . . .

'Forgive him.'

And it's himself he also forgives. His own hands, Ray's hands . . . Both of them wear the stigmata of blood.

'Forgive him . . .'

The window is open and everything that Harland has been searching for, all his life, is here.

Featherstone.

Now the feather drifts again, across the vision of Sonny Johanssen, and of Ray, as Sonny sees him, standing like a graven image, his arms at his sides like the executioner, like the condemned man. Stone, he is stone. Margaret shows the girl the stars and thinks of stone, how she herself has been as stone, but now . . .

*Let me have him,* she prays to the stars, because his heart is stone. His whole body stone from what he has done. As her body was once but now flesh.

*Give him to me.*

Kate Harland moves into place behind her, it's time for her to leave. She's done what she had to do here, and her husband will be needing her. She touches Renee on the arm, goodbye, the mother of the child who can't do anything more now than she can, and they've both done as much as they were able. They all have. They are all here the same. The girl and the three women . . . Kate understands, she's no different from them, all of life to choose if she wants to choose it, this whole night made everything new . . . Quietly she slips away.

Half a mile from where Ray is standing, car headlights create a pattern across the trees. John Carmichael's utility making its way down the steep grassy path leading into the Reserve. When he reaches the gate, John gets out with stealth, like a young boy, to open it, then he starts on foot along the narrow path through the bush. It's like he's tracking down an animal in the dark, hunting something in the wild; he seamlessly moves through the overgrown passage, soundless, eyes alert to any change, any movement. After some minutes, he sees a man's shape; it doesn't startle as he approaches. John comes nearer, says, 'Ray,' and the man looks around at him, without saying a word responds in a couple of steps towards him when John simply says, 'Come on,' and follows through the darkness to the truck where it is waiting, its headlights boring a path of white through the tangle of roots and growth and branches and leaves.

Sonny looks up, the relief is like lightning, the white light of the truck's headlights bringing Ray home. Instantly, he slumps, falls to the ground. Everything is safe. His breathing comes rapid to him, like he can't contain it, and he's never heard breath like this before in his life but no matter, everything's done now, that needed to be done, and what is breath anyway? Only breath, and anyhow he's so tired . . . No matter what breath is, what breath . . . Rhett comes over to where he is lying, sniffs at Sonny's side. Minutes later Harland hears the sound of a vehicle pulling into his driveway by his front door, runs to open it, into the dazzling white of the headlights, to welcome whoever it is there, home.

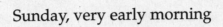

Sunday, very early morning

It begins slowly, the light, does this thing to you, drifts in, kind of, into your room, across your face, it happens, Sonny thinks, while you're sleeping. Of course it's still dark at this time, very early morning, and you'd have to know day is out there somewhere beginning, but know it inside, because if you looked through your window you wouldn't see a thing now except darkness. Sonny has it this way figured. That in his mind the dawn will be forming itself, minute by minute and secretly, a thing coming together out of all the endings, out of night and the moon and the stars . . . like the light has always been there, but hidden, you know, like night has just kept it away from you for a while so you can't see all the lovely colours but they're there, they've always been there and only waiting for you to open your eyes.

'See?'

There's Nona beside him, and little Francie run up the road in her nightgown to take his hand.

'See?'

They both know, always have done, about the colours. Think about things a certain way and they become true, that's what Nona used to tell him. Makes sense, really.

'It's where everything begins.'

Remember, he'd been kneeling on the earth? With his hands deep in where it was warm and he could feel the grains of dirt against his skin and in his fingers the little seeds? Remember? There were the plantings behind him in the garden that he had made, the ground in other places raked over smooth . . .

'Uncle Sonny, it's me!'

That's how it began for him, all right.

Sonny smiles. Like the leaves, really, joined to the branches of the tree growing there outside his window. He can't see them but every one is fastened to a twig with its own little stem. You can think about that sort of thing now, in the dark with time around you. Like about the way there are those soft buds of willows in the spring, and meadow flowers that come up fresh each day through the fields and pasture . . . Each item on this earth is growing, so beautifully made. Just thinking about the green shine on one blade of grass, the way each growing thing is fixed to the ground with its own particular set of roots that answer with each strand to specific need . . . It can be too much to hold, sometimes, the facts of this earth, too much to contain as a kind of knowledge in his mind.

'But still, of course, it all starts that way . . .'

How it can be in a garden. If you're not careful, you'll not get a thing done. The ground won't sift through, the seeds in a seam along your inside pocket will stay. On account of the beauty of the plants that are growing all at once and in profusion you can't settle, how could you, with the different kinds of flowers all breaking out of their earthen beds and Sonny has caused them to be there. Feels like a strange business. To be the one who planted in the first instance the kernel, the pod that holds within it the beginning of something that never before existed. Makes it that you may be in the middle of working on a piece of ground and you just have to rise and go indoors. Fix yourself a hot drink, a bite of lunch. Maybe even have a look at the paper because you're not going to get anything done in that mood, with the feeling of the flowers and the seeds and the tiny roots full up inside you, and the sight of some bit of tangled ragweed in your hand too much to bear . . .

'For goodness' sake, come here,' says Nona. 'There's no need . . .'

For he's weeping now, wouldn't you know it, right here against the soft fabric of her dress.

'Don't take on so,' she says, and she puts her hand on his head, just like he put his own hand upon the minister's head when that man had been crying.

'There, there . . .' she says, like he said.

'I'm right here beside you. Nothing can be that bad.'

So you see? Sure there will be times, certain occasions, and you'll find yourself remembering . . . Best have a lie down then. You're not fit, and besides, the growing things will always be there, whether Sonny Johanssen is out among them or not, makes no difference in the end.

'Uncle Sonny!'

And she would know that, Francie, wouldn't she? That there can always be someone else tending? That the garden itself will continue with its flourishing of leaves, its petals crinkling in the bright wind . . .

She would always know.

*So take the garden first. Take the seeds.*

Dawn will come and the planting can begin again.

For now, though, the dark is still here all around and in a quiet bedroom in the minister's house, Ray's eyes are closed in dreamless rest. It's all exactly as Sonny asked for, the minister's benediction come down also upon his own head. Sonny laid his hand upon him as a sign, seems like a long time ago, but not so long, and now the day is coming in for Sunday and the minister will wake, and Ray will wake, drive over here with John. They'll come in quietly, Sonny knows, for it will be very still here at the house, but calm, and Ray is ready for what he'll see.

'And no need to be wailing.'

Because, look, it's all fine, all of it.

Johnny holding him up, like he held him before, that dear man with tears and trying to brush them away but no need, Sonny's leaning on his arm as they're coming through the willows and it's dark but Sonny knows, really it's all colours there . . .

'So whatever you do, don't be wailing for Sonny . . .'

A funny name when you think about it, Sonny. A name for a boy and Sonny was a man . . .

'Steady on there, Son,' says Johnny. 'I've got you though,' and right enough, just breaking through the fine willow woods you can feel the light starting somewhere for the day, over there, behind the dark shapes of the trees perhaps, and Johnny has him safe to lean on, they're coming through the garden now, and John's there too, and Ray and Nona . . . and look, across the lawn and up the road. The houses are lit up and waiting . . .

*So take them now.*

This feeling of them all around you, the houses and the rooms, take them. This place where you've always lived, in this small town, amongst these people you've loved . . .

*Take them all, the people gathered here . . .*

You don't get so many chances to have your arms around them or feel them next to you, their hand at the back of your neck when you are crying. Not so many chances to hold on to the dear man now, let him carry you. Lay you on the bed . . .

It's all exactly as he said.

For you have to let a thing begin, don't you, then just as easy let it go. Find yourself in a place and you decide to stay. That's how it was for you. Late on a Friday afternoon, a few hours you could call it, and starting there, with the hedge, with the shapes and the light and the flowers. Sonny had looked up then and thought, *I know you . . .*

'So Johnny, don't cry.'

*It's what love teaches us*, Harland is writing. *To let it go.* He's in his study now with the sermon for this morning's service and they'll all be there . . .

The Carmichael family and Gaye looking after the little children. Margaret from the bar, and poor Mickey Parsons with his mother. Ray, Renee Anderson will be there . . .

*Here on earth*, Sonny sees the words appearing, *This is what we learn in life . . . to leave it.* The dark wet of the pen marks the paper, fills it, Harland picks up another page and smooths it down. *Mortal love is all we have*, he writes, *to understand, to know. To love absence, memory, and the hope that memory will keep stealing from us every day a little more, and a little more, until we have left of ourselves but a tiny part, made infinite by absence then, immeasurable by love.*

Harland stands up, stretches. So many words. So much to say now, to speak. To learn to give out words like gesture, like touch . . .

Quietly, so as not to disturb her, he crosses the hall to their bedroom where Kate is sleeping, reaches down and gently lays his hand against her cheek. Many words, but also . . . this.

So there it is, as Nona says, beginning. All colours for old Sonny now. Even with darkness in the air and nowhere near full day yet, still brightness coming slowly in. Across the houses, outlines of trees, behind the shape of the hedge, the edges of the paddock where sheep are sleeping . . . All of the town is here, and the time is coming soon to leave it.

'Uncle Sonny!'

You can't keep things the same, have to let them change, to let them go.

'It's me!'

If he was in his bedroom now, Sonny could raise the blind and see everything he needed in new light, familiar things around him and Rhett lying there beside . . . Yet even with his books on the little table by the bed, the worn fold-back of his striped sheet . . . even with all these things Sonny's fond of and he knows . . .

*You can take it now, everything that is familiar . . .*

Memories, even. All lovely dreams . . .

*Take . . .*

The way Francie would come down the road and into his bedroom first thing in the morning and he'd be sitting up there with a cup of tea.

'Show me!'

And he'd turn the pages of whatever he was reading, library books mostly, but some special ones he'd buy with quite nice pictures there in the pages.

'The one with the gold in it!'

Remember that one, though? He never spoiled her but there was the one she loved that had the gold and silver in it.

'That one!'

She might stay hours with him some mornings. Sitting up on his bed like a little fairy herself from a story, or later, when she was older, playing in the garden while he might, what? Prune the hedge, maybe? Cut back the ivy where it overgrew? She'd just be quietly making patterns with flowers on the concrete steps by the back door, little Francie. Such a clever kid, and reading to him from the newspaper later, while he fixed them up some tea, Nona coming down then and all three of them sitting out there in the sun.

'My two girls, eh?'

That's what he might say. Because they were his beloved, and he belonged to them, and they to him, and he had that for a while.

*But you can take it from me now.*

'Uncle Sonny!'

Even that. It's what she came back to tell them. *You don't hold onto people but you let them go.* Ray knows himself by now, sleeping at the minister's house but soon he'll wake, it's getting light. One morning Margaret will be opening the top windows of the hotel and he'll just be standing there below her on the driveway looking up.

'How long have you been waiting?'

'A while . . .'

Margaret will have her hand up against her eyes to shield the sun, her hair loose down upon her shoulders.

'I didn't see you.'

'You weren't looking.'

'Well,' Ray says. 'I'm looking now.'

So you understand, Sonny, how it's coming to understanding, one by one? A pair of gold shoes by the swings. A mother who stands in the shadow light of her sitting room and now the dawn is breaking.

'Mum!'

Renee hasn't slept all night. Beside her, the television is turned down, pictures but no sound, and behind a glass cabinet full of china figurines, little trinkets from the past, things she doesn't need.

'I know,' she says.

She stands quietly by the television, in this house where she lives. It's in shadows now but light will come later in the day, stream in through the windows and Mary Susan will be off again then, outdoors, you can't hold her . . .

'Mum!'

The light will flow through the grasses outside, run broad across the flat expanses of pasture, across fields. Sun will prick amongst the raspberry canes in Renee's garden and this daughter . . .

'She was beautiful, Mum.'

This daughter . . .

'Who?'

Francie had her eye on her all the time.

'Who?'

Renee turns.

251

'Who was beautiful?'

'You know,' Mary Susan says. 'That lady I was telling you about. Who was watching me before . . .'

'You're the one who's beautiful,' Renee says.

And she is. Look at her, Renee, your little girl walking on ahead. Renee was trying to say something to her but Mary Susan couldn't hear. They don't, Sonny thinks. You can't make them. She's walking down the road ahead of Renee, tall and gold, yellow and red gold, like the same light that is in the leaves of the trees is in her.

'My own girl . . .'

And gold, gold, just nothing but beginnings now. This girl, Renee's own. Her firstborn . . .

'She's going to be fine . . .'

Margaret understands. Margaret knows.

'You do, don't you?' says Mary Susan to her, and Margaret nods, yes. She'll show Renee the way.

The day is truly forming now, breaking into colour, and when you think about it, Sonny is someone who's always lived alone, so not the end of the world to go now, not the end at all, but beginning. It's been fine, the way it's been, it's worked out not a trial and all in all . . . The light is here. There'll be the colours and that will hold him, the thought of so much that's been given. Palest lemon, rose, the tint of violet at the edge of cloud, outlines not clear yet but everything will come through soon . . . The gold rim of a teacup in a tint of sun, a signpost hanging over a shop: 'Ice Cream'. There's a little pin someone's dropped on the floor, a thread from a cotton spool . . . Everything will be shown, it will come through and people will be shown, everywhere, the people Sonny has always known and they know him.

'Hey, Sonny.'

'Hey, Son.'

A strange name for a man and not for a man but for a boy and it's been a long time since he was a boy . . . a long time . . . And he's not in his bedroom now, where he should be when they find him, but Johnny will lay him there on his bed, close his eyes. And dear old Rhett just lying down there beside . . . touch the ears . . . always the softest part . . . And there's Nona saying, 'Let me have them,' the marbles in his mouth, like jam . . . 'Let me . . .' Silly boy . . . and a long time since he was a boy but look, how the day has come in full by then, sunlight all the way through the house, and in the blue air in the distance you can hear church bells ringing . . .

And it's all going now, going, as the light is coming in.

*All going . . .*

Disappearing, all the dear ones, into colour, into time . . . Another day to come, rising clear into the sky and the sun golden. Such gold there is to the grass, turning under the light to show up its yellow grains, gold earth, gold . . . The whole world warmed through with time, as though it may keep the fierce yellow of the sun burning somewhere deep in the earth, in the darkness to keep us all warm. We're all ready now, the fields say, smiling, turning in the light, let it come, darkness, gold is here to be a blanket for the darkest earth and all of us are safe.

*All . . .*

Rhett's muzzle is pressed against Sonny and he wants to reach out and stroke him and he does that, puts out his hand . . .

*Gone . . .*

. . . to stroke him, that dog's soft head . . .

*Into nothing.*

And time, light, the sun streaming in the high church window when they'll come for him, and then the doors of that white building will be open onto the green . . .

'And what is love if it gives us no comfort?' Harland will say, his voice clear through the clear light. 'If it fails to reach out for us, then what is love? If it cannot give us, like a baby's cry, a feeling of its own need for us, a yearning? If we cannot touch or taste it, feel it like the sun upon our backs then what is love now, what is God if He should be so far away . . . ?'

His voice rings out, clear through clear air, and the faces are turned up towards him, shining in the clear light . . .

'No God at all unless there first be love.'

They rise. Together, in rows, and one by one. Johnny and Gaye with the family they have gathered around themselves, Johnny with tears and trying to wipe them away, but no need, his hair wetted down and combed through like Gaye has him do it on a Sunday, and John there of course and the other boys and the kids . . . And what is love, but this? the organ sounds. Old Mr and Mrs Weldon sitting near the front and Ray beside. Bob Alexander from the garage there. Mary Susan, Mickey Parsons with his mother, he takes her hand. Kath Keeley finds her place in the hymn book, touches the words on the page as she sings, 'Love divine, all loves excelling . . .' Renee looks across at Margaret and they smile. What more than this? To let them go now, what more? Now the light's here, colours, the people are here and all along the streets and back roads of Featherstone, the darkness is only left as a shell . . . Go now. Nona would say this is best. To go now, this time of day when there's no one around and you can be quiet. Go now, and no one has to see.

'I waited on the Lord, for the Lord to answer . . .'

Sonny hears Harland's voice in the blue air, the words written down already for them all to hear.

'I waited . . .'

His wife looking up at him with the others, her face in the shining light.

'I waited and I saw you,' Harland says, 'and now I melt away.'

How beautiful it is to be here. The spire of the steeple bright like a cry against the blue sky . . . All happened as Sonny said it would, here he is now, he can go. There are ways you can figure things, Sonny can't know about entire, but some things . . .

He'd looked up and thought . . .

How long ago? Two short days? Some hours? A weekend only . . .

He'd looked up . . .

And the minister will finish his sermon by then, another blue day with flowers . . .

And he thought he'd ask Margaret, too, behind the bar, if there was anyone new in town, a young woman . . .

'Have you seen . . .'

The sweet dry smell of earth in the air, cut grasses . . .

Wiping off a little beer from his mouth where he'd sipped it, ask Johnny Carmichael too if he'd seen anyone new about the place . . .

'Have you seen . . . ?'

And nothing to worry about, nothing. The church bells ringing out, and the doors open, and there they are, all of them, coming through the doors to stand, and how they stand . . .

He'd looked up and thought . . .

It forms a pattern, a round shape on the green. There, outside the white building with its spire you can see it, a circle, for Francie's been, you see, she's been here amongst them . . .

A day? Two days? How long ago that you came in and didn't know that you would stay . . .

And the light was bright, he looked up and thought . . .

But you did stay, you are here now amongst them . . .

Here.

Sonny's eyes are closed. The pattern formed around him complete, a circle and all of them are here, Nona here, and little Francie run down to meet him and he just picks her up . . . 'Uncle Sonny! Uncle Sonny!' and him lifting her up in his arms, she's so light he can't believe it. There on the grass, on the green, he just lifts her up, and she's so light it's like his arms are full of nothing, nothing everywhere, all of them together . . .

He looked up and thought, *I know you*, though the light was bright and upon him bright . . .

And he thought he did know them, though the sun was bright upon them and on their heads bright and at their backs, like foil, and he looked up and he thought at first he could not see but he could see.

KIRSTY GUNN was born in New Zealand and has lived in
Scotland and England. She is the author of several interna-
tionally acclaimed works of fiction, including *The Keepsake*
and the story collection *This Place You Return to Is Home*.
Her first novel, *Rain*, was made into a feature film that was
an official selection at the Sundance and Cannes film festivals. Her books have been published in nine languages.
She lives in London.